The Harvester of Eyes

NEIL CHAMBERLAIN

First published in 2015.

Copyright © John Neil Chamberlain 2015

The right of Neil Chamberlain to be identified as the
author has been asserted by him in accordance
with the Copyright, Designs and Patents Act 1988.

All right reserved. No part of this publication may be reproduced,
stored in or introduced into a retrieval system, or transmitted, in any form,
or by any means (electronic, mechanical, photocopying, recording or otherwise)
without the prior written permission of the author. Any person who does
any unauthorized act in relation to this publication may be liable to
criminal prosecution and civil claims for damages.

This book is a work of fiction. Names, characters, places, organizations
and incidents are either products of the author's imagination or are used fictitiously.
Any resemblance to actual events, places, organizations, or persons,
living or dead, are entirely coincidental.

Typeset in 11pt/13pt Calisto MT.

This book is sold subject to the condition that is shall not, by way
of trade or otherwise, be lent, re-sold, hired out, or otherwise circulated
without the publisher's prior consent in any form of binding or cover other than
that in which it is published and without a similar condition including
this condition being imposed on the subsequent purchaser.

For Victoria & Katie

CHAPTER 1: Bloodletting

Selly Oak, a suburb of Birmingham, is a place in which to disappear. Rows of red brick terraced houses stare at each other across dingy streets. Rented student accommodation changes hands every term and the flotsam of Birmingham's workforce drifts in and out. A Special Branch safe house was, therefore, an easy proposition.

Jayne Quinn needed protection. Her husband's work had suddenly invaded their personal lives more than usual and Jayne was a target. Martin Quinn was a target – but as one of the Branch's finest he could fight his own corner. His wife was merely the potential victim when some Brummie drug barons discovered Quinn was a plant.

And now the druggies wanted blood...

"Tea?" asked Morris.

Jane scowled at her minder as she contemplated the beginning of week five of her confinement holed up in a back street.

"When do I get to see Martin?" Jane grizzled.

"When it's safe. He'll get the bastards. The Branch never wanted you involved," Morris soothed.

"There's no guarantee they'll be caught. And now they're onto me. The first time I realise my husband's involved is when I'm nearly kidnapped," Jane bridled.

"They want to rattle Martin. Martin wants you here... protected...safe," Morris continued.

Bennett shuffled outside the safe house doorway. On watch and 11.40 pm – only another six hours to go. A thin, cold wind wafted the light drizzle into his face as he stood in the porch. Another cigarette. The matchlight briefly outlined his bored features with its transient glow. The street was empty save for a cat diving into a catflap three doors down to curl up on some available washing. Bennett hated this part of the job. A sentry monitoring the shadows.

In less than half a second, his throat was slit from ear to ear. His hands clawed wildly to staunch the red gush. He buckled and crumpled to the floor. And the black shape behind him was in.

Jayne started. "What's that?"

"Didn't hear a thing." Morris busied himself in his twice read paper.

"Downstairs...a creak. Didn't you hear it?"

"Bennett's on the door – he'll buzz if there's a problem."

"What about that tea?"

Morris mumbled something from behind page three.

"OK, I'll get it," Jayne said, confident Morris would be another half-an-hour with nose in newsprint. In the kitchen she rattled the tea things loudly to make the point. Click! The singing kettle sighed and she splooshed the boiling liquid onto the tea bags. One of the mugs was overfilled - hardly enough room for the milk. This meant an overly steady course back into the grimy room laughably called the lounge.

The tray tumbled to the floor. She didn't feel the hot splashes on her legs for something else had caught her attention. There on the sofa, she couldn't make sense of the writhing, twitching bloody mass that was Morris. The dark shape bounded into view. Perhaps she saw the curved, machined blade flash a couple of times as the burning lines of pain slashed back and forth within her.

The carpet came up to meet her. She was lying in a warm ooze but she somehow couldn't focus on anything except a nearby chair leg.

Outside a car pulled up and Martin Quinn emerged. A lean guy - late-thirties, dark-haired and a haunted, drawn face. In the gloom of the damp street a passer-by might have noticed a certain athleticism. Quinn moved towards the inky doorway glancing up and down the street for any inconsistency. He managed to shoehorn a visit to his wife in a spare hour between surveillance and posing as a regular drinker in The Gun Barrels public house. And then a shudder as he discovered Bennett's body. In a trice – alert. A cat. Within the folds of his jacket his hand found the cold metal of the gun and his senses probed the open door beyond.

In the hall he felt for the timer switch – pressed it and immediately rolled to the floor, the snout of the pistol covering the staircase as the light flooded down. Nothing. Silence.

Pad. Pad. Softly up the stairs. And the light popped off.

He inched around the corner of the door jamb into the room beyond – the lights still on. And then the scene – the tight, acid fist of shock squeezed inside his stomach. He gulped air to catch his breath. "Oh Christ…"

Quinn dropped to his knees beside his wife. Amid carnage, love always finds its way to the surface. He tenderly cradled her rocking the bloody bundle silently back and forth.

And then the bubbly rasp. The embers of her life conjoured the energy to recognise the man she had loved for fourteen years. She formed the words, softly, "Martin… I…hate it when you bring your work home…"

Quinn buried his head into her. "Jayne, Jayne." Her name stayed unanswered as the last drop of her life vanished.

CHAPTER 2: Years Passing

The years after Jayne's death had been hard. Quinn had tried throwing himself into his work. He had tried throwing himself into holidays. He tried a couple of dating agencies. He took up a night school course. He had even considered trying to get back into the RAF but he knew that was a non-starter. The Branch became a treadmill. Endless hours sitting in cars and vans waiting for suspects to go out to the corner shop. The damning liaisons never happened on his watch. He got the feeling that they were giving him the boring stuff to avoid any more trauma. What was he going to do? Sue them for a nervous breakdown because the crims were getting too much for him?

What he really needed to get past the awfulness of Jayne's death was a new challenge. Sometimes he would wake up wishing he could really put his life on the line. His instinct for self-preservation was weakened somehow. Without Jayne life did not seem as important as it used to be. No plans for the future because there wasn't one.

He had spoken to his boss. A little more danger would be good. Life more on the edge. And they would see what they could do. That was ten months ago. Shame he would never be able to go back to the air force. He had kept himself fit and sharp nonetheless. The gym, the pool and pounding the pavements were a great way of getting rid of the time between work and sleep. He found that if he didn't make himself physically tired he could not sleep anyway.

He desperately wanted a woman to love but each toe dipped in the water was far away from the intensity he felt with Jayne. Three years now. He had asked the Branch councillor how long the grieving process normally lasted. And the unhelpful answer was that it varied. The rather young psychiatrist did not inspire confidence with his "six months to many years" woolly response. However, the report showed that Quinn's diligence and work rates were undiminished.

His smartphone buzzed – a text from his boss. Yes, he would be able to make the meeting. It was seldom he had to go to meetings trailed as 'interesting' – perhaps, after all this time, there was a lead on the bastard who had murdered Jayne.

Chief Superintendent Tremaine stared bleakly out of his office window as the rain pattered gently against the glass forming fast-tracking rivulets as the droplets combined. He was a spry, watchful man in his late fifties. The battle scars of Special Branch politics were not obvious – perhaps all internal – but they were there.

Cadogan was expected at 10.30 a.m. Tremaine glanced at his watch. A minute to go. Cadogan would be on time to the second – if not it would be Tremaine's watch that would be wrong. Tremaine had never liked the man whom he felt a manipulative chameleon - refined, but moving between being forthright, hard-nosed, obstinate and ambitious as the situation dictated.

The sharp knock preceded Cadogan's instant entry. His black, slick hair was slightly greying upon closer inspection but the bald pate gave away the years. The years of being privy to the most restricted intelligence in the realm had turned him into the ultimate, thin-lipped, cold fish. For Cadogan possessed a high mandarin status in MI6. Only rarely did he visit the Branch in person preferring to send his ill-briefed underlings.

He parked himself alongside Tremaine. The silence of mutual mistrust between 'Six and the Branch was broken by Cadogan.

"Seldom we recruit field men from the Branch, Tremaine."

"So I hear. Special forces exiles tend to be the grist to your mill," Tremaine blandly responded.

"Civvies lack the discipline."

"Never feel the need for a Plod's nose?" Tremaine paused and then carefully introduced his first sales point. "He is ex-RAF, though. Flew Lynx and Tornados."

"Left under a cloud, didn't he?" Cadogan was testing now. "But your man comes highly recommended it seems."

"And he is fiercely loyal to the truth."

"Hardly appropriate for my line of work," Cadogan countered.

"Harldy," Tremaine mused.

The rain intensified a little. The two men stood once again in silence.

Cadogan said, "Lost his wife and two of his officers in a op three years ago, I gather."

"But he put the buggers away single handed," defended Tremaine.

"Ah, yes - the lone avenger that can balance family life with the job. Missed the knife man though…"

"That's unfair, Cadogan..."

Another knock at the door stopped Tremaine in his tracks. He threw an admonishing glance to Cadogan. "Come in," Tremaine snapped.

Quinn stepped into the room. His dark brown hair, tousled and perhaps a little long framed the lean face. His well-cut jeans were of a man at home with not wearing suits in environments where everyone had a tie. The eyes took in everything, evaluated and made ready for a decision if necessary. He looked well in control of himself but there was the wariness of too much exposure to the bad side of human nature.

"Martin, have a seat." Tremaine's gesture was warm and friendly. "This is Cadogan. He may have a pretty hefty role for you working with both 'Five and 'Six – sort of a link man between the two outfits."

Quinn measured Cadogan. "Good afternoon, Sir."

Cadogan returned the blank gaze of a halibut on a fishmonger's block. Perhaps he tilted his head in a greeting.

Tremaine continued. "Martin, you said you wanted more action and involvement than the Branch could give."

Quinn returned a slow nod and cast an eye over to Cadogan. "Some sort of interview I presume."

Cadogan stepped forward with surprising speed going nose to nose with Quinn. "Too bloody right, man!" he roared into his face. Even Tremaine was shocked at the force of it.

Cadogan grabbed a chair and sat directly opposite Quinn. He locked eyes. "I'm here to grill you within a millimetre of your sanity. If I like what I hear we do the physical stuff. Then I decide. Is that clear?"

"Crystal. Sir!" Quinn responded with a military stiffness.

CHAPTER 3: Elements

There was no denying that Harrison was impressed with Niagara Falls. As a child he'd always wanted to see them but, like so many Americans, the rare trips across state borders were an occasion for bragging to the neighbours. For a moment he marvelled at the white, towering horseshoe deluge – nature eating at the drenched cliffs. He was on the 'Maid O'The Mist' tourist boat and sported his plastic spray cape fulfilling a vacation ambition – but on duty. He had been curious why his contact had been so careful. A bizarre location for a meeting but creative nonetheless.

The boat plied its way to the gigantic white wall of water. The noise was deafening. They never mentioned that in the guide books, he thought.

He wandered away from the group of tourists and leant over the rail looking into the foam. He was conscious of another man beside him. He looked up at the hooded figure. A nondescript swarthy face – but the oddest eyes he'd ever seen – the most unnatural, vivid green. The figure spoke, barely audible above the thunderous water crashing down from above, "Mr. Harrison?" The accent a Hispanic edge to it.

Harrison nodded. The man fumbled under his cape and passed a pressed a small piece of paper into his hand. The blue ink started to run in the damp atmosphere. Barely visible in a handwritten scrawl were two words – CORNUCOPIA LIMA. Harrison screwed up the paper and put it in a pocket under his cape.

Just thirty-six hours later...

The desk was black marble – polished to a mirror. Set in the centre was a white enamel kidney dish with a dark blue rim. Within the vessel two bloody human eyes stared vacantly. They were an unnatural, vivid green.

To one side of the dish was a tablet – its screen shone. On it was a list of American surnames with initials. The heading read: 'CIA – New Contacts'.

The hand reached for the touchscreen and highlighted a name – 'Harrison, D.W.'

Simon Hall was late. Lateness is not an option for a British Airways check-in counter clerk. The desks opened at six o'clock on the dot. He was fifty minutes drive away and, with parking, he was normally on station twenty-five minutes after arriving at Heathrow. It was now 5 am exactly. He crunched his car into reverse and started to move off his drive.

The face appeared at the window. His stomach flipped. He knew that wild, mad-eyed look framed by the lightest blond hair pomaded into points, the wide grin and the yellow teeth. He opened the window. Slitz leered into his face. He caught the stench of a late night pizza.

The face spoke, "Go to work, scum. Get those seats assigned right, right? Not a word – or you, your wife, your kid..." He drew a finger across his throat.

"Yes! Yes! Yes!" quivered the counter clerk. The curved, machined cheese knife blade rose into view – Simon fixed his gaze on the glittering point.

In a flash, Slitz took the knife to work on Simon's cheek. A diamond-shaped nick started to gently bleed. "Should be more careful shaving…"

Simon drew himself into the car and sped off. He knew what he had to do. He knew that he would do it as before.

The street was quiet save for the distant rumble of the car. Slitz turned on his heel, about to walk off. A tall-stemmed potted plant caught his eye. He paused and threw the knife towards the pot. The plant shook briefly and then, in a delicate mirrored parting, the split stem, cut perfectly in two, parted and flopped earthwards. Satisfied with his accuracy, Slitz retrieved the weapon and calmly walked away.

Chironex fleckeri is about the size of a human head when fully grown. It drifts in warm seas – particularly off the Australian eastern coasts – but is found across the Pacific and around Hawaii. And it should be avoided at all costs. For the box jellyfish is, quite simply, the most venomous creature on this earth. A brush with its many three-metre long, diaphanous tentacles means extreme burns on the skin followed by certain death after a series of extraordinarily painful neurotoxic convulsions and cardiac arrest - unless an antidote is administered in minutes.

At sea, it is extremely difficult to spot being almost transparent. The trailing filaments are covered with millions of stinging cells each about half a millimetre long. On contact with skin they fire their tiny needles in just three thousandths of a second. A mature example has enough venom to kill sixty adults.

One such specimen floated aimlessly in the laboratory tank. Doc glanced at the fatal tendrils hanging under the pale blue, milky canopy while he filled syringes from phials containing a pale orange fluid. The completed syringes were placed, the long, sturdy needles exposed, in a concealed foam compartment in a small attaché case.

Doc shut the case. He stood in a tall, bird-like stance with a shock of prematurely white hair. His sour features framed a mouth set into thin line of distaste. The 'mad professor' look was finished with a pair of modern, rimless spectacles perched on the acuminate beak. He paused in thought for a second and left the lab, softly closing the door behind him.

The conical, verdant mountains of Peru's tropical cloud forest basked in the evening sun. Like some gigantic inverted eggbox, the lush, velvet-clad peaks jostled for position. Layers of mist hung mid-way up the sides. Screeches of birds and wildlife punctuated the awesome green stillness.

A distant commotion – shouts and the sounds of foliage being hacked with machetes – broke the calm.

A small band of Quechua men hacked their way through the dense vegetation. They wore paramilitary garb – oddly modern for today's Inca stock. The leader shouted back – his bowl of black hair catching up with his round, tanned South American face a split second after he turned. To Western ears the language would have been completely unfamiliar.

"Stop! Ahead – look – it is the place."

Ancient carved stonework peeped through the tangled creepers. They raced to the spot and hacked away the leafy cover to reveal a stone slab. A lump hammer crashed down and the rock split apart – dust hanging in the motionless air.

The leader spoke again, this time softly, reverentially. "This is the place. May the Senderos be forgiven for defiling this grave."

Where the slab was, a gaping hole stared back. The leader flicked on a powerful torch and stepped into the inky passage. Reflections glittered off the slimy olive Inca walls, each stone in perfect union such that a piece of paper could not be slid between the joints. Ahead a chamber beckoned. The beam settled on the socketed face of an Inca mummy – shards of hair hung off the yellow-brown parchment flesh which, in turn, still clung in places to the skull.

But adorning this long forgotten warrior was a headdress – glinting and shimmering – a lavish gold and beaded affair and exquisitely wrought. In a swift move the leader grabbed the artefact and pocketed it.

CHAPTER 4: Instinct

The wall clock impassively stared out. Three twenty-five.

"A.m." Quinn grumbled to himself as he glanced at it. The left side of his neck ached as he hadn't moved from the computer screen for ten hours. A dark stubble had formed on his face and his jacket lay crumpled over the back of his chair. The terminal displayed photos of a myriad of criminals helpfully displayed in response to any number of nested keyword searches.

He leaned back, stretched and became conscious of the four other men who also sat trawling the records. He'd been so absorbed he'd forgotten they were there.

In one of the unending Secret Service abbreviations, TPMS stood for Terrorist Profile Matching System. Rushed in during the wake of 9-11 with unusual speed for computer installations, TPMS was, even to the initial doubters, extraordinarily powerful. With care lavished on its inception by GCHQ's brightest, it combined links from the PNC (Police National Computer), DHSS, HMRC and DVLA meshed with feeds from lesser know data sources from the Doughnut (the tag given to the UK Government's Gloucester-based surveillance centre). This information was then cross-referenced with GTAC, MI5's email and Internet surveillance system, MI5 and MI6 records and foreign systems. The security services had been characteristically slow to share the resultant sum of the parts to 'friendly' foreign powers and UK government Ministers as was the norm when such major breakthroughs occurred.

And so the punishingly tedious data mining continued.

Edmondson breezed in. "Any progress, gentlemen? Cadogan's getting impatient."

Cadogan always was, thought Quinn. There were only so many combinations of '+neurotoxin +aircraft +murder' you could search on.

Smith spoke up, "Nothing's connecting yet, we're trying everything."

Edmondson continued, "News from the CIA at Langley. Another of their field guys, Harrison, disappeared on a flight to Peru."

"They'll probably find him pickled in the hold like before. That'll be the sixth man the CIA have lost," Quinn muttered.

"Where the hell's Wilcox?" Edmondson started noticing an empty chair.

"Out on the first flight to New York. Had to get packed," Quinn said.

"Wilcox will get more info when he gets Stateside," Smith mumbled from behind his screen.

"Keep at it, chaps. No more losses on this one." And Edmondson was gone.

Beaconsfield is the first bastion of English market town life on the A40 out of London. It prides itself on its antique shops, tea rooms and over-inflated house prices. The Chiltern line is one of the few railway networks to run on time into London and life is altogether soft and ordered.

Wilcox lived down a leafy avenue with accountants, marketing directors and systems analysts. They all thought he was nearly something in the city.

The MI6 car purred up to his house at 5 am.

"Mornin', Mr. Wilcox. I 'ate these early starts. I was booked late last night. Anywhere nice?" the driver chattered.

"Hello, Norman. New York – again. Terminal 4, British Airways." Wilcox got in as Norman slammed the boot. Wilcox wanted to ask Norman not to slam the boot for fear of waking the neighbours.

The United Airlines 747 was well into its descent into Heathrow. The fuselage and leading edges glowed reflecting the ball of copper fire that was the morning sun. The flight from Washington had been uneventful and nearly empty. Another loss-making flight but United, like all transatlantic carriers, had to keep appearances up in the schedules. Breakfast had been served and the underworked flight attendants started making preparations for making a fast getaway from the plane when they landed.

The intercom crackled into life, "Ladies and Gentlemen, we'll shortly be arriving at London's Heathrow. So please fasten your seatbelts and make sure that your seat is in the upright position..."

An old lady passenger exchanged the briefest of glances with a suited businessman. He, in turn, nodded gently across an aisle to a woman with two small children.

Devereux sat sleepily in his seat towards the back of the rear cabin. His mind wandered, thinking about what his first meeting with MI6 would be like. The Brits he'd met in Langley had all been charming if a little perfunctory.

The old lady suddenly clutched her chest in a gasping

seizure. Nearby passengers frantically pressed the call buttons.

One of the small children decided to throw up all over a well-dressed lady passenger. She too pressed her call bell.

The suited businessman knocked a half-full cup of coffee to the floor – ringing for assistance.

Stewardesses rushed out of the rear galley past Devereux to sort out the commotion. Other passengers craned forward to see what all the fuss was about.

In the quiet, empty row directly behind Devereux, Doc silently popped the catches on his small attaché case. He took the syringe and, in a powerful move, drove the needle right through the seat back deep into Devereux's torso.

Devereux jolted upright – his face contorted into silent agony as the toxin simultaneously stopped his heart and sent instructions via most of his nerves to contract all his muscles into intense spasm. The poison hadn't quite reached his brain so he was aware of a unique, searing helplessness just before the torture was quenched by the black cloak of oblivion.

Like some leopard, Doc swung round, unbelted the body and dragged it behind the galley curtain. A firm tug lifted the carpet to reveal a metal hatch flush with the floor. With his free hand, Doc found a small power screwdriver in his pocket and engaged the bit into the hatch screws. In less than thirty seconds the hatch was up and the corpse bundled into the opening. Another twenty and the hatch was closed and sealed.

Doc returned to Devereux's seat and started to fumble in the dead man's jacket. In a deft move, a wallet was swapped...

And still the other passengers were occupied with the bustle ahead. The whole episode had taken one minute and twenty-four seconds. The fastest yet, mused Doc.

The glittering eye of a polished, intricate, golden statuette of a Chinese dragon stared blankly. It was sitting on an opulent, carved wooden stand and, because it was the only ornament, dominated the low-ceilinged room. Otherwise the space was clear of furniture. Restrained Chinese paintings in simple frames were scattered on the plain walls. The floor was a pale polished parquet. And upon it a large square of plain, but definitely Chinese, carpet lay in the centre.

The highly muscular male arm and chest was oiled and glistening. The sculpted form almost glowed. Beads of perspiration stood out on the yellow flesh. The arm flicked straight in a flash of a practised karate blow. The sinewy, extremely fit body belonged to Zhenxi Thaxoi warming up before what appeared to be a work out. He was young, Chinese, with a shock of black hair in a bandanna. Naked save for a brief embroidered loin cloth he performed a series of very complex martial arts moves - hissing quietly through his teeth as he snapped into each movement sequence.

With the sound of a distant gong he moved to the centre of the carpet and sat cross-legged. Then, closing his eyes he drifted into a trance.

A wall panel slid open into the room and a karate dan entered clad in the typical loose fitting white suit. His black belt was festooned with gold and red embroidery signifying a very high status. He bowed towards Zhenxi Thaxoi.

Zhenxi Thaxoi's eyes flashed open, fully alert. In a split second he was on his feet and gave a cursory bow.

They locked into a fight - high kicks and hard punches in the classical Shoto-Khan karate style. The moves were complicated and very vicious as the opponents wheeled around each other - arms, fists and legs flying. This was no sporting contest. This was a fight for real.

Zhenxi Thaxoi's fighting style began to change - more kick-boxing - but the aerial moves somehow seemed more subtle - more deadly...

As the fight continued, Zhenxi Thaxoi's mastery became obvious. Although his adversary was very skilled, the new moves completely outclassed him. A kick from Zhenxi Thaxoi connected with the karate dan's temple sending him spinning to the floor and, in a swift arm lock move, the neck of the dan broke with a sickening, muffled crunch. Life exited the dan's body and all was still.

Zhenxi Thaxoi returned to his meditation as two Chinese servants entered the chamber and removed the heap before him. He hissed again and whispered something in Chinese to himself, "Nothing compares to live practice."

Back in MI6 records, five men were still hard at work over their screens. Quinn blinked and rubbed his eyes. The word 'SEARCHING' flashed on his screen. He was getting to the point where any result wouldn't make sense. A photo popped up – a white haired, wiry individual. The image was poor – obviously a grabbed surveillance video frame. A name appeared underneath – 'QUENTIN DONOVAN [KNOWN ALIAS(ES): 'Doc']. Another flashing word appeared – 'LINKING'. A new grainy picture popped up alongside Doc. The round head with close-cropped red hair sat on a barrel of a chest. The face gazed angrily from the screen. A name – 'Nipper'. Quinn was on his feet, his chair crashing to the floor as he turned on his heel for the lift. The lift doors opened and Quinn nearly crashed into the emerging Edmondson.

"Where the hell are you going, Quinn?" Edmondson blurted in surprise.

"Instinct."

"You know how Cadogan approves of your instinct."

But Quinn was gone as the lift doors hissed closed.

Wilcox walked up to the check-in desk gratified that there was no queue. Simon Hall took over from the female counter clerk who muttered thanks as it was well after her coffee break.

Wilcox proffered his tickets and passport. "New York, please."

The usual banter regarding who packed your bags and did you have any sharp objects ensued. Hall tapped the keyboard and gave Wilcox a brief glance.

"Thank you, Mr Wilcox. I'm afraid it's rather a full flight but I can get you a non-smoking aisle seat towards the back. It'll be quieter there."

Another man stood waiting behind Wilcox – a barrel of a man with close-cropped red hair. He conveyed the impression of an ill-tempered pitbull terrier. His grey, dull eyes tended to fix unerringly on the subject in hand - here onto Wilcox's back. He sported in an overly-tight, dark, three-piece suit. His real name had long fallen into obscurity. He was now known by his masters as Nipper.

As Quinn raced out of London on the A4 in a company Jag he gave scant regard for the speed cameras that flashed in his wake.

Weary passengers with trolleys of luggage exited customs into the Arrivals Hall at Terminal 3. The usual crowd waited to meet them. Amongst the forest of drivers' signs for various companies and names of their representatives one in particular went completely unnoticed in the mêlée. It read 'Petersfield Haulage'. The driver was pleased that he'd managed to combine both a drop off at Terminal 4 and a pick up at Terminal 3 – and had the chance to have a breakfast in between.

A white-haired, bird-like man appeared walking amongst the new arrivals. His beady eyes spotted the 'Petersfield Haulage' sign in an instant and he strode towards it.

Doc, with a perfect American accent, spoke to the MI6 driver, "Hi, transport for the transport business!"

The driver responded with the well-used line, "Indeed. Was your flight on time?"

"Sat on the tarmac for a while - but they made up the delay in the air."

The driver sometimes wondered what the procedure was in case people didn't get the introductory conversation right – but this one was word perfect.

"Welcome to London, Mr. Devereux. Mr. Cadogan's looking forward to meeting you. I'm to take you straight to Chequers. Must be an important meeting. Can I take your bags for you?"

Two cars passed each other on the perimeter road – a black Jaguar going faster than was reasonably safe and one supposedly belonging to Petersfield Haulage with a white-haired man sitting in the back.

In the British Airways 747-400, passengers were taking their seats. The rear cabin was strangely empty. Wilcox is put his hand baggage in the overhead locker. As he snapped the door shut his eyes met Nipper sitting in the seat directly behind him. Nipper returned a faint, wintry smile.

At the set down area outside Terminal 4 Departures Quinn's car screeched to a halt and Quinn raced in towards the check-in desks pushing past queuing passengers.

"I must see the passenger list for flight 173. Has a Mr Wilcox checked in?"

The startled check-in clerk switched into auto-pilot. "Sorry, sir, I can't give out passenger names. I suggest you see Customer Services. You're probably too late as the flight has been closed and cleared for departure." Then, becoming indignant, "Now, perhaps you'll allow me to help this passenger who you barged in front of."

Quinn's eyes flashed around and settled on a counter clerk staring directly at him. As their eyes met, Simon Hall averted his gaze with a trace of unease.

This was enough for Quinn's antennae. He span round, pelted out of the departures hall and got into the car, engine still running. Punching the stubby selector into sports mode, he jabbed the accelerator with his toe and catapulted the Jaguar forwards into the traffic. The car lurched from side to side weaving through the dithering vehicles. And it began to rain. "An omen?" thought Quinn.

He leant forward and pressed a combination of buttons on his radio panel. Heathrow's ground control airband frequency crackled into life, "Speedbird 173, cleared for standard instrument departure, runway twenty-seven left, after the Iberia Airbus has crossed the runway taxiing from your right to left."

"Thank you, tower. Speedbird 173 cleared for take off after crossing traffic," the pilot curtly acknowledged.

"You'll need to execute your right turn quickly to miss the thunder clouds, 173."

"173, roger that. I can see them from the cockpit."

Quinn gunned the Jaguar along a perimeter road, slithered round a corner - and burst through fencing. He was onto the apron. The rain was heavier now. A flash – forked lightning rent the grey sky in two followed almost instantly by a sharp crack of thunder.

The big whale of the BA 747 held its position at the runway threshold as the Iberia Airbus trundled across its path – wipers flicking back and forth across the cockpit windows. The rain sheeted across the tarmac like some giant net curtains caught in an open window. The aircraft lights shimmered off the soaked 27L runway.

Quinn's car sped across the apron underneath a parked aircraft towards the take-off runway narrowly missing a convoy of baggage trailers.

The Iberia Airbus moved out of the path of Speedbird 173 to New York revealing the shiny black tarmac disappearing into the distance. The Jumbo's engine revs increased - the throttles pushed wide open. The captain held the beast on the brakes until the tower gave final clearance.

"Speedbird 173. Cleared for take off, twenty-seven left. S.I.D. heading three-twenty. Climb out to one-eight-zero."

"173, cleared and rolling. S.I.D. three-twenty. Climb one-eight-zero."

Imperceptibly at first, the nosewheel started to turn. The take off run had begun. On the flightdeck, the Captain and co-pilot, both their hands clasped to the levers, eased the four throttles open and the muted Rolls-Royce roar started to move the giant bird down its track.

The Jaguar was coming up fast alongside the jet. Quinn slewed the car round to a stop, got out of the car and ran towards the moving nosewheel - barely keeping up. Grimacing with the effort, Quinn made it to the nosewheel attempting to clamber on the undercarriage leg between the spinning wheels. But his foot slipped on the wet surface and sending him tumbling to the ground. The main wheels accelerated directly towards him certain to crush him to a pulp. Summoning more power from the adrenalin rush,

Quinn was up on his feet and running once more.

The aircraft's speed increased as the deafening turbofans ate the air. With an almighty lunge, he hurled himself onto the metalwork grabbing the structure - his legs trailing along the ground. Inch by inch he heaved himself up the gear, the wheels rotating ever quicker.

The nose undercarriage began to lift off the runway as the plane became airborne. Already, strong turbulence from the bad weather started to slam the plane from side to side. Quinn looked up trying to assess how the gear would collapse as it retracted. He might be caught in the mechanism. He clambered further up the undercarriage leg as the ground slipped away beneath him – the wind tearing at his body.

With a groan, the hydraulics then sprang into life. The wheel started to retract. A support arm moved toward the main leg. Quinn had to move out of its way with no choice but to swing his legs free just holding on with his arms. And then his left hand slipped - just clinging on only with his right.

The undercarriage doors started to close and Quinn was hanging free - but in their path. They'd chop him in two as they met. He started to swing frantically back and forth just managing to get a hand-hold with his left arm.

But the effort was too much. He looked upward to see both hands slipping with the strain - his face desperate. He could hold on no longer. The hands parted and Quinn was falling.

With a supreme effort, Quinn managed to land with one foot on either side of the closing undercarriage doors. As the doors closed his legs were brought together until he stood upright on the shut panels. He was glad of the comparative respite from the thundering wind.

He looked round. There was no way into the aircraft

from the gear bay so he tried banging on the roof. In the first class cabin above, fruit juices, salted nuts and champagne were being served as the plane commenced its climb. And not the vaguest sound from Quinn's hammering.

Back in the cramped nose gear compartment, Quinn started to look over the hydraulic mechanisms. He paused and shivered. Starting to pant a little, he checked his breathing – then held his nose trying to equalise the decreasing pressure in his ears.

In the cockpit all was proceeding normally. Using the T-scan technique, the captain checked his prime gauges. The altimeter's digital readout showed that the plane was just passing through six thousand feet as it climbed at two thousand feet per minute.

Humans do not perform well at altitude. Anoxia progressively slows and confuses the brain. The feeling preceding coma and death has been described by many who have experienced depressurisation in a hyperbaric chamber as euphoric. Anoxia symptoms can manifest themselves at altitudes as low as eight thousand feet

Quinn sat back from his investigations - breathless and gulping for air. He knew his time of consciousness was limited. He clutched himself, shivering as the temperature fell. He started to swallow frantically as he wagged a finger in each painful ear.

And still the plane rocked back and forth in the turbulence. One particular air pocket slammed Quinn into a wire loom. His mind was racing.

As the plane passed eleven thousand feet, the co-pilot idly worked out that they would be reaching their cruising altitude of 33,000 feet in eleven minutes.

Although he wasn't aware of it, Quinn was becoming delirious. His RAF training told him he must only have minutes left. He glanced at his watch and struggled to make a mental note of when five minutes would be up – the maximum time he'd have left before passing out.

By his head, near the wire loom, he noticed a cable splitter – a junction point for the bundle of wires. There were labels by a number of spurs off the main loom. Struggling to read the labels, he paused at one that read 'MASTER CYLINDER ACTUATOR WARNING LIGHT'. He couldn't be sure of its meaning through his addled brain but hoped it had some significance. He tugged, softly at first and then building to the manic wrenching of a desperate man. He knew it was his last chance. His last memory was of the wire giving a little but not breaking as he slipped into unconsciousness.

The co-pilot leant forward slightly.

"Nosewheel warning light, captain." The pilot tilted his head. Indeed the red glow of the text 'NOSEWHEEL WARNING' was the only light on amongst a forest of indicators.

"Must be an electrical fault."

"Do we cross the pond with it or turn back?" asked the co-pilot.

"Mmm. We could complete the flight - though it'll be easier for engineering at Heathrow to check it out. We've only been in the air for ten minutes." The captain decided. "But I don't fancy doing the trip with it. Get onto LHR and tell 'em we're turning back. Something or nothing but let's have the fire services stand by."

The captain flicked the cabin p/a switch. "Sorry to disturb you, ladies and gentlemen. I have made a decision to return to Heathrow - we have a minor warning light on. Nothing to worry about but I'd rather it was checked before we do the full seven hours with it..."

In seat row 56, Wilcox reacted to the message with

mild irritation. Nipper's face purpled with rage – a man with a thwarted mission.

Quinn's motionless body lay across the closed undercarriage doors.

"Commencing go around procedure, tower," said the captain calmly into his headset. "Descending to level two-zero for ILS approach."

Quinn very slowly started to stir.

The co-pilots's fingers hovered over the 'Gear Down' button.

Quinn's eyes flickered open.

The 'Gear Down' button was activated.

The undercarriage mechanisms hissed and wheezed and the nose-wheel doors started to part. A crack of daylight opened up letting the wind come rushing into the nosewheel bay. The doors parted further and Quinn began to slip through.

As he fell between the opening doors, he just managed to catch hold of one along an interior side bracing strut with a hand. Swinging free by one hand hold from the edge of the door the pounding gale tore his body buffeting him from side to side.

In panic, Quinn jerked his head upwards to see the massive nose wheel assembly start to drop heading straight for him. The air blast shoved him wildly about.

"Nosewheel down and locked," the co-pilot announced.

"Good. I knew it'd be the bloody electrics," said the captain. Three green undercarriage lights glowed reassuringly.

A 747 on final approach is a majestic sight. Fully extended, the flaps and leading edge slats increase the wing area by over a third. The first Jumbo pilots had to be specially trained using double-decker buses to get used to the fact that the flight deck was seven metres off the ground. The standing joke in pilots briefing rooms is that the nose wheel touches the ground two minutes after the main undercarriage – and that the flight crew know they have landed two minutes after that.

The electronic cockpit voice snapped, "One hundred – minimums" as the aircraft sank over the glittering landing lights. Fifty...twenty-five...and touchdown just beyond the white parallel threshold lines. Blue tyre smoke billowed from the main wheels as the rubber hit tarmac travelling at exactly 135 knots.

Quinn was sitting astride the nosewheel leg as the ground rushed up to greet him up. A thump and squeal and the nosewheel was down. The engines bellowed their reverse thrust and four fire tenders chased the plane down the runway.

The aircraft came to a stop surrounded by fire tenders. Firemen clambered out. Quinn carefully climbed off the nose wheel, brushing himself down.

"Gentlemen, good morning," Quinn greeted them with alacrity.

The firemen looked on in astonishment.

Quinn continued, "Undercarriage seems to be working fine."

There, by the runway, stood Quinn's Jaguar where he had left it just seventeen minutes before. Quinn walked over and got in. Just before he closed the door, he shouted nonchalantly across, "Can you get a message to a passenger - a Mr. Wilcox - tell him to call the office..."

And with that he drove off.

CHAPTER 5: Actions

The brass catches of a black leather attaché case were slid back by thumbs encased in surgical gloves. There was no sign of the night's storm abating as the driving wind and rain lashed the dark saloon. Comfortable in the back seat, the man with the case opened the lid. Torchlight played on the neatly bundled, high denomination US dollars.

The lid closed and the velvet Dutch-Canadian voice spoke softly, "If there is one dollar short, you are a dead man. Do you understand?"

A gloved thumb gently tapped on the leather.

The courier of indeterminate Middle-Eastern origin turned in the front seat to face the man.

"I trust the information will be reliable, Harvester."

A purred response, "Quality costs. Goodnight."

The meeting was over. The courier popped the door handle and the gale whipped the door open from his hand. He got out, slammed the door shut and made his way, leaning into the horizontal rain, up the deserted track to his own car.

He fumbled with the lock while his other arm shielded his face from the wind. He clambered in happy to be out the weather.

The headlights of the dark saloon ahead were turned

on, temporarily dazzlingly the courier. It reversed away.

He found the ignition and turned the key. WHUMMPH! His car was engulfed by the fireball sending panels and shattered glass high into the air. The bright, convulsive flash gave way to angry flames biting into the blackened shell of the vehicle. Of the courier there was no trace.

In the back seat of the other car, a gloved hand opened the case and peeled a banknote from a bundle. A gold cigarette lighter was flicked into life and its tiny, steady flame caught the note. The burning dollar bill rose to meet the tip of a cheroot clamped between the letterbox lips. The tobacco was puffed into life and the hand crushed the bill extinguishing the flame.

The silky voice spoke again, "One dollar short..."

The President of the United States of America sat facing Senator Craig Cline. The President's hands were splayed flat on the polished oak in front of him. Cline sat powerfully and comfortably and obviously well at ease with the President though his visits to the Oval Office were infrequent. Cline was the archetypal statesman, late middle age, with eyes that twinkled from under the hooded lids.

The President broke the silence. "Craig, thanks for getting in so fast. I know you're under pressure."

He's edgy, thought Cline.

"Mr President, always good to see you."

"You're sure security was strapped down?"

"CIA at Langley thought I was a flight courier."

"So...?" The President leaned forward.

Cline paused briefly wondering how to break the difficult news but decided that a direct approach was best in the circumstances.

"Sir, we've lost a seventh man."

"What, after Harrison?" The President remained surprisingly controlled. "Who?"

And now the difficult bit, thought Cline. "It's Dave Lesko... missing... we presume dead. He's not reported in - he always does."

The President's finger slipped into his collar. "So, it's terrorism - but who? How did they know Lesko's involvement? It must be from the inside."

Cline shifted uneasily.

The President continued, "The public feels unsafe - threatened. Terror cannot beat us. The media are having a field day. Any demands?"

"Not yet. The Brits say they might have a trace of a lead. Cadogan says it's only based on a field op's hunch."

The President's mind was made up, "Craig, get on the line. Tell 'em to follow anything. Go direct - personally. By now, Devereux will be in London - meet up when you arrive." He paused considering his next words carefully. "There's a problem... Lesko was on a nuclear committee for the NSA Inner Circle. He knew certain 'structures' to enable weapons systems to become live. Can't risk this kind of thing getting out."

Cline stood up to leave. "You have my very best shot, Mr President."

The olive and white Presidential helicopter, a Sikorsky VH-60N, immaculately polished, swung in to land on the White House lawn, its rotors scything the air in a techno beat of sharp thuds. Cline raced out to meet it and climbed in.

Inside, Cline sat down in a beige leather seat and donned a pair of headphones. He feet settled in the deep pile of the maroon carpet.

The pilot's voice crackled through over the noise.

"Welcome aboard Marine One, Senator. Not long to JFK so relax and enjoy the ride."

Cline knew the hour's trip well. He always sat on the right to look right down Chesapeake Bay with its complex inlets and islands - and then across the Delaware River as it widened into its bay. New Jersey would slide beneath them finally revealing the world's most famous skyline before lazily curving into New York's biggest airport. He thought briefly about the two teeth of the Twin Towers so brutally extracted and pondered on whether the States would ever be the impenetrable citadel against terror again. Now the US had declared war on the world's madmen he felt that the Land of the Free had confirmed itself a target.

Three miles to the north west of the heart of Washington's government nerve centre, lies the Glenwood Cemetery. The sprawl of the city starts to thin and people here live normal lives. Between Lincoln Avenue and Douglas Street is Lincoln Park - an area of green in the midst of suburbia. Locals sit and eat lunch, jog, cycle and generally meet up there. There is a children's play area with swings, roundabouts and ice cream 'n' soda stands. Young mothers watch their offspring tear across the pale red rubberised 'SafeTec' surface in between the climbing frames. The extreme northern edge of the park is quite wooded. Mature trees create the perfect environment for kissing couples on a long summer evening. The area backs onto part of the Glenwood Cemetery and the trees seem to go on forever even though a quiet road acts as a boundary.

Parked up on this lane was a five year old Buick station wagon, rented from one of the cheap independent car hire garages. A fat, swarthy gentleman sat in the driver's seat with the engine running. He sweated profusely as the aircon had given up some weeks ago. His greasy, open-necked, polyamide shirt offered little comfort. An open rusty gate was close by leading into the park.

Being a Tuesday and most people out at work or looking after their children, the clearing was deserted. Deserted except for two olive-skinned, black-haired men perhaps in their late twenties. Each had a handgun loosely tucked into their belts. They were wary but exuded the quiet confidence of the well-rehearsed.

They stood by an upright grey metal pipe mounted onto a wheeled trolly. The pipe was perhaps two-and-a-half metres tall. The men listened to the drone of a distant helicopter. The noise got steadily louder when the thinner of the two crouched down and busied himself with the controls.

Suddenly a little girl skipped into the clearing. She was no more than six. The standing man loped towards here. She stopped noticing his ill-concealed pistol.

The man leered at her – his eyes showing manically white around the pupil. In a thick Yemeni accent he spoke to the petrified child.

"Now listen, Little Miss. Go back to mamma. These woods aren't safe for little girls." He gave a grimace and the child instantly turned on her heel screaming into the trees.

The crouching man did not look up. "Should have killed her," he said in surprisingly cultivated Arabic. The other man ignored the comment listening as the sound of the whirring blades grew louder.

The silhouette of the Sikorsky appeared through the trees.

"Get back," shouted the control man. With a muted 'pffuddd' the surface-to-air missile lifted itself from its cylinder sitting on its tail of flame and smoke. It arced skywards seeking its target.

In the cockpit, the pilot saw the air attack warning lights and heard the electronic "Engage counter measures" dinning in his ears. But only for a moment. The VH-60N had some of the most sophisticated missile evasion systems available – but useless if they were not engaged because of a 'hitch' in the maintenance schedules of the high security projects department at Sikorsky in Connecticut. The weapon found its target – urged on with its electro-mechanical desire to find the hot engine exhausts. Cline was briefly aware of a bright sheet of flame before the Presidential helicopter burst into a million fiery pieces.

With practised ease, the launcher was collapsed and the two men man-handled it towards the waiting car. Seconds later, the Buick drifted out anonymously into the traffic on Lincoln Avenue.

The South American sun roasted the run down back street alongside the Presidential Palace. A man in a crumpled, lightweight, sand-coloured jacket emerged from the inky shadows into the noon brightness. He heard the sound of distant cheering.

The man wore a hearing aid. He lifted his hand to his mouth. The big palm concealed a tiny walkie-talkie.

The crumpled man spoke as he glanced at his watch, "Twelve noon. Mark."

He paused to listen to the response. "Five minutes and forty-seven seconds. Mark."

Around the front of the Palace in the main square of this particular South American city, the sound of the cheering was overwhelming. A waving hand clad in a white glove acknowledged the thronging masses from under the green and white striped awning. El Presidente was in his full ceremonial garb. It felt good 'connecting' with his people. He feasted on the sea of faces packed into the Plaza de Republica – all wildly cheering and fluttering flags.

An aide moved alongside the President. "Your people love you..."

The President turned to look at the aide through his dark glasses set under his peaked, braided cap and beamed. "Jose, I'm starting to believe it."

"Sir, your car is ready. We must go."

"Yes, yes! Let's make a move." The President's medals clinked as he turned to give a final salute to his adoring crowd and then strode back to the open doorway that led out from the balcony.

The Presidential limousine waited, door held open, in the baking sun. Police cars sandwiched the vehicle in the forecourt. The President swept into the car joined by a couple of military personnel. The door was closed and the convoy moved off.

A pair of sturdy gates set into the palace wall swung open into the back street. The crumpled man watched impassively from directly opposite the gates.

The presidential convoy emerged and turned into the street.

From the doorways that lined the street at least twenty armed men with automatic weapons appeared. And a cacophony of gunfire...

The police cars, peppered with bullets careered off the road, their occupants killed within the first seconds of the crackling Kalashnikovs.

However, the limousine was bullet-proof and started to accelerate away. But at the end of the street, an ancient lorry trundled into its path blocking its exit route.

More gunmen appeared from the shadows as the limousine drew to a halt by the lorry. The driver of the limousine tried to turn it round but the vehicle was surrounded by spitting weapons.

Inside the President sat paralysed by fear as bullets clattered off the car. The bullet-proof glass began to craze. One gunman fired a stream of shots into the door handle locking mechanism on the President's side of the limousine. The President's and the gunman's eyes met through the cracked window.

The door started to give. The gunman stopped firing and tugged at the door. The President recoiled as the door opened. An aide reached for his gun but the interior was sprayed with soft-nosed bullets.

In a few short seconds, the interior of the car was a red mush of barely recognisable bodies sprawled in a cloud of gun smoke.

The gunmen in the street raced towards the lorry and jumped in the back. And the lorry was gone.

A small group of Presidential staff spilled from the gates and fired lamely at where the lorry had been.

And the crumpled man simply stepped back into the shadows.

Two days later, massive orchestral chords burst from the overture of Mozart's 'The Magic Flute' and filled London's Royal Opera House with the rich sound. The splendour was matched by the glittering finery adorning the audience.

The house lights went down. There was an empty seat in a row near the front of the circle. A man in black tie sat looking anxiously for his partner to join him. The sharp, dark evening suit and crisp white wing-collared dress shirt was a contrast to his preferred sand-coloured, crumpled jacket.

A extraordinarily attractive and perfectly attired woman appeared at the end of the row. Those who had worked with her were sure she was much older owning to her calculating, mature outlook on life.

Anastasia Montero was a beauty. Ever since her early teens her combination of looks and wit made her irresistible to men. And she used it. Even now, approaching her thirtieth year, she was still amazed at what charm and a pretty face had got her. Moving to the UK from Spain when she was just five meant she suddenly was different from her peers – noticeable. Academically she performed flawlessly reading law at Cambridge. Along the way, she started to find male power intensely fascinating. She started to set monetary goals as to how much she could fleece from her adoring lap dogs for as little involvement as possible. By the time she was twenty-four she was a tabloid darling – the woman to be seen with. A string of broken hearts and promises had netted her well over six figures.

Jewellery, particularly, produced large amounts of cash when sold. And there was no better place to offload diamonds than the Jewellery Quarter in Birmingham. Her dalliances with a 'pharmaceutical entrepreneur' based in the second city not only yielded string of fabulous gems but an introduction to a hit man who went by the nickname of Nipper.

For all Nipper's thuggishness, he was intelligent. He, too, used his gifts to maintain a comfortable lifestyle. And this Anastasia admired. Nipper kept the lowest of profiles. He methodically covered all his tracks and clearly thought out all possible outcomes. He had killed many times but he was hardly known to the authorities.

And then Nipper got an invitation to work for someone in a different league. Someone with a more international outlook. And Nipper thought Anastasia might like an introduction...

Even in the darkness of the theatre, eyes flashed at her

checking whether it was really possible for a woman to possess such physical perfection. It was. With an air of confidence and muttered 'excuse me's', she made her way along the row to her seat. People instantly moved out of the way with deference – especially when her tight black satin and velvet number rubbed the knees of thrilled males.

The man by the empty seat rose and kissed her on the cheek, obviously relieved she made it to the opera. Settling in their seats, Mozart engulfed their senses.

Halfway through act two, the man reached into his jacket pocket. The perfectly natural move went unnoticed – as was the small black drawstring pouch he now concealed in his hand. Carefully, he passed it across to her lap. Her hand was waiting and withdrew it into her evening bag.

Within the evening bag, she opened the pouch and her eyes moved gently downwards. The sparkling cut diamonds winked from within the blackness.

Reaching further into her bag for a pair of opera glasses, she opened the hinged front lenses and inserted two diamonds taken at random into them. She closed the lenses and brought them up to her eyes as if watching the opera.

The opera glasses had been modified such that jewellers' eyepieces replaced the original optics. She put the glasses back into her bag, looked across at the man and nodded almost imperceptibly. The man could not conceal relief. The stones had passed inspection.

The second act drew to a close and the theatre rang with applause. The man, however, sat perfectly still staring forward. She got up made her way to the aisle. The syringe containing the pale orange fluid was safely back in her bag. Moments later she had hailed a taxi and was making her way back to her hotel where she would then be checking out to catch the late flight.

CHAPTER 6: Reactions

A shiny, official car swept to halt with two police outriders, lights flashing, at the main security checkpoint at Chequers. Armed police attended the vehicles. One pushed a lit 'mirror trolley' underneath the car to inspect for 'devices'. Documents were checked.

Quinn and Cadogan sat in the back seat in their best suits for the meeting with the Prime Minister.

"Good morning, gentlemen. Please can I have your weapons," said the fresh-faced constable.

This was normal procedure. Quinn produced his pistol. Cadogan fumbled in his jacket and another gun was produced. Cadogan looked sternly down towards Quinn's feet. Quinn, instantly realising, found the small, flat-bladed throwing knife from a strap on his calf under his trouser leg. The knife and guns were taken by the security guard. The car was waved through.

Chequers is the British Prime Minister's country residence. Set at the foot of the Chilterns it nestles between two shapely hills - Coombe Hill to the east, covered with trees and low bushes topped with a monument to the Boer

War – and the grassy Beacon Hill to the west. The ancient path of the Ridgeway defines its southern boundary. To the north is the village of Ellesborough – the pub is often frequented by visiting heads of state who are given a taste of English village life when they are being entertained at Chequers. The towered church, set on a hill, was where Margaret Thatcher commented on the 'day she was not meant to see' after the IRA failed to kill her in Brighton.

The pink gravel drive up to the house is perhaps half a mile long after the checkpoint. The building itself is a red-brick Tudor mansion – the main façade was built in 1535. The roofs pitch at sharp angles jostling together like a house of cards. Tall chimney stacks jut skywards from between the roof valleys.

The heavy, oaken plug of the main door was swung open and a flunky emerged to meet the car.

Cadogan and Quinn stood waiting in the Great Hall. Cadogan stared ahead at some point in space. He would have been here many times, Quinn thought.

Quinn looked around examining the ornate detail. A dark place – the tall leaded windows struggled to light up the dark wood panelling. Various gloomy oils hung as testament to the forgotten great and the good. A number of heraldic shields studded the walls along with mounted crossed swords and helmets. A heavy staircase ran up to a galleried first floor.

Another suited flunky entered. "The P.M.'s ready for you now. Follow me."

Up the stairs and down a short corridor was the Prime Minister's private office. Quinn was amazed at how small it was as the door was pushed open for them. More dark pictures. More panelling. This was, however, altogether a less bleak place as lights in brass fittings shone yellowly about the place casting a warm, intimate glow. A couple of maroon leather button-back chairs were casually placed in front of the heavy desk. He looked up from his state paperwork, stood and proffered a much shaken hand.

For once, Quinn noticed, Cadogan was everso slightly deferential.

"Welcome to Chequers." The Prime Minister gave a thin, worried smile. "Please - sit down. With any luck there'll be some coffee on its way."

They sat. The P.M. hunched over his intercom and flicked a switch. "Jean, can you send Mr. Devereux in." He leant back and looked at Cadogan then Quinn. "CIA man sent to liaise," he confided unnecessarily.

With a soft knock, Doc appeared from behind the door.

It took Quinn less than a second to recognise the drawn face, the glasses and prematurely white hair. He hoped he hadn't leaked his complete surprise at seeing in the flesh the digital face that had stared out from the TPMS just hours ago. His mind started racing and judged it best not to act instantly.

The imposter pulled up a chair and joined Quinn and Cadogan.

The P.M. spoke. "The U.S. still haven't a shred of a lead. Missing field agents, random terrorist attacks - all seriously undermining public confidence. The administration's containment of the situation is stressed to the limit." A pause. "But still no demands."

"It's clear different terrorist groups - as yet unidentified - are involved," said Cadogan. "Seems most of these episodes must have been based on inside information."

"And there's the worry," responded the P.M. "Cadogan, you had contact with Lesko. I hope he's given you enough to be going on with. However, now he's missing, we can only assume the worst."

Cadogan looked stung by this fact. "Lesko?"

Doc shifted to speak. "The victims get more senior. Lesko is, perhaps was, a very good man. There has been no word."

"America expects our support. We must not disappoint," growled the P.M. The intercom buzzed on his desk. He picked up the telephone receiver listening intently. For a full minute he said nothing. Then, with a quiet, "I see, thanks for letting me know," he returned the handset to its cradle. He spread his hands on the table as if for support and looked across at the three men. "Senator Craig Cline was killed an hour ago. Ground-to-air missile on the Presidential helicopter. He was on his way to catch a flight over here. Disturbing, wouldn't you agree?"

Cadogan blurted, "We've got our Terrorist Profile Matching systems working overtime, sir. I've enlisted Edmondson's section to look though what it's throwing out. There may be patterns beyond what the computer can provide..."

"And..." encouraged the P.M.

Cadogan darted a look over to Quinn. Carefully, Cadogan continued. "Nothing concrete, sir... except... Quinn thought he had a link. Couple of two-bit, freelance thugs connected with murders using syringes full of a rather untraceable death cocktail." Then, dismissively, "Nothing proven."

Quinn felt he had to speak. "They'd slipped through the net thirty-six hours before the bodies were discovered. Wilcox's flight to New York this morning was water-tight. We think one of the suspects was on that flight - but clean."

Cadogan disliked having his train derailed. Drily, containing his annoyance, he said, "Yes... Quinn recalled the jumbo by some rather unconventional techniques, shall we say. We've had to placate British Airways." He cast an admonishing gaze over to Quinn. "Wilcox is now on an RAF Dominie out of Northolt - just as a precaution." He obviously felt that the decision was against his better judgement.

For a few seconds, Doc began to look just a little uncomfortable.

Quinn, suppressing disrespect, added, "With respect, sir, it is still all we have."

The P.M. steepled his fingers. "We owe the U.S. a number of favours." He had made a decision. "Cadogan, perhaps Quinn needs a little fieldwork. Can you spare him?"

"Sir, his desk is rather full..."

The P.M. moved fractionally in his seat but Cadogan read it correctly.

"We can put his work on ice, perhaps, for a while?" said the P.M.

There was a short silence. Cadogan had been overridden. He snapped at Quinn. "Let's speak back in London."

The Prime Minister felt he had achieved something and Devereux would report back to the President's staff that the Brits were being very co-operative. He spoke, "Good - for the moment. Mr Devereux can fill you in on the CIA's views. Please brief him on as much as you can. There's an office directly across the corridor for your use."

They had been dismissed. The P.M.'s head dropped back to the contents of his red briefcase.

Cadogan sat at the head of a table - Quinn was to his right and Doc to his left. Quinn and Doc eyed each other carefully.

"Now, gentlemen, to business." Cadogan felt back in

control. "Mr Devereux...."

Meanwhile, Wilcox sat drinking a coffee at thirty-nine thousand feet in the RAF 'exec jet'. He was only slightly irritated that powdered milk had been used. He imagined it must save weight. Actually it was so the crew didn't have to traipse over to the mess to get the fresh stuff.

"...well, that's been most useful, Mr Devereux." Cadogan brought the meeting to a close.

Doc was enjoying his new role. In his confident drawl he said, "If anything develops, I'll be right on the line. Vice versa - catch me at my hotel."

"Where have they booked you in?" Quinn casually enquired.

"Gee, great little place - The Green Man Inn near Wendover."

Quinn thought it was time to rattle Doc's cage a little. "Sounds good. Perhaps we could have a drink. They serve lethal cocktails. Inject a little spirit into the proceedings."

"Perhaps..." Doc said without enthusiasm.

Cadogan stood up to go. No time for small talk. He liked the CIA man's brusqueness towards Quinn.

Out of the office, they set foot down the Great Hall staircase - Quinn behind the other two.

Perhaps a third of the way down Quinn spotted an old brass helmet and crossed swords adorning the wall of the panelled stairway. No time like the present, he thought. As he passed, he gently grabbed the sword. It slid out easily and noiselessly from the display. He hid the sword vertically behind his back and planned his moves.

The group reached the bottom. Cadogan turned round as if to speak to Quinn. Quinn put his finger to his lips to keep him silent and brought the weapon into view. Quinn signalled to Cadogan to move out of the way. Cadogan's brow knitted in incomprehension but stepped aside. The off beat of the step caused Doc to turn round. Quinn lunged, the sword aimed directly for Doc's heart.

But Doc was too quick. He dropped to the floor and the sword caught air. As Quinn withdrew for another lunge, Doc rolled over and got back on his feet.

Quinn rounded and lunged but his opponent was again too swift, side-stepping out of the way. Cadogan stepped back to the safety of a corner as the fight commenced.

Doc, noticing another sword display on an opposite wall, dived across Quinn's path. Another lunge from Quinn missed its target again. Doc scampered to the wall and removed the blade - wheeling round to face Quinn. They circled, staring at each other like some black and white swashbucking movie.

Doc made the first move, Quinn parrying confidently. A swift interchange of crossed swords ensued - neither man having the advantage. Once more they circled.

Another vigorous exchange ended in a powerful thrust from Doc which just missed Quinn's torso - the blade, however, went inside Quinn's suit jacket and emerged through the back of the cloth. Quinn's confidence lost a notch as he realised he had an effective opponent.

Quinn span round extricating his jacket off the blade. As he turned to face Doc, he ducked avoiding another lunge. Coming out of this move, Quinn rugby-tackled Doc who crashed to the floor. They grappled on the polished planks - the blades too long to be effective at close quarters. Each man, however, held onto their sword - the only weapons they had.

A flunky entered the hall. He eyes wide in surprise at the commotion.

Doc managed to plant a fist into Quinn's face. Quinn

recoiled, stunned for a second.

Doc was back on his feet. He bounded towards the flunky now rigid in shock. Without a break in his movement, Doc speared the man through his heart. The dying flunkly pitched forward, Doc withdrawing the blade as its victim keeled earthwards.

Doc instantly returned to the dazed Quinn who was clambering to his feet – the bloodied steel poised rock solid in Doc's unwavering hand. Before Quinn was up, Doc started lunging. Quinn parried from his off-balance stance but was forced backwards towards the stairs. Quinn tumbled as he stepped backward into the unseen bottom step of the staircase.

Again, Doc thrusted just missing Quinn's chest as Quinn was effectively pinned to the stairs. Another frantic exchange and Doc started to have the upper hand - Quinn having to parry more and more, scrabbling from side-to-side to avoid the thrusts.

Slowly Quinn gained some purchase and kicked Doc's legs from under him. Doc crashed forwards to the floor and Quinn was now up on his feet. And then onto the second step - higher than Doc - and in a more commanding position. But Doc thrust upward stabbing Quinn in the thigh. Quinn crumpled as he lost balance and fell forward onto Doc. Once more they writhed, rolling into the centre of the hall knocking chairs and ornaments off pedestals as they fought.

Quinn was suddenly conscious of the pain and wetness around his thigh.

The grapple continued, each man landing punches and chops. They rolled towards a wall - Doc on top. His free hand smashed Quinn's head against the panelling. Quinn blacked out momentarily - but it was enough for Doc, yet again, to be on his feet. Quinn flickered back to consciousness and Doc had the sword at his throat. A flicker of a winning smile crossed Doc's face; staring into Quinn's limpid eyes. The point of the blade pressed Quinn's flesh. Doc started to push the steel home into the soft, yielding flesh of the throat.

Smash! Cadogan crashed an urn over Doc's head – at that moment Quinn slid sideways as the blade met carpet. And Doc appeared to be out cold.

Quinn sat up. "I'm constantly grateful for intervention by my superiors."

They stared at each other. Perhaps they had reached a new understanding - even mutual respect.

The main doors burst open into the hall and two policemen put in a late appearance. Moving over to Doc, they were ready to handcuff him. Suddenly Doc lashed out with both hands, semi-closed fists contacting the lethal pressure point between their top lip and under their nose. Both men were floored. In that split second Doc was up and through the open door.

Outside Doc sprinted towards a police bike - now no longer occupied. He climbed on - it started and he was off towards the main drive.

Quinn had emerged, limping, from the building. The car driver from Quinn and Cadogan's earlier arrival at Chequers stood frozen, leaning against the saloon. Quinn rounded on him, "Get in. Start the bloody engine!"

The driver snapped out of it. Quinn shuffled towards the front passenger side and got in – his thigh preventing any control of the car. "Just give it all you've got!" Quinn bellowed.

The police motor bike screamed up the drive, crashing through the checkpoint barrier - the car following.

The motor bike sped left onto the country road, the car about a second and a half behind. The motor bike roared down the sunlit tubes of wooded Buckinghamshire roads - the leafy canopies dappling the grey asphalt with broken shade - the car on the bike's tail.

A motorbike will always outperform a car in a straight line but the bike's weakness is traction - two tyres in contact with the road with a patch no bigger than a lady's hand. A car has a four comparatively wide wheels – each tyre kissing the road surface with much more area than the bike. Any bends in the road start to swing the advantage to the car.

Through twists and turns the vehicles lurched and leaned. On they raced slowing to no less than eighty for the bends.
There was an opportunity for Doc - a fork in the road was coming up fast. He glanced in the mirror. The car had not yet emerged from around the last bend. He decided right. Still at full speed, he checked his mirror. No car.
And again. Still no car.
He permitted himself a small, satisfied smile. Glancing down once more at the mirror the car appeared in the far distance. The smile was replaced with a renewed, grim resolve. He accelerated even harder.
Inside the car, Quinn was surprised by the driver's skill. If anything, the car was gaining on the bike.
Doc slewed the bike off to the left into fairly dense woodland - the roar of its engine echoing through the trees as it traced a path between the trunks.
Quinn's car followed, lurching over the rough woodland floor. The route to follow the bike was longer as they could not cut though the trees so easily.
Doc pressed on – ahead, an ancient ditch. He powered on throwing the bike into mid-air crossing the twenty foot

wide dip. Quinn grabbed the wheel to take a detour to a shallower point. Doc just made it onto another road cutting through the trees. A look back and he saw Quinn's car emerging onto the road in the distance behind him.

Doc's right hand twisted squeezing out maximum power only to slam on the brakes to make a sharp left hander - the bike slewed round, control nearly lost but he just made it into another side road. Quinn's car got to the turning and squealed round.

Up ahead a three way fork loomed - but which way to go? Doc had to choose the middle – too fast to make the other turns. The car hurtled on, past farms and finally into open countryside. The road stretched out clearly up a hill in front of them.

In another part of the wood just further back all was peaceful. Birds were singing. A police motor bike lay partly hidden in the undergrowth - the cooling metal ticking. Dead still. Doc nowhere to be seen...

CHAPTER 7: Spanbauer

A thumb tapped on a stylish smartphone. A round head set on a thick neck sat on shoulders covered by an exquisitely cut jacket. The vulgar letterbox mouth pulsated into the device. A half-smoked cheroot was jammed between the stubby fingers.

To the back of the head - a small pony tail, the jet black hair was just too short to make a proper one, was held in place by what appeared to be a cluster of blue sapphires.

The face was tanned and wrinkled from expensive travel but very healthy. The eyes, though handsome, were unsettlingly too far apart - the right one very blue; a steely gaze into nothing. The left eye was false. It is as though someone had inserted a dark blue, shiny orb into the socket. There was no white or pupil to this eye. The opening between the lids just showed an area of polished, disturbing, glinting navy. The eyebrows were as though pencilled to the thinnest black arches.

A pair of rimless, square-lensed spectacles perched on the end of the nose. The right lens was normal, small - as though just for reading. The left lens matched the weird eye - a piece of opaque dark blue glass.

His tie was held by a chic, very opulent gold tie pin. The crisp white shirt, the tie pin also holding down the collar, and a suit of somewhat futuristic cut - dark and businesslike – enhanced his presence. The body was very powerful, athletic and muscular.

His fingers were festooned with ornate rings - one with a stone carved into an eye set into it.

His journey to where he was now had been complicated. An Austrian by birth he had suffered a lack of parental attention as his father's work for an oil company had taken his family all over the world. Making friends was not a life skill he had acquired – rather an ability to use people he met. An only child – and a lonely child – he had had to find ways to amuse himself for many a long day and night. As he grew the Devil found work for his idle hands. In an effort to get a buzz out of life he became involved with, what his parents would have called, the wrong type of people. From an early age he understood that life was based on money and money was obtained through business. His business acumen became noticed – particularly by the Mafia during a stint in Italy. There came a point when power became more intoxicating than money.

And then he found a business model that meant he could work for himself. It proved extremely successful...

He sat in a polished black leather, gold trimmed executive chair behind a marble desk...

In an unconcerned monotone, Dr Marius Spanbauer breathed into the phone. "Ah yes, his car exploded. You know the higher cost of dealing direct. You have your security to protect. So do I. Goodbye."

The accent was basically Canadian but with an almost Dutch lilt. The words were spaced somehow unnaturally. The voice precise, measured and deep - lowering in pitch on the last two syllables of each sentence.

He placed the smartphone on the desk and spread his hands on the angular dark marble - polished to a mirror. There was only a single sheet of paper in front of him.

The rest of the office was capacious. Half closed black blinds covered an enormous window. There were floor standing sculptures dotted around of very good quality, some plants, deep carpet, polished wood cabinets and waist high, polished dark wood panelling on the wall. And discreet light fittings.

There was a small control panel on the desk. It gently buzzed into life.

"Dr. Spanbauer, Fitzner arrives in fifteen."

Spanbauer rose from his desk towards some lift doors in his office. They slid open and he entered. The doors closed and the fast lift descended for a full six seconds. The doors then opened onto a small room with three big leather chairs with four-way, centre-buckle seat belts. There was a small desk, control panel and intercom. Spanbauer exited the lift, sat in a seat and fastened his belt. Pressing a button on his desk an inner door slid across the lift doors. He was in a small underground shuttle. A display on the wall showed 'km/h' and 'km'.

He pressed another button. The capsule was on the move - Spanbauer pressed back in his seat with the acceleration.

The shuttle floated on a 'MagLev' linear motor track. There was a sign saying 'DANGER - High Intensity Magnetic Field'. The craft was shaped aerodynamically; designed to move through the tunnel at great speed - the tunnel diameter only just big enough to allow the passage of the craft.

The displays showed 'km/h' reading 205 and rising. Elapsed 'km' was 1.6 and rising.

The capsule hurtled through the tunnel. The speed

indicator then dropped right down as the vehicle slowed. It stopped. 57 kilometres from the start.

And Spanbauer was inside another office, dimly lit. A false wall partition noiselessly slid back to cover the closed lift doors. There was a low table, chairs each side. To the side of one seat another control panel was set into a plinth. He sat by it. Another door was on the other side of the room opposite the lift.

Then a soft knock.

Two men entered. A wiry, hard-bitten individual – the other very frightened, pale and drawn. Spanbauer fixed the first man with his eye. The letterbox spoke, "Andreas Fitzner, welcome."

"Harvester, good-day. May I present Mr. Dave Lesko. He has had his operation. You wished to tell him its purpose."

"Andreas, thank you." Spanbauer moved his gaze to the timid wreck. "Mr. Lesko, since your capture you have been sedated for good reason. A little surgery was completed. You have a small device screwed to the underside of your collar bone."

Spanbauer reached for a switch and a monitor screen on the back wall behind Spanbauer flickered into life showing a map with a small flashing red dot. "This shows you current location, Mr. Lesko."

Lesko recoiled in horror. Spanbauer continued, "Your implant is also connected to certain spinal nerves direct to pain centres in your brain. Which reminds me of another feature..."

Spanbauer's hand reached for another switch.

Lesko jolted upright, eyes bulging and staring forward - his mouth contorted into a silent scream. Quivering and shuddering he couldn't breathe. Pure, agonising pain.

Spanbauer flicked off the switch and Lesko slumped

forward, gulping for air and slowly recovering.

Spanbauer's gaze did not move. "It also causes this temporary seizure. Interestingly, there is also a low frequency microphone transmitter embedded. We monitor all conversation." Spanbauer paused. "Oh, another setting causes instant death. Now, the question is, Mr. Lesko: do you feel the need to die for your country? Or will you join my 'virtual network' to share your information? Indecision is not an option."

Lesko barely summoned an angry, exhausted response, "Who the hell are you?"

Spanbauer steepled his fingers. "They call me 'Harvester'. In reality, I need no name. The world over, there are people with similar devices - often highly placed in governments and covert organisations. These people are my 'eyes' on the world's security. I am the 'Harvester of Eyes'. Spanbauer hardened. "To ensure your demise - feed me inaccuracies or explain your predicament to colleagues. You will surely die at my convenience."

Spanbauer looked at his watch. "By now, your Senator Craig Cline is dead through useful information - though the organisation which produced that spectacular was, of course, completely unconnected with me."

Lesko looked unnerved but curious. Spanbauer continued, "I will give you a little time to ponder loyalty - to your country - or to your life. Andreas, Mr. Lesko, thank you."

Fitzner stood and showed Lesko the door.

CHAPTER 8: Ladies & Bidding

In a stylish, expensive, Swiss coffee shop, Anastasia sat alone at a table looking at a menu. She was expertly dressed, her hair and make up beautifully executed. She exuded that confidence that comes with money and great beauty.

Another exquisite woman approached the table. She too looked calm and assured. Her name was Ghina Cunningham. Anastasia did not even look up as Ghina sat at the table.

Anastasia said, still without looking up, "Hello Ghina. Marius is very pleased with the diamonds. He got far more than the expected yield."

"Oh, that's good, Anastasia," Ghina replied with mock warmth.

A waiter approached. "Are you ready to order, Mesdames?"

Anastasia was. "Espresso, please. I'll also have the Chantilly Meringue."

He turned to Ghina.

"Espresso. And a ripe pear, thank you."

"God, you'll waste away," Anastasia proffered.

"You certainly won't." Ghina paused. "Marius has asked me to go to London on a 'very delicate mission'."

Still their eyes have not met. Anastasia tried to appear uninterested. "Doc was blown at Chequers. London is not 'favourite' at the moment. The British Secret Service knows."

"Marius is not happy. A certain Martin Quinn is involved. He comes highly recommended."

"So what?" Anastasia nearly grizzled.

There was a silence. The coffee arrived.

"So, I'm to trap him," Ghina almost crowed. "Quite a prize for Marius, wouldn't you agree?"

A tiny flicker of frosty disdain crossed Anastasia's face as she took the coffee cup to her lips. Ghina was the thorn in her side – a competitor who had followed much the same track as she had done in life - wealthy men succumbing to great beauty. Ghina's introduction had been through Doc. Apparently they had a fling – but Spanbauer was rather taken with Ghina...

The large room was almost dark. Tiny red and green lights created a small constellation on a wall. Suddenly, the wall was alive with a bank of screens as they switched into life. On each of the monitors was a face - a disturbing gallery of men and a couple of women. The faces displayed a broad ethnic mix – the only common factor could only be described as evil. The monitors formed a vaulting cathedral of faces.

The screens showed the jerky frame rate characteristic of video conferencing and webcams. Each had a red light underneath the screen and a sign on it saying 'BID'. The monitors were numbered – around forty of them.

Spanbauer stood erect at a lectern in the centre - almost

an 'altar'. He was not lit forming a silhouette against the bright monitors. He had the demeanour of a captain at the controls of some huge ocean liner.

He spoke, "Gentlemen...and Ladies...I would like to welcome some new customers joining my Auction of Intelligence Data... The Red Mafia, some Real IRA splinter groups, four new Middle Eastern Fundamentalist organisations, a couple of Japanese 'companies' and, in particular, a new representative from China. Welcome, one and all."

On the mention of China a face on a screen moved slightly with the recognition - an oriental man, youngish with a shock of black hair. He was clean shaven and looked extremely myopic wearing thick-lensed spectacles with heavy, chunky, black frames. It was Zhenxi Thaxoi.

Spanbauer collected himself. "Let us begin. Firstly, UK Trident submarines - schedules and routings for the next two calendar months. Shall we start at three hundred thousand US dollars?"

A number of 'BID' lights came on.

"Three-fifty?"

Most of the lights went out. Three remained.

"Four hundred thousand?" No lights. "Mmm, a little expensive, perhaps. There is no reserve on this one. Three-seven-five?" A single light came on from a swarthy Far-Eastern face. "Ah, Number 23. Sold. Thank you. Next, a rather engaging primer on the production of the USA's Delta 50 nerve agent. This describes in detail its safe production and mechanisms for clandestine release. Shall we start at six hundred thousand?" Spanbauer waited a second, invitingly, "It is the USA's most deadly compound..."

Around twelve lights came on. "Aah, a good level of interest." Then as a statement rather than an offer, "Seven hundred thousand."

Still twelve lights remained.

"Eight-fifty."

Only three lights blinked off.

"Gentlemen... ...and Lady." Then with a measured gravitas, "One million US dollars."

Five lights extinguished.

"A million, one-fifty?"

Only two remained.

"One million, three."

A single light glowed - a Middle Eastern gentleman. "Done - and worth every cent, Number 34. Now, drugs. Interpol, the CIA and a number of Far Eastern drug enforcement agencies regularly pool information. This..." Spanbauer held up a manila folder, "...is their latest report. Examine your trafficking risks at leisure. A quarter of a million."

A forest of lights came on.

"Mmm, more popular than I had imagined. Six hundred thousand dollars it shall be..."

And so the auction of terror continued. After fifty minutes of bidding on various tasty morsels of intelligence Spanbauer started to wind up the session.

"I've a selection of packages relevant to some particular groups' interests. Those who've purchased will be switched through to after-sales to arrange payment. To you good people, I *bid* you good-day. We will be in touch through the usual channels. Thank you."

Some of the screens flicked out.

Sunlight streamed through the floor-to-ceiling window. Anastasia contemplated the mountainous Peruvian cloud forest – the Urabamba valley stretched far into the east. It was a view to rank with the top ten in the world. Ghina found more to see in a glossy magazine as she lounged across a soft pale leather settee. Spanbauer appeared. "Ladies, enchanting to see you."

The women sprang over to clutch Spanbauer - an arm each. They planted fawning kisses on his cheeks. He was in heaven but he checked his thoughts reminding himself that the two of them had few values - except money and power. "I have presents for you both..."

Anastasia and Ghina yelped with delight. Spanbauer produced an obscenely large diamond twin set. "Anastasia, I couldn't sell all the diamonds."

He passed her the jewellery and dug in his pocket to retrieve a tiny black velvet pouch. "And I thought a few loose stones for you might be acceptable."

Anastasia was beside herself. "Marius, you are such a sweetie!"

Ghina is struggled to conceal the green within. But then her eyes lit up as Spanbauer produced a large fistful of high denomination bonds. "Ghina, my dear. Some negotiable bearer bonds to the value of around eight hundred thousand," he purred. Ghina reached for them. "No, Ghina, not yet. You have a task..."

Ghina's eyes blazed with purpose.

CHAPTER 9: London & Threats

In London the rain hammered on Cadogan's office window. Busy with papers at his desk, without looking up, he gestured the waiting Quinn into the chair opposite. "You're late, Quinn."

"I was waiting for the laserprinter."

"Lame, Quinn." He didn't believe the excuse – then he realised the pun. "How is the leg?"

"No real damage. Fine in a couple of days, according to the M.O."

"They found the real Devereux's body. I'm going to let you off the leash."

"To where, exactly?" probed Quinn. There were few leads.

Cadogan leant back. "Some infiltration, don't you think? Who is this 'Doc-Devereux' character? What about the link to your man 'Nipper'?"

Quinn précised from a file. "In summary, Doc was a brilliant pharmacology student - forced to leave after being caught with a selection of human body parts from dissection cadavers. Apparently, he was selling these to Birmingham gangsters who used them to frighten their victims' families. Very sick. In and out of prison...returned to gangland...manufacturing, selling lethal and addictive drugs. Real name: Quentin Donovan. Not much else. This was eight years ago. Nothing since."

"Birmingham? Home turf, eh?"

Quinn controlled himself at this unnecessary reference. Cadogan continued, "And Nipper?"

Quinn opened another file. "Less clear. Nipper...small time, nasty thug. Started as a night club bouncer - in Birmingham -" Quinn made the point, "- hence the link to Doc. Not very bright. A long history of damaging people rather inelegantly - the precise term is 'pithing'. Never been convicted - but he's linked to a number of killings. No word about him for over seven years."

"All the passengers on Wilcox's jumbo checked out. But Wilcox swears he saw Nipper," Cadogan ventured.

"Something told me that Wilcox might have been a target - especially as he was on his way to New York on this very matter."

Quinn's hunches were painful to Cadogan. Cadogan moved on. "And now Doc's flown. Must've had very high levels of inside knowledge to play Devereux. He knew all the background to this sporadic terrorist activity - and he knows we've got nothing."

"Therefore not working alone."

"Granted. His masters can't be happy with his blown cover. He'll have gone to ground."

"Perhaps Nipper's a better lead," said Quinn.

"Make sure your old chums in the Branch are onto it. Go home this afternoon - wrap a hot towel round your head and see if your instincts can come up with something more solid." Cadogan finished the meeting, his nose back in the papers.

Spanbauer steepled his fingers. He leaned back in his

chair, eyes closed facing the window behind his desk.

In front of his desk Doc sat looking blank..

Spanbauer talked to the window, the back of his chair faced Doc. "Difficult situation, isn't it, Doc? Through your errors, the British are sensitised. The quality of the information provided to our customers will suffer." Spanbauer spun round. "Any suggestions, Doc?"

Doc stared back blankly.

"For more than six years you have not failed me, Doc. You agreed at the start - everything at your own risk. This was made very clear. But we can only continue without mistakes."

Doc started to become nervous.

"I have devised a simple test of your resolve to continue. Ghina is tasked with the entrapment of Martin Quinn. Your job is to kill him. You love the human body so much. Bring me his eyes. If Ghina succeeds before you, Quinn becomes implanted and works for me. You die by my choice of one of your ingenious methods. Then I will take your eyes. Kill Quinn - then none of this happens. Is this clear?"

Doc just managed a shaky nod.

"Get out of my sight - you're losing time already," Spanbauer bellowed. And then, as Doc reached the lift door, "Test Lesko on your way. He's in the care of Fitzner."

Quinn swept out of a doorway into the bustling street, hand raised ready to hail a taxi. The tablet in his hand started to take his attention. As he crossed the pavement, he crashed into a woman. She was carrying an armful of paperwork and box files - these fell to the ground under the impact strewing paper everywhere over the paving slabs.

"Oh God. I'm most terribly sorry. Really, I didn't see you."

He helped her gather her things. She looked up into his eyes holding his entranced stare.

"It's all right. I wasn't looking. If you can just give me a hand with this lot," said Ghina Cunningham. She had made contact.

Quinn and Ghina, on hands and knees, picked up the papers. Passers by stepped over and around them. Quinn gave her the last few items as they stood up.

"I do apologise," Quinn said again.

A taxi pulled up from Quinn's initial hailing.

"Honestly, it's fine. Where's your cab going to? I need one too."

"Belgravia." The cab stopped – the driver poised for a destination. Quinn gestured towards the car for her to take it.

"Well, I'm off to Knightsbridge. We could share..." Ghina was exploring.

Quinn was smitten. He thought he somehow recognised her. He stood looking at her lost in thought. Then the bolt hit him. She reminded him of Jayne. His beloved Jayne. It was uncanny.

"Hello? We could share..." she said.

Quinn snapped out of it. "Sorry, yes. Er... please, after you..."

"Where to?" asked the cabbie.

"Knightsbridge," responded Quinn.

"Belgravia," said Ghina simultaneously. They laughed.

Quinn turned to the driver. "Knightbridge first, then Belgravia."

They got in. "So, what do you do...?" They both spoke together. Another laugh.

"No, you first," said Ghina.

"I was going to ask what you do when you're not having strange men crashing into you."

"Well, you're not *that* strange. I work for a Law Firm - desperately dull. My boss is away today - the rest of them promised they'd cover for me. And you?"

Quinn didn't want to stop being intoxicated. "Oh, we're an export consultancy. It's greasing the skids for businesses who want to sell stuff around the world."

"You get to travel a lot?"

"Yes, but the novelty wore off some years ago. Twenty-four hour delays in Jakarta are not recommended." Quinn inwardly cursed himself for using a standard recognition line.

So the engaging conversation continued without a pause until the taxi pulled up outside Harrods. Ghina got out. She was about to close the door. "What's your name?" She was suddenly very serious.

"Martin... ...Quinn." Again he checked himself. Never use the real name.

She smiled. "I don't normally do this to strange men - but here's my card. Call me - if you want. Thanks for the ride." And she was gone. Quinn held the card tightly – and surveyed it minutely...

Ghina D. Cunningham
Personal Assistant to Advocate Harvey Andrews
Blackwell, Andrews, Coleman, Scott
Great Clarendon Square
Regents Park
London NW2 6SG
Tel: 020-7493-7953
Fax: 020-7493-9831
Email: GhinaC@BACSlaw.co.uk

He turned the card over. There was a scribbled number on the back – 020-7323-2379. He put the card to his lips and his face broke into a broad smile.

The cab taxi pulled up outside an anonymous Georgian terrace. Quinn got out to pay the driver.

He put the key in his front door and went in. The hallway was tastefully appointed though not extravagant. "Hello, Avril. Back earlier than I'd expected," he called.

A voice came from within. "Ooh, Mr. Martin. Hello. I've just this minute finished. I'm in your drawing room." Quinn entered the room. Avril stood holding a duster in her hand. She was middle aged - straggly, white hair flowed down to her shoulders. As Quinn's trusted housekeeper she took great pride in 'doing for' the nice batchelor man. Houseproud, to Avril, was defined in the true nineteen-fifties way.

Quinn's 'drawing room' was restrained. Decorated with precision, one wall was covered with a neatly kept bookcase. There were some traditional paintings and a few ornaments and artefacts from around the world. A discreet sound system and television were to be seen. The furniture; limed oak and modern. A drinks cabinet dominated a bay window.

"Mr. Martin, I'm just off. Is there anything else?"

"Avril, what would I do without you? Thanks, but that's all. I'll see you tomorrow. Have a nice evening."

She bustled past. "Well, I'll be off then. Cheerio."

Quinn slumped into the sofa. He closed his eyes. There was the familiar click of the front door as Avril departed. He opened his eyes and grabbed a small picture frame from under a lamp on the coffee table. It was a photograph of a woman. Quinn stared at the picture - close to tears. His late wife, Jayne, smiled back – frozen in time. He studied her face. The similarity with Ghina was remarkable. He reached towards the telephone and then decided against it clutching the picture to his chest and stared into space.

CHAPTER 10: Extracting information

It was a room nightmares were made of. Dark, damp, airless and silent. The cool, wet walls were covered in green algae. The floor was partly mud and foetid. An ancient rusty metal door was the only access. To one side covering around a third of the floor area was a single bed. On it lay a mainly wet thin mush that must have once resembled a mattress. Lesko sat naked save for some slimy boxers – his head in his hands. It was a dark, frightening and gloomy space. Lesko sat on the corner of the bed, head in hands.

There came an echoey metallic grind and the cell door opened. Already, Doc, Fitzner and a heavy were onto him frogmarching him into a passage and into another room. A dull click and neon striplights flashed into life. The room was completely white.

In the centre stood a sturdy wooden chair bolted to the floor. Numerous leather restraining straps hung from it. To one side was a small table with a small black attaché case on it. Doc spoke, "Sit down, Mr. Lesko."

Fitzner and the heavy crashed Lesko into the seat with

gross force. And then, as though instructing a dog, "Stay..." With that, Lesko was buckled in – strapped and immobile.

Doc moved to the small table. "Mr. Lesko, allow me to introduce you to two of my friends, sodium amytal and sodium pentathol. Truth drugs have, historically, been an unreliable interrogation method - but in the hands of an expert can show a remarkable record of success." He opened the case and removed some phials and syringes. "Narcoanalysis, as this procedure should properly be called, is performed in phases. The drugs used are kept in a complex balance." He started to fill a number of syringes. Lesko recoiled in horror.

Doc continued, "First chlorpromazine..."

He grabbed Lesko's greasy, pinioned arm. Doc produced a leather lace and tied a tourniquet - the vein stood out. "This is a relatively old drug used for the treatment of psychotic illnesses working directly on the brain. It is particularly effective in calming the violently disturbed..." Doc pierced the proud vein and commenced injecting the fluid. "...without tranquillising. On a normal individual, however, fear diminishes and a feeling of alert relaxation follows."

Doc returned to the table. "Now for my two friends. These substances are administered to steer the subject towards unconsciousness whereupon a highly suggestible, childlike state ensues. At this point there is very little resistance to questioning. I will be using atropine and adrenaline to preserve the balance between sleep and wakefulness."

Lesko was nearly in shock with fear. Doc proceeded to inject him again as Lesko tried vainly to struggle. Doc gave him a toothy grin, "There's little point fighting it. This has not failed yet."

It is a sad fact that in any country with a copious archaeological heritage and weak government you will find shops selling treasures of antiquity to anyone who asks and has some dollars. Peru had too many of these 'outlets' haemorrhaging wonderful pieces even before the history professors and cataloguers could even guess their existence. Here was a display cabinet, beautifully lit, in one of these emporia in a Lima suburb. Ancient Inca treasure glittered under the pin spots - small stylised sculptures and dishes, some in gold. Gold ceremonial jewellery, polished and finely made. Rings, necklaces and bracelets; brooches and ornaments.

A sweaty, chubby American tourist intensely studied the items. He was standing in, essentially, a high class antique shop. It was dim but shafts of bright sunlight streamed through gaps in the shuttered windows. The floor was polished wood - but the general feel was a little dusty in the corners. A selection of ancient artefacts littered the place, some on stands; others propped up against the walls and more on shelves. Chubby tourist drawled a big Texan accent whilst his nose pressed the glass, "Say, these are just fabulous. Why don't you rent retail space in the centre of Lima - these would sell a treat. How much for the gold necklace with the eyes set in it?"

"These are priceless. Original Inca of course," said Spanbauer.

The American looked round - somewhat startled by Spanbauer's appearance. "What are they on display for if you're not selling them?"

"I did not say they were not for sale. They are only for sale to the right people. Are you a collector?"

The American became quickly irritated as one used to service and deference. "You're saying my money's not good enough? Hey, I'm collecting!" Then posturing, "So, how much?"

"I would have expected you to suggest a price. These are not factory outlet goods; these are antiquities."

"OK, Wise-ass. I give ya six hundred dollars U.S."

"I fear that you are a factor of a thousand out."

Another man entered the shop. Spanbauer noticed. He needed the American out of the shop. "Good-day. I trust you'll have an enjoyable holiday here with us in Peru. Now, if you'll excuse me..."

"Well excuse me!" Chubby indignantly stalked out of the shop an turned to look back at the discreet shop-front. He wanted to remember the name to tell his friends to avoid it if they ever found themselves in Lima. It was called 'Cornucopia'. "Well excuse me," he muttered to himself as a coca tea beckoned.

The man who entered the shop waited by a small table with a chair either side of it. He carried two well-used plastic carrier bags. They were full. He looked a little simple. He was young, local and his clothes were old and torn. He had an agricultural feel about him - very Peruvian Quechua. He made himself known. "Escuse. Sendero Luminoso."

Spanbauer turned. "So, you must be Diego, my friend sent from the Shining Path. What have you for me?"

They sat at the table opposite each other. Diego dug around in the bags and excitedly produced a bundle wrapped in yellowing newspaper. He proceeded to unwrap the object. It was a spectacular golden Inca headpiece. Spanbauer looked on, almost bored – emotionless.

Diego's eyes lit up. "See, is beautiful, no? Original head-dress. Inca gold. Made long time ago. Forty thousand dollars – U.S."

"It is certainly old," said Spanbauer casually examining the piece.

"The price. Is good? Yes?"

"The price is reasonable," Spanbauer replied dully.

"My elders sent me. I check money moved OK into elders' banco before you have gold."

"Of course, Diego. That was the agreement. Come!"

Spanbauer got up motioning Diego to follow. They moved towards the back of the shop. Spanbauer pulled a curtain across revealing a pair of shiny steel lift doors - incongruous against the old, faintly shabby shop. Spanbauer touched a panel by the lift. "Harvester," he said softly. The doors slid apart - the voice had been identified. They entered the lift and the doors closed. Diego felt uneasy - he never expected to be in such a high-tech place. As the lift rose, Spanbauer gave him an encouraging grin.

The lift stopped. The doors hissed open into an office of considerable elegance. Diego was agog – never during his life had he imagined such places existed - especially in a shop in the back streets of Lima.

"Diego, please be seated." Spanbauer gestured to a carved chair by a desk. "Your masters need proof that the money is transferred." A screen on the desk glowed. There was a telephone by the side of it. A menu for electronic cash transfer appeared on the monitor. "Diego, pick up the telephone. Describe what you see."

Spanbauer tapped away at a keyboard. The screen showed the following:

   H a/c 004366102: Credit : Debit

The text 'Credit' was highlighted. This highlighting then moved to 'Debit'.

A new line appeared:

   Enter currency:

Spanbauer keyed in: US$

> Enter amount:
> 40000
> Target A/c's   SP a/c 01808375

A whole string of account numbers appeared:

> 001235673
> 001235674
> 001235675
> 001235676
> 001235677
> 001235678
> 001235679
> 001808363
> 001808364

Meanwhile, Diego described the screens in Spanish down the phone line. He stopped. Then, to Spanbauer, "They say to give you a number." Spanbauer nodded acknowledgement. Diego continued, "Zero, zero, one, six, one, eight, eight, three, zero."

Spanbauer typed this in and it appeared on screen...

> H a/c 004366102   Debit
> 40000 US$
> SP A/c 001618830   Credit
> 40000 US$
> Press ENTER to irrevocably complete transaction:

Spanbauer pressed ENTER. Another message

appeared:

> Transaction confirmed and completed

"They say the money has appeared in banco," said Diego, the telephone still pressed to his ear.

"Good. Hang up, Diego."

"They say I not say anything about you. Is OK. I not say anything."

Spanbauer mimicked Diego's accent, "Is OK, Diego. You not say anything."

In a swift move, Slitz appeared silently behind Diego. Slitz had his blade ready. He grabbed Diego across the chest from behind. In a sudden move, he slashed Diego's throat deeply almost decapitating the man. Diego, blood gushing from his neck, slumped forward onto the carpet.

Some small drops of blood had splashed onto Spanbauer's desk. A single droplet landed on Spanbauer's cheek. He pulled a crisp white silk handkerchief from his suit breast pocket. Without a flinch, he wiped the blood from his cheek and then, in a casual manner, from the desk, he threw the silk onto the body and returned to his papers.

Slitz pulled Diego's chair aside. He knelt and pulled at the carpet. A inset in the main carpet lifted and the body was rolled up into the resultant section of rubber-backed material. Slitz picked up the body rolled up in the carpet and made for the lift.

Nipper appeared carrying a new piece of carpet which was set back on the floor. Nipper withdrew and, without a word or any emotion, Spanbauer continued his paperwork.

CHAPTER 11: Forensics

The two pathologists, Kingsley and Ferrante were in the midst of a post-mortem. It was a spotless, brightly lit, well-equipped path lab – the CIA's best. Kingsley was the more senior. As he bent over the body Ferrante had a clipboard taking notes. A microphone hung over the slab. "Most of us crave a quick, painless death, Ferrante. However, Harrison's was fast enough but agonising. I'll start the report and insert the toxicology stuff later when we're through." Kingsley busied himself with the body. "Deceased poisoned intravenously. Needle entry below left scapula into chest cavity. Obviously some very fast acting neurotoxin - and powerful. Signs of massive heart failure and general muscular seizure in the torso."

He straightened up and looked at Ferrante. "Suggest toxicology looks for naturally occurring substances - tetrodotoxin, curare and the like. Death would have occurred within two minutes owing to shock and lack of oxygen to the brain." He turned back to the body on the slab...

"He would have felt it all but unable to move or

scream," Ferrante noted.

Kingsley continued, "Injuries sustained in keeping with being bundled into the aircraft hold where the body was finally found. Body still in good shape since death. The Peruvian morgues look after their guests well."

The lab door opened. A female laboratory assistant entered. She too carried a clipboard. Without looking up Kingsley said, "Hello, Miss Cooper. Is it or is it not curare?"

Miss Cooper answered carefully, "If it was curare, the amount would never have killed him. The residuals would point to a lethal dose some eight hundred times smaller. Have you ever heard of a Box Jellyfish?"

Kingsley carried on - again without looking up. His eyebrows raised skywards.

A Beefeater (a Yeoman Warder correctly) escorted a party of tourists around The Tower of London. "And this is Traitors' Gate. You probably can't imagine the awful sense of foreboding when arriving here from the Thames. Many of the condemned would turn to see their last view of London as they entered – and they knew only a miracle could save them from the executioner's axe." The tour continued.

Ghina loitered trying not to be noticed. A clock struck in the middle distance. She glanced at her watch. A Yeoman Warder approached her. "Can I help you, Madam?"

Ghina started, "Oh...er...yes. This is Traitors' Gate, isn't it?"

"Yes, my dear."

"Oh, good. I'm waiting for my friend. He was desperate for a coffee. I said I'd wait here. Soak up the atmosphere and all that...oh, here he is now."

Doc approached carrying a steaming coffee in a polystyrene cup. He acknowledged Ghina.

"Sorry to disturb you, madam. Enjoy the Tower." The Warder walked away.

"Where were you? It's gone 11 o'clock," Ghina hissed.

"Spanbauer said we should meet," said Doc.

They moved off joining another group of visitors – their conversation low...

"Oh, really? I've never seen him more angry. Why are you back in England?" Ghina probed.

"A support role. If the going gets too hot for you, I might be around to save you neck." He leered at her. He did not conceal that he was infatuated with her. And she did not want the attention.

"I can look after myself, I'm a big girl now."

"Reckon you'll catch Quinn, eh? Not much of a catch really. Let me sort it out for you."

"Marius gave me specific instructions. Quinn is to be implanted. Marius will use him as fit and sell his information. That's it," Ghina countered.

"You need some lunch. I've found a great little place not far from here. Then we might find a hotel room..."

Ghina nearly wretched. "I think not, Doc. You're just a lecherous misfit. Find someone else to play with while I get on with my job." She turned to walk off. Doc viciously grabbed her by the arm. Ghina locked eyes with him. "Take your fucking hand off me right now. Even Quinn has more charm than you ever had."

Doc was wide-eyed, "Listen to me, Ghina. We had something. I'm not out to let it go."

"Are you threatening me? Why don't you clear off back to your drugs?" This cut through and, after a beat, Doc released her arm.

He turned to walk off. "I'm not done yet."

Ghina stared, rooted to the spot.

An RAF Dominie taxied up to the Washington Dulles general aviation terminal building. A black sedan raced out to meet it. The aircraft door opened as the car stopped. As the driver got out he donned a pair of sunglasses. Wilcox breezed down the aircraft steps and greeted the driver who extended a hand to carry the bags. In a flawless American accent, Nipper smiled his line, "Mr. Wilcox, hi! Welcome to sunny New York."

"Where are we off to?" Wilcox basked in the moment as he seldom got to fly by private jet.

"We've got a fair drive to the Le Parker Meridien on 57th. You'll meet the reception committee then - meantimes, make yourself comfortable. Just relax and enjoy the ride." Nipper was enjoying his part as the driver.

Wilcox climbed in the back of the car and Nipper went round the back of the vehicle to open the trunk for the luggage. A face of a man stared blankly out - partly covered by the bags. The original driver looked like a broken rag doll, legs and arms at crazy angles. Nipper had to break the limbs to fit the body in. With the trunk slammed shut, Nipper got in and drove off.

CHAPTER 12: Employment history

Three receptionists answered a stream of calls behind a low counter in fairly modern, but average, offices - a law firm. It was pleasant enough with plants, sofas, the occasional picture and an awards cabinet. A few people waited for their appointments. The mantra of answering the phone bubbled across the foyer - "Good afternoon, Blackwell, Andrews, Coleman, Scott; can I help you?"

Swing doors connected the reception area to the London street. A well dressed, middle-aged lady entered. She walked purposefully up to the desk. A receptionist caught her eye as she finished taking a call. "Hello, madam. Can I help you?"

"Yes, I've an appointment with Mr. Coleman. My name is Miss Marion Moffat. I'm sorry but I'm a few minutes late. It's about Moffat versus Eclipse Decorating Services."

"If you'd like to sign in, Miss Moffat..."

Harvey Andrews, a partner, put his head around an adjoining door and in true doctor's surgery fashion announced, "Mr. Balfour?"

Mr. Balfour got up from a sofa. "Mr. Andrews. And how are you? Cases going well I trust?" They greeted each other shaking hands.

A receptionist picked up a call, "Good Afternoon, Blackwell, Andrews, Coleman, Scott. Can I help you? ..... I'm sorry, but Mr. Andrews has just gone into a meeting. Can I take a message? ..... No, you're out of luck again, Ghina Cunningham is on holiday today. ..... I'll see what I can do. Please hold for a moment." Another pause and she made an internal call. "Hello, Violet. It's Tina on reception. I've got the tax office on the line - something connected with a tax refund. ..... I'll put him through." She switched back to original call. "Sorry to keep you, I'm transferring you to Violet Evans. She'll help you."

A small, rather tatty office was occupied by a bewigged dragon of a woman. It was a rather portly Violet Evans. Surrounded by filing cabinets, she wore pointy, fifties, horn-rimmed glasses with a gold spectacle chain. There was a vaguely untrustworthy air about her. She prided herself on being the HR scourge of the unjustified expenses claim. Wearing a telephone headset she picked up the call. "Hello, can I help, Mr..er...?" A pause. "Oh, I see, Mr. Quartermain. A tax error? Well let's hope it's in her favour. Let me call up her details on screen." She typed in 'Cunningham' and the record popped up. Then a flashing message: 'Associate: MS'. Evans' attitude visibly changed when she saw this. Evan's responded in the flattest tone she could muster, "Joined us six years ago at the beginning of this month. Is that all you require, Mr. Quartermain? ..... Good, well I'm sure Miss Cunningham will look forward to hearing from you. Goodbye."

She rocked gently back in her chair thinking for a moment – then leaned forward and dialled an international number.

'Paris House' is an oak beamed folly set in the grounds of Woburn Abbey, Bedfordshire. It is a truly spectacular restaurant set amongst trees and deer. It is accessed by a long, sweeping drive beyond a walled arched gate with a lodge house. The food is stunning.

Quinn's black Jaguar purred through the arch and along the expanse of gravel. A glorious evening, the sun was setting and the heat of the day was just cooling to comfortable levels.

The car stopped by the building. Quinn and Ghina got out to be greeted by the chef de maison, Peter Carter.

"Peter, lovely to see you again. This is Ghina."

"Enchanted," said Carter as he kissed her hand. "Mr. Quinn, we've a fabulous meal for you this evening. Perhaps some champagne on the terrace. There are menus waiting."

Quinn whispered in Ghina's ear, "Peter Carter is the finest chef in all England - or so he tells me."

They laughed.

On the small terrace, the champagne had been poured. The terrace was bounded by carved, stone balustrades adorned with small statues. The deer barked in the distance and the Tudor black beams set amongst the red brickwork formed a classic backdrop. Quinn and Ghina sat on white enamelled, cast iron chairs looking out across the grounds. The table, in the same style, had a white parasol erected through its centre.

They clinked glasses and sipped. Ghina gazed across the grounds. "Martin, this is simply wonderful." The deer grazed nearby, the trees hushed in the warm breeze, the pale orange sky turned deep blue and the evening birds sang. A group of bats flitted in tight circles and wheeling swifts screeched as they grabbed insects on the wing.

A waiter approached.

Quinn studied the menu. "I know what I'm having tonight." He didn't look up but Ghina cast a small, knowing glance at him. "OK, I'll start with the wild mushrooms and foie gras set in the puff pastry shells with tarragon cream. The sole parcels seem appropriate to follow. Then the cherry Madeira duck."

"Excellent choice, sir. And for Madam?"

Ghina fixed her eyes on Quinn. "Mmm, terrific." And then to the waiter, "The same, please."

The sommelier appeared at the waiter's side. "Chef has a case of very special Sancerre just in. Very young, very flinty - a spectacular wine for this glorious evening. Then, a particularly excellent, well-aged, 1982 Premier Cru Margaux."

"Tell Peter I override his choice at my peril," but Quinn's mind was elsewhere.

The sommelier nodded acknowledgement and departed.

They brought the champagne glasses to their lips simultaneously.

An hour or so later Ghina finished a sip of coffee. "That was the best meal." Her face furrowed. Quinn seemed distant. "Martin, are you OK?"

He snapped out of it. "Sorry. It's just that... ...you remind me of someone I once knew."

Ghina flashed a hurt frown.

"No, no, it's OK, she was a wonderful person. She died a few years ago. It's a compliment, believe me."

Ghina took Quinn's hand and kissed it. Quinn grabbed her hand across the table and squeezed it as though drawing comfort. Quinn renewed his energy, "I almost forgot. Can you get away for a long weekend...this weekend?"

"I'd nothing on."

Quinn fumbled inside his jacket pocket and produced two plane tickets. "It seems as though we're off to Edinburgh."

"Oh, Martin. That's so sweet of you."

"I was hoping you'd have nothing on..."

They exchanged a knowing glance.

Back in Belgravia, Quinn's car was parked outside the terrace. It was quiet - but two upstairs windows were lit - the curtains drawn.

Doc appeared from the shadows. He wore a dark, close fitting suit. He extracted a balaclava and pulled it on - just eyeholes and a mouth-hole. He dashed silently over to the frontage looking intently for ways up to the lit window. He spotted a drainpipe and darted over towards it. From his belt he withdrew an automatic pistol with a silencer attached.

Inside, Ghina and Quinn were entwined on the sofa, gently kissing. They began to undress each other.

Doc shinned up the drainpipe.

Quinn began nibbling Ghina's earlobe whilst Doc settled on a ledge outside the window.

"Martin?"

Quinn nuzzled into her neck. "Mmm, yes?"

"We need a drink." They break the clinch.

"Good idea. What do you fancy?"

"A long G and T would lubricate nicely!" Quinn gave her a sideways look and got up and walked towards the drinks cabinet by the window.

Doc produced two small objects from a pocket. One was a small rubber sucker which he stuck to the window. The other was a small device - much like a pen - with a length of thread attached. He wound some of the tread around the now stuck suction cup and took the cap off the 'pen'. It looked like a white tipped marker. He used the thread like a compass to scribe a circle about twenty centimetres in diameter with the 'pen' around the sucker onto the glass. As the tip touched the glass the fluid it deposited started to smoke and fizz. The pen contained a liquid which ate into glass.

Shadows moved behind the window curtain. Quinn was fixing the drink, facing the drinks cabinet – and the window. He turned to Ghina. "Lemon?"

Ghina lay on the sofa, eyes closed. "Mmm. Please."

Outside Doc gently tugged on the sucker. It came away silently, complete with a circle of glass – it's rim still fizzing. The shadow was still at the window. Doc carefully set the glass down on the other side of the ledge and retrieved the silenced gun from his belt.

Quinn placed slices of lemon in two gin and tonics.

Doc's gloved hand inserted the snout of the gun through the hole in the window. The hole was directly behind the shadow. He flicked the safety catch to 'off.'

Quinn was about to pick up the glasses. Ghina subconsciously licked her lips with expectancy of the drink. Quinn paused to swirl the ice round to cool the drinks.

Outside, Doc's forefinger of his right hand repeatedly squeezed the trigger...

PHUD! PHUD! PHUD! PHUD! PHUD! PHUD! PHUD! PHUD! PHUD! PHUD! PHUD! PHUD!

Twelve silenced shots blasted the curtain. The automatic spent its load. The shadow slumped to the floor. Doc slid down the drainpipe, jumping the last couple of metres and silently pelted across the road.

He made it round the corner of an adjoining street and climbed into a car. The key was in the ignition and he pulled away gently into the night, switching on his lights after he had moved off.

The disused quarry was a huge flooded amphitheatre. 'DEEP WATER' notices surrounded the boundary paths on the vertical sides of the workings. Abandoned quarrying equipment rusted quietly. 1-800-PLANT had no use for it any longer. The breeze whipped up puffs of white dust. The nearest human life might have been in the buildings that formed the Manhattan skyline over the other side of the Hudson Bay.

A black sedan appeared and pulled to a halt at the edge of a precipitous bank. All its windows buzzed down.

Nipper got out and stretched in the sun. Wilcox's body sprawled across the back seat - he has been pithed through the back of the head.

Before Nipper closed his door, he peeled off his sunglasses and threw them into the body of the car. He reached in, released the handbrake and slammed the door. The car started to move almost imperceptibly, gathered a little more momentum and rolled over the edge. Nipper gave it a helping foot.

The car plummeted down into the water briefly catching the side of the gigantic pit with a sickening crunch. It hit the thick, muddy water with a deep splash - and sank with surprising rapidity. Nipper, squinting against the sunlight and the dust, leaned over the edge to check that the car had disappeared. The only visible evidence was a stream of dying bubbles breaking the murky surface. He walked off wiping the dust from his hands.

The last 32B London Transport bus of the night trundled past a nondescript office building. On the fifth floor Cadogan was still at his paperwork. His second marriage had broken down and, truth be told, he was a very lonely man. Outside of his work he found interacting with people difficult and, frankly, to be avoided if possible. So he sought solace in his work. He gave everything to it. His staff, however, did not understand these reasons for his seemingly endless dedication to duty. By the water coolers it was sometimes noted that no-one had met any of his family. Some ventured that he had refused invitations to dinner. The only thing that was agreed was that working for Cadogan was oppressive - he was brilliant at ruining his subordinates' home life and very tiring owing to his boundless attention to detail and process.

Edmondson, face lined and in shirt sleeves burst in...
Cadogan jolted round. "Edmondson?!"
"Thank God you're still here. I think we've lost one."
"No. Can't be, surely..."

The sky was only just brightening with a steely dawn. A number of police vehicles were parked around Quinn's car. White-suited forensic experts examined the holed window on an extended cherry picker.

Policemen went in and out of the terrace entrance. There was a policeman on duty guarding the doorway.

In Quinn's kitchen Ghina was fully dressed. She looked pressured. She opened the refrigerator, whipped out a carton of orange juice and poured some into a glass. She swigged down the liquid at speed, looked at her watch and grimaced.

She turned on her heel walking swiftly out of the kitchen into Quinn's bedroom. She pulled back the curtains without looking out. The dull light penetrated the darkness a little. Quinn was still languishing in bed, face partly buried in a pillow. He had just been woken.

"Martin, got to go. It's late."
"I thought you'd need some breakfast."

Ghina grabbed her handbag. "No, I've had some juice." She walked over to the bed and planted an affectionate kiss on him. "All hell's going to break loose if I miss this morning's meeting." She made her way to the bedroom door. "Thanks for a wonderful evening, Martin. Got to dash."

Ghina went down to the front door and pulled it open. Standing on the other side were two uniformed policemen about to ring the doorbell.

"Oh, good morning, madam. Is, er, Mr. Quinn in?" asked one of them.

Ghina was surprised and shocked but controlled herself well. "Er, yes." She turned back into the house. "Martin, there are a couple of policemen here."

Quinn appeared in the hallway in a dressing gown, tousled.

"Mr. Quinn? Sorry to intrude..."

Quinn gestured them in and lead them all from the hallway to the kitchen. He started a coffee machine going. The policemen and Ghina sat round the kitchen table. Ghina hid her nervousness convincingly.

"Coffee?"

There were murmurs of acceptance.

The second policeman began. "Anything strange happen last night, sir?"

"No, we went for a meal yesterday evening. Got back around one-thirty. Had a nightcap and went to bed."

Ghina began to look more relieved.

"And you both stayed here all last night?"

"Yes."

She motioned to leave.

The policeman instantly picked up on this. "Madam, can you leave an address and a number with my colleague in case we have to contact you again?"

"Why of course." She produced a card from her bag. "What's happened? Is there a problem?"

"There was an incident in another flat last night. We're just checking if anyone heard anything."

"Incident?" Ghina calmly enquired.

"I can't say at present. You'll get to hear the full details later I'm sure. Thank you, madam."

"I can go to work then?"

"Please do. And thank you for your co-operation."

Ghina tossed a mystified look across to Quinn who returned the same.

Quinn spoke, "Ghina, I'll call." And she was gone. "Now, gentlemen, what can I do for you?"

The policemen looked across at each other. "Er, Mr. Quinn... ...I've some bad news for you. There's never an easy way to do this. We were called in the small hours from another resident downstairs. There was a commotion... ...your housekeeper was murdered last night. We were told how close you were."

"Avril?" Nothing had sunk in yet. "But..." His brow creased. He froze. Thoughts crossed his face. He began to realise how important Avril was to him - the fundamental part of the stability of the 'normal' side to his life.

The policemen looked on sympathetically. One of them got up and poured Quinn a black coffee. Quinn sipped it staring into space.

Avril's lounge was swarming with forensic men and police. A white-suited photographer stood taking flash photos. The curtains closed - there was a series of nasty burnt holes in the material. Avril lay motionless, face down and riddled with bullets in pools of blood. The flashes continued.

Doc would have been annoyed at shooting the wrong target.

CHAPTER 13: Tattoo

Cadogan and Quinn sat opposite each other in Cadogan's office. Quinn looked shattered clutching a drink in his hand. Cadogan had to speak. "I know it's tough." He paused. "D'you think you were the target?"

Quinn looked down into the cup. "Possibly... ...probably. As Wilcox failed to report he could have been captured. He knew where I live. There are plenty who need to settle debts."

"And what about this woman, Ghina Cunningham?"

"No, she checked out OK. I confirmed she'd been working as a P.A. at some law firm for six years. I was discreet. I made a tax enquiry."

"A sleeper?" Cadogan probed.

"Who knows? Who ever knows?"

"Quentin Donovan - our friend Doc?"

Quinn looked up at Cadogan. "Blown. I wouldn't expect him to surface so quickly. Perhaps he's been sent back into the breech to finish the job."

"Mmm... he thinks he's done the deed. Let's keep it that way for a while. You need to disappear for a few days -

come to terms with things. We won't issue anything about Avril just yet. Better that way, eh? In case you were the target."

"I had thought about Edinburgh. That's where Avril was born. London was never good enough for her." Quinn got to his feet.

"Stay in touch." Cadogan didn't look up.

A British Airways 737 taxied to its pier at Edinburgh Airport.

There are many romantic things that can be done in the city. Holyrood House has some spectacular gardens. Jenner's department store can lighten any wallet in the most traditional way. The Firth of Forth coastal path offers some remarkable views of the bridges. Excellent lunches are served at the Acanthus Bistro. The National Gallery of Scotland rivals the Tate for the quality of the works on display. Arthur's Seat boasts a simply breathtaking panorama from the top. And Quinn and Ghina managed to do all of these things.

"What shall we do this evening, Martin?" asked Ghina as they got back to the foot of Arthur's Seat.

"Oh, sorry, I forgot to mention, there's a Tattoo we must attend."

"You've got tickets??? You never said!!"

Edinburgh's Military Tattoo is held within the main square of Edinburgh Castle – a dramatic monument at any time but particularly impressive at dusk when the façade is lit by the floodlights of the Tattoo against the darkening blue sky. The performances running nightly through most of August each year are an orgy of military entertainment from Britain and the Commonwealth. 'Acts' include massed pipe and drum bands marching in complex patterns across the castle esplanade. Or flashy Gurkha Kukuri routines or the ever popular gun carriage races where teams of enormously fit young men carry the component parts of weighty gun carriages over impossible obstacles culminating in their assembly and firing. It is a noisy, glittering couple of hours and good seats are hard to come by even a year out. Temporary arena seating is erected in the fashion of a steep-raked, squared-off horseshoe on three sides surrounding the sand covered esplanade. The horseshoe is divided into seventeen sections of seating reaching a dizzy height of some twenty-eight rows. The organisers try to arrange an orderly queuing system at the castle entrance but it always ends up as a frustrating wait.

Crowds were milling around trying to jump the lines of patient 'tattooists'. Quinn had paid rather more than the usual market rate to ensure some 'fast track' service through some of his old military contacts.

People poured through the ticket booths and into the maze of staircases under the seating. Quinn and Ghina made their way to Block 13, G22 and G23. Security staff checked tickets and helped to guide the crowds to their places. Some way behind Quinn and Ghina, one of these operatives checked the tickets of a young family and sent them on their way. Then a middle aged couple and then Doc...

Quinn and Ghina chatted as the dimming floodlights curtailed their conversation. The main arena lights came up – dazzling tracks of red, white and blue. The castle gates swung open and an ear-splitting roll of snare drums announced the arrival of a massed pipe band playing 'Scotland the Brave.' The men marched and wheeled to the continuous applause of the crowd. There was a spare seat directly behind Quinn. A man muttered 'excuse mes' along the row as people stood to let him pass to the unoccupied H22. Doc had made it – the seat flipped down as he sat and he permitted himself a broad smile.

Another marching band entered – this time the white-helmeted Marines. More cheers and applause. The drumstick tips left the drummers' nostrils as they made contact with the taut snare skins – the white leather gauntlets a blur as showy rolls announced the next number. Quinn and Ghina sat enthralled - Quinn's usual guard down a few notches from the norm.

Doc tilted slightly forward in his seat. There was the glint of a hollow needle – the syringe held concealed - but ready. The Marines tracked directly past block thirteen – Quinn was transfixed.

In the blink of an eye, Doc lunged stabbing Quinn in the back with the deadly needle. But the jab was not quite centred and the needle bent, then collapsed - breaking to the left. The jellyfish toxin dribbled out harmlessly on the back of Quinn's jacket.

Quinn whipped round grabbing Doc's arm. Quinn dragged him forward using the momentum. Ghina started. Quinn's move was so powerful that Doc tumbled head-over-heels into the people in the row in front of Quinn. There was surprise and annoyance in the audience around the incident.

Doc recovered quickly and clambered back to grapple with Quinn. Quinn broke free and shuffled along the row to an aisle. Doc followed lashing out at people in his way.

Quinn raced up the aisle towards the back, highest row. Doc chased, gun already out. In one smooth movement Quinn flipped himself over the rails at the top of the aisle so that he was underneath the temporary seating. It had a tubular steel scaffolding structure forming the supporting gantry. It was dark save for many shafts of light leaking through the seating floor planks. Quinn hanging free, swung crazily to get a foothold under the seats.

THUD! THUD! THUD! Doc started firing shots though the flooring. Quinn jinked madly underneath to avoid the bullets. The audience in the vicinity started to react to the pandemonium.

Doc stood still, head cocked unconcerned knowing time was on his side whilst onlookers tried to assimilate what was happening. He was not certain he had shot Quinn. Quinn hung motionless. Slowly, Doc carefully peered over the top rail to see if he could make out anything underneath but it was too dark.

Very gingerly, Doc launched himself over the top rail. Just as he got underneath, Quinn swung a kick into Doc's chest. Doc lost his grip and started to fall but managed to grab hold of some structure below.

Doc, now fixed on Quinn, started to climb towards him. Quinn managed a foothold and climbed downwards and inwards under the seating but he was still hanging - his back facing the ground as he clawed for hand holds.

THUD! PZZING! A shot ricocheted off a steel tube. Doc took aim and fired again - THUD! PZZANG!

Quinn's mind raced. He had to get down to ground level to at least have a chance. He made it down another tier. THUD!

Doc was now gaining on him. THUD! THUD! PZZING! Quinn lost his grip - he fell but landed awkwardly groaning into a crumpled heap. THUD! THUD! Still Doc's shots rang out.

Doc paused to climb down further. Quinn was not up yet. THUD! Quinn managed to muster the energy to roll out of the bullet's path. He rolled again. THUD! Another shot just missed him.

Doc, now down on the ground, brandished the weapon straight at Quinn. "Looks like this is it, Quinn." Doc allowed himself a sneer. The gun was pointing directly at Quinn's head from about three metres.

"Kill a man when he's down, would you?" Quinn said almost to himself.

"Oh yes, without the slightest hesitation..." Doc moved slowly towards Quinn. "But I always like to minimise the chances of failure." The dull snout of the gun wandered ever closer to Quinn. Doc was now upon him, putting his knee in Quinn's back and jabbing the weapon into Quinn's temple - Quinn pinned face down.

"Failed to needle me, eh?" Quinn ventured.

"It's a shame. I wanted something far more lingering for you." Doc's index finger started to apply pressure on the trigger. Quinn thought about preparing to die. The military music swelled and swirled as the trigger started to move the tiny bar of metal within the gun mechanism a whisker away from releasing the sprung pin into the back of the bullet casing.

Doc decided and the finger pulled all the way...

...click...

"It was twelve," Quinn confirmed to Doc.

Incensed, Doc launched a boot into Quinn. Quinn groaned.

Doc drew himself up to his full height ready to kick once more. This time Quinn struck out, lashing his legs into Doc's. Doc toppled to the ground and Quinn was up. Quinn kicked into Doc's back but Doc was up on his feet too.

A frenzy of fists ensued - no man really gaining any advantage except both were starting to tire.

Doc ducked to avoid a right cross from Quinn. As

Quinn missed it sent him slightly off balance whilst Doc decided to make a run for it.

Doc sprinted off towards the castle diving to dodge the supporting seating poles. Quinn was close on his tail. They lurched through the surreal steel scaffolding uprights of the underseating area amongst darting shafts of light. Pipes and drums washed over like an ocean.

Ahead, Doc saw a small open door in the castle wall. The official sitting by it to prevent unauthorised entry was already half on his feet. Doc delivered a massive uppercut flooring the man – dived for the aperture and he was in. Quinn followed.

Through the door was a gloomy spiral staircase going up – footsteps drowned by the pomp from the esplanade. The steps ended at a door set into a wall behind some glass display cases with mannequins dressed in period military uniforms – part of the castle museum. Doc entered first. The room was only dimly lit with emergency lighting. He stopped briefly to get his bearings. There was a pike propped in the hand of a model soldier in a display case. He grabbed a chair and smashed the cabinet to retrieve the weapon. Alarm sirens instantly sounded. He dashed to the far side of the room and crouched behind a display. He could just see the open door through the glass between the exhibits.

Quinn entered and stopped dead. Instantly wary he noticed the smashed cabinet and empty-handed mannequin.

Quinn started to pace carefully along the rows of cabinets. Doc still had sight lines. Quinn walked towards him - not realising the unseen danger.

Suddenly Quinn sidestepped momentarily out of Doc's view and Quinn found himself by a full size dummy of a soldier with a rifle and bayonet attached. It was not in a case. In a silent, swift move, Quinn released the bayonet and carried it dagger fashion.

Quinn continued to move across the rows of cabinets - still very wary. Doc got a glimpse and then lost sight of him again. Quinn now changed direction again - and again. He stopped. Below, Doc's feet were protruding from behind a plinth.

Very carefully, Quinn motioned closer to the feet - crouching as he went. Now on all-fours, he slowly crawled forward. Level with the feet and, inch-by-inch, he leaned forward putting his head round the corner of the plinth to see Doc's back. Quinn readied the bayonet.

A small polished brass corner fitting in front of Doc reflected Quinn's head. Doc span round but was too close to Quinn to use the pike. Doc saw the bayonet and lunged grabbing Quinn's wrist to prevent him stabbing with the blade. They grappled on the floor, rolling and crashing side-to-side. A display cabinet fell away from them smashing to the floor. They rolled back and forth toppling two nearby suits of armour.

The alarm sirens were still squealing and now three quite burly security guards were in the room from another door. They bounded over to the commotion and attempted to split up the protagonists, each one taking on a man. They manage to prise Quinn and Doc apart and were joined by three more men who instantly assisted.

After a short struggle Quinn and Doc were effectively separated and disarmed.

A guard spoke, "What have we here? A couple of tearaways old enough to know better."

Suddenly, Doc made a drop, spinning this way and that - he broke free and darted through the door through which the security men entered. A couple of his captors gave chase.

"Let me go! British Secret Service. That man's a terrorist," Quinn shouted.

"Yeah, and my auntie's Bin Laden," came the reply.

Doc pelted past a series of displays. Out of sight of the security men, he dived into a shadowy corner. The guards raced past missing him.

The sound of military music swelled.

Doc sat thinking. He was by a life size model of a hussar, complete with helmet. He grabbed the helmet and started taking off his jacket.

Outside, the forecourt was full of ceremonially-clad Tattoo performers milling around waiting for their appearance in the main arena.

A small door opened onto the forecourt Doc emerged with the helmet and the swapped military jacket on. He walked casually into the mêlée lost in the crowd.

By the same door, Quinn and three security men entered the forecourt straining to find Doc. He had convinced them of his authenticity but lost precious time.

Across the other side of the forecourt, a shadowy figure appeared from the crowd - minus ceremonial helmet - making his way up the steps to the ramparts.

Quinn scanned the area. He just noticed the figure disappearing up the steps. "Gotcha!" he said under his breath. He broke from the security men and plunged into the mass of uniformed soldiers. After what seemed an eternity of bustling through, Quinn made it across the forecourt. He bounded up the steps to the ramparts.

Doc sat in an alcove dimly lit by the castle floodlights. Gun in hand, he slipped in a new clip.

Quinn paused at the top of the steps on the ramparts. Cold, dark, save for the odd sweep of a floodlight, and it was windy. It started to rain. He strode onto the battlements following his man...

The Tattoo was still in full swing. Patriotic, stirring music from the marching bands echoed up from below.

Elsewhere from a high vantage point overlooking the esplanade, an unusual view of the Tattoo was played out - through a telescopic sight of a muzzled high velocity rifle. The cross hairs lingered for a while on some musicians in their dress uniforms. Small artillery guns were wheeled into the arena ready to fire blanks to punctuate the music. To the shooter, the loud music had all but disappeared with the concentration on the job to be done. The view through the gun sight crawled up into the watching audience searching for its target.

Up on the ramparts Quinn walked stealthily, checking alcoves and shadows.

Doc sat hidden nursing his loaded gun.

The rifle sight lazily moved up an aisle between the seats to the top back row. Ghina stood at the top, one minute looking over the railing at the back - the next scanning the crowds. She looked worried.

The cross-hairs settled on Ghina's head.

Back on the ramparts Quinn's shadow fell across the crouching Doc. Quinn had unwittingly overtaken him. Doc rose gently from his hiding place and stood aiming squarely at Quinn as Quinn walked further on. Doc held the pistol two-handed police style, legs spread – he was not going to miss.

The rifle cross-hairs were still centred on the anxious Ghina. The sniper appeared in no hurry.

Artillery guns were being ceremonially manned and loaded. Still the sniper waited. A sergeant gave the all clear to fire.

Doc still stood rock solid, gun aimed. He yelled above the wind, "Put your hands right up into the air and turn round very slowly. New clip and a dozen to shoot."

Quinn froze then turned around, hands aloft. "I'd hate to think you were bluffing."

THUD! PZZING! Doc loosed one off at Quinn's feet. "Only eleven now."

"Get to keep your job if you kill me, eh?" said Quinn.

"Either way you lose, Quinn. Ghina's your honey trap. Edinburgh's great this time of year - 'Let's have a long weekend.' This'll be your longest. In seconds, Cunningham is dead meat too."

BOOM! Back down on the esplanade the first blank of the artillery gun barrage was set off. CRACK! Almost simultaneously the rifle fired, the recoil causing the view through the sight to flip upwards. The sight was controlled back to the target.

BOOM! BOOM! The barrage continued.

Still through the sight, Ghina was now on the floor of the aisle - obviously hit. The audience nearby had sensed she was in trouble. The cross-hairs settled once again on Ghina.

BOOM! spoke the artillery guns. CRACK! answered the rifle. The shooter brought the smoking rifle down from her eye. Anastasia, perched high on the battlements folded the rifle ready to make good her escape. A satisfied smile played on her lips.

BOOM! The barrage continued. Doc fired – THUD! Quinn dropped. Doc missed - he fired another - THUD! Missed again.

Quinn dummied and threw himself into a recess in the wall. Doc wheeled round to see the opening. It was in total darkness. Doc fired madly into the void. THUD! THUD! THUD! THUD! - he paused - waiting.

There was no movement for a full ten seconds. The wind lashed the rain onto the dark stone blocks – drops fizzing off the surface as they hit. Doc moved slowly close to the alcove and then realised it was an unlit passageway.

Quinn felt his way along the winding stony enclosed corridor until he found himself on the other side of – and at the base of – an octagonal tower – now clearly lit by the battlement floodlights. He followed a path skirting the base of the structure. Suddenly he found himself round the other side by the passageway entrance – arriving directly behind Doc.

Quinn sprang onto his opponent's back bringing him crashing to the floor. Surprise gave Quinn the second he needed to grab Doc's right wrist. He tried to shake the gun free but to no avail. THUD! The gun went off accidentally.

They rolled across the rampart walkway until they were stopped by a battlement next to a floodlight. As they struggled, they gradually stood up against the low wall. They were starkly lit by the floodlight shining up onto the corner tower. Quinn, still holding Doc's gun wrist away from him, pushed him slowly up onto the top of the wall. They were face to face.

The top of the wall was flat and about a metre across.

Doc lost his grip on the gun and it skittered across the top of the wall and over the edge down into the void. The distant clatter of metal on stone was heard seconds after the gun left the edge.

Quinn wrestled Doc further over the edge. Doc's head was now unsupported in space directly over the intense, blinding floodlight set into the wall a metre-and-a-half below on the outside surface of the wall. They were now in a mutual stranglehold. Quinn was on top of him on top of the wall.

The struggle continued, until, with a supreme effort, Doc violently arched his back sending Quinn over the wall, head over heels, into the abyss.

Doc slowly climbed off the wall onto the safety of the

rampart walkway. He closed his eyes in relief. Turning back to the wall, almost out of curiosity, he carefully leant over to look down. A pair of knuckles were holding onto the floodlight mounting bracket. Quinn hung in space buffeted by the wind – his sinews tearing with the effort to support his body weight.

Doc returned to the rampart from the flat top of the wall. He spotted a small sign on a post. The notice, on a round metal plate, announced 'DANGER: SHEER DROP. KEEP CHILDREN UNDER CONTROL'. He gave the post a series of animal tugs. It came free like some big lollipop. He went back to the edge and leant over the wall again. He held the sign by the end of the post, sign downwards, like some swinging sword of Damacles. He brought the metal edge of the sign across the white, unprotected knuckles. He scythed away like an axe on a pendulum. Quinn yelled with pain as his fingers became bloody.

The white knuckle bones were now visible sitting in their little red pools. Pain swamped the strength of the tendons in his hands. The fingers began to uncurl. Doc jabbed the metal circle down again and again.

Quinn let go...

Doc allowed himself a moment's rest. He lay on the wall. Subconsciously he wanted to check Quinn had gone. He peered down.

Below, Quinn was now dangling from the electrical cable from the wall to underneath the floodlight. He had managed to make a successful grab at the wire as he lost his grip in the mounting bracket.

In a wild fury Doc started to swing the signpost again but it was not long enough to reach Quinn's hands. He threw the sign down into the abyss and proceeded to climb down onto the floodlight.

Quinn looked up as Doc's toe made it onto the lamp housing. The cable began to pull out of the casing as the electrical connections stretched and the grommets failed with the weight.

Doc was now sitting on the floodlight, soaked in the rain. He began to ease himself down to Quinn.

With a sickening jolt the cable tore away from the floodlight extinguishing it. Quinn swung free holding only onto the wet cable. His fingers started to slip - his feet flailing. He managed the tiniest foothold against the castle wall relieving some of the weight on his hands.

There were some bare wires at the end of the cable. Quinn desperately scrabbled to try and gain some height. With a gargantuan effort, holding onto the cable with one hand, he gripped the bare end of the cable and rammed it against the floodlight housing. Nothing happened. Doc smirked – closer than ever.

Quinn clenched his teeth. "For Avril..."

He tried the cable again contacting the lamp casing. A spark, then a blue and white glow, as rivulets of high voltage arcing traced around the metalwork and Doc. Doc screamed, stiffened as the current burst through his body. He toppled off the floodlight into the blackness beneath. A few seconds later a sickening crunch - Doc's motionless, shattered body was dashed on the sharp rocks below - quite dead.

Quinn assessed the climb back onto rampart wall as thoughts of Ghina started to return...

By now the Tattoo was over. Quinn sprinted across the main arena towards an empty seating stand save for a solitary policeman sitting at the top of the aisle. From the centre of the arena Quinn shouted, "Where's Ghina Cunningham?"

"Do you know the lady, sir?" the constable returned.

"I was with her tonight. What happened?"
"You're best enquiring at the Infirmary, sir."

Ghina lay on the bed seriously shot up. Hooked up to life support the heart trace was worryingly erratic. A nurse sat by her side.

Through the window into the room, Quinn's distraught face appeared. The heart trace flatlined triggering alarms. The nurse jumped to her feet and hit an alarm button on the wall.

The room instantly filled with the resuscitation team. Quinn looked on through the glass - helpless. The medics got on with their work – a well-oiled machine. Ghina's body arched as the defibrilator sent its voltage into her chest.

The electrocardiograph display stayed flat. Another shock. Still flat. The whine of the thyristors readied the next charge. The medics gave each other that terrible knowing glance as the defib unsuccessfully spent its power again.

Quinn leant against the window into Ghina's room. "Jayne... ...no!!" he roared with despair, bashing his fist against the window frame. Turning on his heel he ran out of the hospital into the night.

CHAPTER 14: Langley & Lima

McLean, West Virginia is a pleasant suburb. Near Piedmont and Washington DC there are worse places to live for top ranking government executives. A good percentage of the seventeen thousand plus homes are occupied by government officials and, for those that can afford the relatively high cost of living, a large number of CIA employees. Langley is on the very doorstep of McLean making it a perfect, short commute dormitory town.

One inhabitant of McLean was Lisa Harrison. Her husband used to work for the CIA until he went on a visit to Niagara Falls and then to Peru. She sat on a sofa clutching a sopping handkerchief. Her face was puffy and red after much crying. There were two men with her, Doug Kramer, a CIA case officer and a British secret service man by the name of Martin Quinn.

Kramer shifted in his seat with practised concern. "Mrs. Harrison. If there's anything we can do..."

Lisa Harrison regained some control. "Mr. Kramer, he... we knew the risks of being in the field. I thought I'd be or this day. I mean, it's been weeks since he died - pain... somehow... ...it just keeps on."

Quinn gently interrupted, "We've got to bring the people who did it to justice. You owe it to your husband to see this through, Mrs. Harrison."

Lisa spoke calmly, "I know. He'd want it this way, but I just can't think of anything strange before his trip to Peru. At the time, I didn't even know he was going - they never tell you where or when - that's hard. Like the time before he went up to Niagara Falls. He didn't tell me he'd been there until he got back with a suitcase full of damp clothes."

Quinn stiffened a little – his interest piqued. "You said 'Niagara'?" And then to Kramer, "Did the Agency know?"

"News to me," said Kramer truthfully.

"Lisa, have you still got that clothing?"

"I'm not sure. The suit was ruined. I think it might have gone in a bundle to the charity store - but I'll have a look."

She got up and was back in less than a minute.

"Gentlemen, you're in luck."

Quinn took the suit jacket and went through the pockets. Kramer went through the trousers. Nothing to find, apparently.

Kramer handed the trousers back to Lisa. "Bit of a long shot, but worth it. Thanks for your co-operation, Mrs. Harrison. It's appreciated."

Quinn got out of a cab as it pulled up in front of his hotel - The Inn at Langley. Kramer remained in the back seat.

"Be seeing you, Kramer. Take care," said Quinn.

He walked up to reception – the receptionist quite liked the few Brits that passed through 'The Inn'.

"Your suite key, Mr. Quinn. There are no messages.

Have a nice day, now." It was unnerving how the receptionist remembered his name thought Quinn.

Quinn took his key and walked towards the elevator. With his other hand he retrieved a ball of paper from his jacket. He sleighted it at Mrs. Harrison's house. Opening it out in smeared blue ink, hardly visible, it said:

CORNUCOPIA LIMA

"Sorry, Langley - personal business," said Quinn under his breath.

An American Airlines Boeing 777 started its push back from a pier at Newark Airport. In the passenger cabin, the soothing poetry from the captain seeped its way into Quinns head. "Welcome aboard this American flight to Lima, Peru. If you want to get yourself comfortable, we should be on our way shortly..."

Quinn settled further into his seat.

"Flying time this fight is on schedule at a little under eight hours. I'll be giving you more details once we're airborne. Thank you for your attention."

A woman appeared, late, and motioned to sit in the empty seat next to Quinn. They sat in silence. For some impulsive reason, Quinn engaged the woman, "Hello, this is my first trip to Peru. My name's Quinn."

She turned. The face behind the sniper's rifle in Edinburgh beamed at Quinn. "Hello. I better introduce myself if we're to spend a few hours together. I'm Anastasia... Anastasia Montero."

They shook hands. "Erm, Martin, if you prefer." Quinn was fascinated.

Directly behind Quinn, a disguised Nipper quietly took his seat.

Seven-and-a-half hours later at 19:32 local time, the American 777 touched down just beyond the threshold marks on the main runway at Jorge Chávez International Airport on the west side of Lima, Peru.

Quinn and Anastasia walked together through the zoo that was International Arrivals. The airport, though refurbished a few years ago, was already getting tatty - and very hot and sticky owing to the badly maintained air conditioning systems. Quinn was not accustomed to this inefficiency and it showed. They were lucky enough to find a trolley – useful as a ram to make their way through the bustling, shouting crowds. A large gaggle of taxi drivers aggressively plied their business.

"If you've never been to Peru before, you'll need looking after, Martin. Are you staying in Lima?"

"Yes, at the Sheraton," replied Quinn.

"Oh, that's on my way. I'll give you a lift."

Nipper casually walked with his bags some distance behind.

Quinn fended off hordes of aggressive porters and marched with Anastasia to the main exit. They emerged into the dark, thick heat of evening. Quinn crinkled his nose at the stale outside air. A battered maroon Toyota Hiace pulled up by them.

"Our transport..." said Anastasia.

The MPV lurched out of the airport main exit and into the battlefield of the main road towards central Lima.

They drove through the tawdry lights of the outskirts. Garish, flickering neon advertised Norky's Chicken and the Texas Casino and then past ornate floodlit colonial facades - people milling everywhere on the roadsides.

Quinn looked around the battered interior of the Toyota. "Nice motor," he commented almost to himself.

"If you want to keep your wheels in Lima this is what

you drive," retorted Anastasia. The driver gave a wry, toothy grin.

"Any In-ca entertainment?" ventured Quinn.

Anastasia ignored the pun.

The MPV ground to a halt outside the main entrance to the towering Sheraton Hotel.

Quinn got out of the vehicle. The back door clicked open and a porter retrieved his bags. Quinn closed the door and leant into the window. "Anastasia, thanks. Shall we be seeing each other again?"

"I think I'll decide, Mr. Quinn. Try the Rotunda, tomorrow, three p.m." And the battered MPV sped off into the darkness. Quinn stood watching the vehicle disappear. A hint of a smile played upon his lips.

CHAPTER 15: Valuable Information

Dr. Marius Spanbauer sat alone in his chair. It was silent - save for the gentle whirring of the slim laptop on the desk. He read data from the screen. It showed much tightly typed text. The title was 'Lesko Interview #16 - Transcript'.

He continued to read. The words hardly conveyed the terror of the way the information was obtained – sitting blandly, black on white - the screams, the chilling breathlessness of someone close to death were not part of the text.

It read:

```
LESKO: No! No!...Please let me
die.....nothing to say... please...
(inaudible) I cannot tell... Security
clearance - level Chrysanthemum... no...
no... must fight it... exact frequency
required... (inaudible) ...one - one - three
point six megahertz... identifier
sequence ...Johnson's Field, Arizona silos...
...fifty-four warheads, nineteen launchers...
(inaudible)...then arming sequence... ...oh
God! God! My head, my head... ...
(inaudible)...then target co-
ordinates... ...latitude first to seconds
```

precision... pulse at 550.3 confirms... then longitude...same confirmation. Launch sequence initiated by...

Spanbauer hurriedly made notes:

Johnson's Field, Arizona:
US Nuclear Base. 18 silos, approx 54 warheads, 19 launchers. Missiles targeted and triggered either by direct or remote command. Remote command as series of radio transmissions. To activate, Presidential clearance required to cease base jamming capability.

Specific frequencies containing pulse sequences assign warheads, define targets and initiate launches.

Security clearance – Level CHRYSANTHEMUM.

Warhead number and launcher combined in simple four-digit code.

Carrier: 113.6mhz; Overlay sine wave...

Spanbauer steepled his fingers. He switched the laptop to a speadsheet and typed at the foot of a list:

Lesko PROJECT: Information nett worth: $500,000,000

He sucked his teeth in thought. His fingers dropped to the keyboard once more and altered the on-screen figure to $750,000,000. He paused. Still not content he then changed the figure to $1,000,000,000.

In his room at the Lima Sheraton, Quinn ran his finger down a grubby telephone directory page. It stopped at 'Cornucopia, rua San Martin 150'. His eyes narrowed.

Spanbauer continued hunched over the screen. There was a soft knock at the door. Anastasia entered. Without looking up Spanbauer said, "What happened in Scotland?"

Anastasia, fearful but controlled, gave her well rehearsed reply, "Doc killed Ghina. He said she was getting too involved with Quinn. It wasn't secure. Quinn killed Doc. Nipper and I then tracked Quinn to the CIA, Langley. Now he's in Lima. I shall bring him to you."

"Hmm. Unfortunate. Two dead operatives. But then who isn't expendable in the scheme of things..." Still not looking up, Spanbauer allowed the threat to hang in the air.

Anastasia leaked a tiny amount of fear. Spanbauer was recording her every reaction on his computer. He turned and fixed her with a dull stare. "My dear, I'm relying on you now to get him here. Let's hope it's worth it after all this trouble."

"Marius, you know Doc had eyes for Ghina," blurted Anastasia. She bit her lip with the *faux pas* of mentioning 'eyes'. His expression did not change. "Don't you grieve for her?" she continued.

"You hated her. She knew the risks. You know the risks. Enjoy your afternoon tea." Spanbauer's conversation was over.

Anastasia departed. Spanbauer returned to his screen.

Next morning a taxi swept up to the ornate colonial frontage of the Gran Hotel Bolívar. Quinn paid off the driver and entered the main door. There was a discreet sign pointing to ROTUNDA, GRAN HOTEL BOLÍVAR.

The Rotunda is a splendid, old colonial tea room. Tall, corinthian pillars support a stained glass dome in the ceiling which sends shafts of coloured light onto a dusty string quartet playing light chamber music. There are tables scattered around with visitors taking tea and cakes in grand fashion. There is a bar in case of the need for something stronger. The plain, curved plaster walls are a tribute to magnolia paint.

Anastasia sat alone studying a menu.
Quinn spotted her. "Hello. Earl Grey, gently suffused in an individual teapot?"
"With thin cucumber sandwiches with the crusts cut off and a selection of cream cakes. This is afternoon tea 'Rotunda-style'."
Quinn sat down. "You've no objection to my joining you then."
Coyly, Anastasia gave him an inviting stare. "Mr Quinn, you are quite forward. I hardly know you."
They exchanged a smile. A waiter approached with a tray of tea things.

The debris of the afternoon tea littered the table. Quinn glanced at his watch. "I have to be going I'm afraid."
"Martin, you never said. Can I come?" Anastasia flashed her round, brown eyes.
"Got to do some shopping. I don't want to leave it too late. You could give me your number..."
"That's settled. I'll look after you and get the best prices. You don't speak much Spanish - they'll rip you off otherwise."
Quinn paused for a while, thinking. He studied her. She

might be a good cover. He decided. "I told you I was in the export business. I have to go to an address. I don't know what to expect. There could be a deal... It's not without...risk."

She studied her nails intently and then, "You never said exactly what you did. Import...export...what is that?"

"My company searches out opportunities. In Chinese they have the same word for 'risk' and 'opportunity' - it's only the context that tells you the difference. International trade is not without...opportunities."

Her eyes narrowed. "You're not quite what you seem, Martin, are you?"

Quinn ignored the comment and ploughed on, brighter. "OK, tag along if you want. But let me do the talking if it gets interesting. We must behave like tourists. I just need to check an address out."

"This sounds so exciting." She giggled conspiratorially. "Where are we going?"

"Rua San Martin, number 150. You know it?"

"That's a little out of the way. The area used to be controlled by the Shining Path some years ago. You know about Sendero Luminoso?"

"A little, actually. Near-defunct terrorist group. Their leader was imprisoned in 1989. They still do some sporadic stunts. But they're no more corrupt than the military...or the government for that matter. It's a sort of eternal triangle of hate I suppose."

She was rather taken aback by his detailed knowledge. "My, Martin, you've been doing your homework! Come on, let's go. There's a great little antiquities shop on San Martin. 'Cornucopia' it's called. Nice things. Very expensive. Collectors only."

Quinn felt a stab of suspicion but covered perfectly. "Odd. That's the name of the place I was going to."

"OK. I understand. Illegal exports. Inca gold, eh?" she said off hand.

Quinn feigned sheepishness. Best to let her believe that one.

Anastasia happened to be driving herself that day. Her battered Toyota pulled up outside the frontage of 'Cornucopia'. Once out of the vehicle Quinn surveyed the place like a hawk. He walked up to the shuttered windows to see if he can make anything out.

"Shall we go in, Martin?"

A far off bell tinkled as the door from the street was pushed open and Quinn and Anastasia entered. A series of beautifully lit glass cabinets housed the shining Peruvian antiquities. Bracelets, necklaces, vases. Quinn started to peruse them intently.

Towards the far side of the dimly lit shop Nipper stepped back into the shadows. Slitz watched through a beaded curtain. Silence. Quinn suddenly moved to a larger cabinet containing a particularly fine head-dress – unbeknownst to Quinn, recently raided from an Inca tomb.

A soft, deep, clear voice came from the back of the shop. "Can I help you, sir?"

Quinn whirled round on the balls of his feet to see Spanbauer towering over him, his one eye staring, unblinking, into Quinn's eyes.

Quinn gently raised himself to his full height and a little unnerved by Spanbauer's appearance.

"No prices - so I assume expensive and negotiable," Quinn replied, flatly.

Spanbauer beamed. "Right... and wrong... But certainly for sale. Are you a collector?"

"No. Dealer. But I have a range of interested contacts." Quinn produced a card - which Spanbauer studied.

"All the way from England no less. Tell me, how on

earth did you hear of us?"

Quinn's mind raced. "Shall we say by the...er... Way of Light."

Spanbauer's eyebrows raised perhaps half a millimetre. "The Shining Path. You keep questionable company, Mr... er..." He glanced at the card. "...Quinn."

"Not me directly. Via my company's associates."

Spanbauer gently turned away. "But then the only company to keep is questionable I find. May I introduce Nipper and Slitz."

Nipper and Slitz appeared behind Quinn with pistols trained unerringly on Quinn's head. Quinn turned slowly. He looked at Slitz first, then Nipper. A flash of recognition crossed Quinn's face.

"Highly questionable, I'm sure. Do you do this to all your customers?" Quinn asked.

"Please raise your hands. Both Nipper and Slitz enjoy a good view of them," said Spanbauer.

Quinn looked across at Anastasia. She, too, had a gun trained on his head. Quinn felt satisfied that his intuition had not let him down yet. "Oh, Anastasia. Just too good to be true, eh?"

Anastasia placed her gun on a nearby display case. She opened her handbag and extracted a syringe. She stepped forward towards Quinn. He he didn't dare move because of the weapons trained on him. She stabbed him in the thigh emptying the syringe.

"Welcome to Peru, Mr. Quinn," smiled Anastasia.

"I'm sure you must miss Doc dreadfully. Such a shame he had to duck out."

Spanbauer spoke – a harder edge to his voice, "Unfortunately, your Mr. Wilcox can't be here either. Rather uncooperative. Harrison you may have known too. And I'm sure you've heard of Dave Lesko. Most of the

Pentagon has. He's not available right now. Senator Craig Cline also sends his apologies.

Quinn started to lose control. A fog of barbiturate enveloped him. His eyes started to close and he swayed from side to side. With all his remaining focus he forced some words out, "It's Ghina I miss the most. You kill your own too."

"Only in exceptional circumstances. But, sadly, Doc was insistent that she'd fallen for your charms," responded Spanbauer casually.

Fear fleetingly crossed Anastasia's face.

Quinn was fighting for consciousness now and, through gritted teeth, he spat out, "Who the hell are you?"

"My goodness. I'm genuinely surprised you don't know. I'd have credited the British Secret Service with more... intelligence." Spanbauer laughed heartily at his joke. He looked Anastasia in the eye. "My dear, you've done a wonderful job."

Anastasia lowered her eyes avoiding Quinn's hazy gaze.

Quinn keeled over and slumped to the floor. Nipper and Slitz picked him up and man-handled him towards some lift doors - dragging his limp body into the lift. They were in and the doors closed.

CHAPTER 16: Power & Control

In the corner of a damp, dark cell, Lesko stared at the single, dim, uncovered light bulb hanging from the ceiling. His broken body was racked with pain. The walls appeared to be hewn straight out of damp rock and thick, galvanised bars lined the fourth side to the cell - darkness beyond.

His half-closed eyes were bloodshot – unblinking. His skin was clammy, pale and grey. He seemed to have lost all control of his facial muscles - his sunken features drooped. And he moaned softly rocking very gently from side to side - his consciousness is shattered. The price for sharing high security information was high for Dave Lesko.

But Lesko's cell was not the only one. Opposite in another cell in near darkness, Quinn was lying face down in the recovery position on a basic bed. He was out cold. Suddenly he stirred as though shaken from a deep sleep by a nightmare. He sat bolt upright rubbing his eyes. Putting his head in his hands he nursed a severe headache. Slowly he started to get accustomed to his surroundings.

Getting up stiffly he paced round the cell. There was no air vent in this one. The bars were solid. He felt around the cool, wet rough hewn walls – then stopping, he listened intently.

Lesko's moaning was just audible. Quinn peered through the bars into the corridor beyond. It is dark, save for the dimly lit cell opposite. Through the bars Quinn could see the crumpled, battered man. A flicker of recognition crossed Quinn's face.

"Lesko?" said Quinn in a stage whisper.

Lesko rocked gently from side to side.

"Lesko!" Quinn was louder this time. Lesko stopped moving. "Lesko. Can you hear me?"

Lesko, infinitely slowly, moved his head to focus on the source of the sound.

"Lesko, wake up! Listen to me!"

Lesko gave a slightly questioning louder moan towards Quinn.

"Lesko, my name's Quinn from British Intelligence. Can you understand what I'm saying?"

Lesko managed a slight nod.

"Can you speak?"

Lesko started mumbling as though he'd had a mouthful of major dental work. "Mmmm... ...yeth..."

"You've got to try and tell me what's going on. What's happened to you?"

Lesko gathered what was left of any strength he had. "Captured... ...truth drugs... ...don't know what I've said... ...Doc said the pain would pass... ...I answered... ...don't know what I said..." His eyes started to close with the effort.

"Go on, Lesko. I can help."

"Implant... ...the Harvester is... ...Dr. Marius Spanbauer... ...sells information to terrorists... ...don't know what I said... ...he has conferences wi..."

Lesko's sentence was interrupted by a silent scream.

His body stiffened and jerked upright - his eyes wide open, his lips drawn in agony back from his teeth. He quivered for some time. At last the shaking stopped. His glaring eyes were motionless as his body toppled onto the floor. He didn't attempt to break his fall. He was dead. His body a crumpled, bloodied staring heap.

Quinn watched with horror. In the stress reflex, his finger went into his collar. He stopped as his fingers caught something - a neat row of stitches running from the lower part of the left hand side of his neck along and into the depression behind his collar bone. The scar was only a few centimetres long. He was puzzled.

Then, a distant commotion. Quinn strained to see what was happening. A clanking of doors ensued and Slitz and Nipper entered the corridor. They walked purposefully to Quinn's cell, completely ignoring the ragged body that was Lesko. They stopped outside Quinn's cell - Nipper's gun trained on him. Slitz held his weird knife in one hand, a bunch of keys in the other. Slitz unlocked Quinn's cell.

Slitz barked, "He wants you. You come with us. Any slight move and it's over."

"So, I'm expected," muttered Quinn.

"Shut it, Quinn," breathed Nipper.

They grabbed Quinn by each arm, either side, and frog-marched him out and down the corridor. Quinn thought it best to co-operate. The odds might get better later. Nipper and Slitz manhandled Quinn along to a heavy iron door. They pushed it open. Beyond was a pair of polished steel lift doors. The doors opened and they entered.

The doors swished to. Quinn relaxed, waiting for the opportunity. Extremely nonchalant, he gazed about the lift, unconcerned - waiting. He caught Nipper's eye. He smiled.

With a powerful crash, Quinn dropped to the floor

breaking the grip of his captors. He then lunged upwards with his elbows into their respective groins. Off guard and Nipper and Slitz doubled up in pain and surprise. Quinn's fists connected with their jaws as they bent over. They reeled backwards. Quinn snatched Nipper's gun in the commotion and trained it on them both as they recovered.

Quinn was in control. "Get in that corner both of you, NOW! Kneel, hands on top of your heads NOW! Believe me, I'll shoot."

Quinn suddenly stiffened and shook. He screamed. Something had taken over his body. He couldn't move. His eyes glared as his face froze into a painful grimace. He crumpled to his knees.

Nipper and Slitz got to their feet. They realised they had nothing now to fear as Quinn has been implanted.

The lift doors opened onto a unique room - Spanbauer's lounge - his relaxation and study area. The carpet was a very dark rich blue with gold stars, moons and planets woven as a motif pattern. The walls were lined with nooks with lamps shining onto dark blue leather-topped desks. Much of the walls were covered with bookshelves with many volumes stuffed in.

There was rich polished, carved wood everywhere. Small wine tables, beautifully veneered as display stands for Inca and pre-Inca treasures were lit from focused eyeball spots set into the navy ceiling.

Spiral staircases swirled down from the ceiling and connected to balconies and aerial walkways in front of yet more bookshelves. There were sumptuous pictures adorning the walls - each properly lit. Suspended galleries (similar to minstrels' galleries in mediaeval halls) were fashioned from the same, polished, carved wood.

Deep leather button-back chairs and sofas in rich maroon were arranged around the place. The ceiling was low. There were discreet screens dotted around the place - none of them was on.

Overall, there was a sense of oppressive opulence.

In a central, wide, high-backed sofa, surrounded with integral tables and screens sat Spanbauer.

He steepled his fingers as Quinn was dragged out of the lift in front of him.

"Mr. Quinn, a very warm welcome. You may sit down when you have recovered. You have the pleasure of meeting Dr Marius Spanbauer." Spanbauer gestured to a nearby chair.

Quinn scowled across at Spanbauer as he pulled himself to his feet and hobbled over to the chair. Quinn fought and succeeded at regaining his composure. He sat, relaxed, opposite Spanbauer.

Spanbauer continued, "You seem to have a notable prowess at winning against the odds, my friend. Doc was an extraordinary individual. Ruthless with a sublime economy of purpose and highly intelligent. Until he met you he had a one hundred per cent kill rate. I am surprised that British Secret Service can afford to keep a man of your skills." There was a pause. "You've just experienced your implant."

Quinn's fingers found the small, fresh scar.

"Mr Lesko did too, terminally, when he decided to try and expand on some details about my operations. I constantly monitor the speech and position of anyone carrying such a device. Like you, for example. Put a foot wrong and you will be going to the same party as Mr Lesko.".

Quinn fixed Spanbauer's eerie gaze. "What's it all about, Spanbauer?"

"Oh, it just might be to your advantage." Spanbauer changed gear. "What do they pay you? A British Civil

Service pittance? Preferential membership of a motoring organisation? Get real. The world has changed completely. What is the UK nowadays? It's a rather sad, average, European state - it's lost its influence - an entire empire gone. Who really cares what Britain thinks on the global stage? How can you possibly be motivated taking orders from masters who simply have no international mandate? You put your life on the line for... for what?"

"One can derive a certain satisfaction from putting psychos away. One could say how much pleasure I get from my imminent prospects for doing exactly that."

"Surely you're a misfit, Mr Quinn. You have to be to play in your murky trade. *I* may even be mad - if anyone can define what that condition is. I get my kicks from money, power and control - in roughly equal measure. Any other pleasures I require come with these three elements as standard." Spanbauer relaxed. "Anyway, enough semantics. First and foremost, I am a businessman. Working with my organisation, a man like you could do well... very well. Think of it - no reports, no desks, no hectoring superiors, no office politics - just action."

Spanbauer waited – his good eye boring into Quinn's eyes. "Sounds tempting, doesn't it? On reflection, I doubt if you have a choice." He leant back waiting for Quinn to answer.

Inside, Quinn was rattled. His face showed the weariness of endless assignments. His mind was racing but self doubt crossed his face. He stared at Spanbauer implacably as if trying to read the man.

At length Quinn spoke, "I...er..."

Spanbauer leaned forward slightly - his attention caught.

"...don't seem to have a choice..." Quinn continued.

A certain relief surged through Quinn as he shed the

responsibilities of the past.

Spanbauer closed the conversation. "The wise man always acts to save his own life - yours has now been extended...for a while. But now to work. I have a task to test your new-found loyalty. Nipper, come join us in the Operations Room."

CHAPTER 17: Zoo, Awards & Payroll

Animated parties of schoolchildren went through the turnstiles at a zoo. It was a hot, sunny day but not too busy. The chaperoning teachers were glad of the weather and thankful they had missed the crowds. Of particular interest to the enthusiastic children were the big cats – not far from the entrance. An adult tiger growled as it demolished a side of meat. There were six fully grown tigers in their lush pen. Spectator viewing was at ground level at one end through thick glass. The area was set into a bowl such that the other end of the enclosure was raised into a steep, sheer-sided wall. Here visitors peered over a wall down into the tiger pit. There was much excitement among the big cats as it was feeding time.

At the raised spectator wall a pudgy, touristy looking man with a bulky DSLR and telephoto lens swinging round his neck appeared. He leant over. He looked a little comical in his overly tight shorts and a T-shirt. He was dark - perhaps Italian. He carried a small, heavy, brightly coloured rucksack which he placed on the floor beside him.

He was joined by a woman – her face obscured by a headscarf and large sunglasses. They were alone on the parapet. The man with the camera used his foot to gently push the rucksack across to the woman standing next to him. The woman picked up the heavy rucksack and took off her sunglasses. It was Anastasia. She fumbled in the bag, ostensibly to retrieve a compact camera. However, Anastasia's downward glance confirmed the bag's real pupose – to conceal two bars of gold. Anastasia took a picture of the tigers and casually walked away carrying the rucksack.

The man stayed and started to take more photos - fiddling intently with his camera. Silently, Slitz appeared behind him. There was no one about. Slitz squatted down behind the man and, in one swift movement, grabbed his legs and hoisted him up and over the wall.

The man tumbled over, screaming, into the tiger pit. He was on the floor. The tigers stopped dead still - watching. Injured from the fall he struggled to get up but they were upon him, all six cats, slashing and biting, pinning him to the floor. The screams died into a bloody burble below the noises of the satisfied growls.

A seemingly endless convoy of black limousines dropped off dignitaries and their wives to the main reception doors of the ballroom complex at the Hotel Elegance in Brussels. All the guests were in full evening attire ready for what promised to be a glittering evening with the great and the good. At the awards ceremony later that evening the meal was in full swing as waiters scurried around a sea of heavily bedecked tables.

An M.C. appeared on the stage. "Mesdames et Messieurs, bienvenue and welcome to this year's EuroTech Awards ceremony. We are particularly honoured to have so many government ministers from across Europe to join us here this evening. In just a few short minutes we shall begin the formal proceedings - in the meantime, Bon Appetit!"

From a low hill opposite the hotel, two men in night fatigues lay prone looking through infrared binoculars at an excellent view the hotel. A car paused to leave the hotel to join the main stream of traffic in the road in front of the building. The binoculars focused on this car. Because of the infra-red, the driver was fairly clear to see. He gestured with his hand making a signal.

The first man spoke quietly but clearly to his colleague, "Signal seen and noted."

The second man responded into a small walkie-talkie. "Seen and noted, go, go, go."

An unseen hand dialled a mobile number which simultaneously triggered a series of detonators setting off the exothermic reaction that stared the deadly chain reaction in an unfeasibly large mass of Semtex.

The entire frontage of the hotel lit up with an enormous explosion from the interior. The entire facade burst out and billowed into a gigantic ball of fire. The men watched the explosion until the smoke began to clear to reveal a sea of blackened, flaming rubble. The building had been levelled. The men sprinted off into the night.

The room was clean and white. A large screen filled one wall. There was a round table in the centre surrounded by some comfortable leather-backed chairs. An array of switches on the table in front of Spanbauer glowed ready. Also at the table were Quinn and Nipper.

Spanbauer spoke, "Remember the Brussels Bomb?" Footage of the grisly aftermath appeared on a big screen. "Seventeen high ranking Government ministers from across Europe were killed along with twenty-six senior industrialists. This spectacular was carried out by a Mafia splinter group who wanted to make a point that they weren't getting enough action. I supplied all the details as to who would be there, the venue - which changed at the last moment - and information required to plant explosive under the noses of the unusually vigilant security mandarins.

"You see, I don't kill. I merely supply others with information. They use it how they wish. However, for this operation, I was underpaid. The gold supplied was only a third of the agreed amount. Any underpayment I regard as terminal. As luck would have it, the skinflint Mafioso with whom I agreed the deal is currently holidaying here in Peru on one of those sickening Inca tours. His name is Massimo Colombo."

Spanbauer had made his decision. "I think it appropriate that you and Nipper take a look at Machu Picchu the day after tomorrow. That is when Colombo visits the site." Massimo Colombo's face appeared on the screen alongside some surveillance footage. "He will have his usual bodyguards and his family with him. There will be tourists around so the method has to be ingenious. He is dangerous and used to looking after himself. Don't for one minute think this easy, Mr Quinn - or may I call you Martin?"

CHAPTER 18: Machu Picchu

The sun rose over the majesty of the Inca ruins at Machu Picchu, Peru - perched on steep, green terraces atop the lush tropical cloud forest. The light played around the site and surrounding mountains sending eerie shafts between the stones. Layers of cloud caught the dark green velvet of the forest clad mountains. The ruined city seemed to hang in mid air – the flush cut stones basked in the yellow-orange glow of the morning sun and sent dramatic, violet shadows across the ancient site.

There was a distant drone of a helicopter. An Aerospatiale Twin Squirrel moved between the peaks, glinting in the dawn light. It crabbed over the central ruins, descended and hovered at about 50 feet. A rope ladder dropped from on open door and two figures climbed down.

Quinn and Nipper were in black military garb and laden with kit. Jumping off the bottom of the ladder onto the ground, Quinn sprinted across into a fairly well preserved, small, windowless, roofless ruin. The walls were just higher than a man so a person would be concealed within it. Nipper, dropping his bags off, raced away.

Quinn unzipped a long, black padded container - not

unlike a large sports bag. Out of it came something like a rolled up wooden exercise mat made up of thin slats. This opened into an area of about a metre by two metres. Quinn hung it up over the ruin opening. It was a false door which fitted across the aperture. There was a notice on it in Spanish, English and Quechuan:

>Keep out - Drainage Control
>Dangerous machinery

The false door was suitably battered and aged. And completely convincing.

Hiram Picchu is a small area slightly below the main site. It is the location of a small hut that sells tickets, brochures and souvenirs to visitors arriving on foot. Nipper arrived outside the apparently locked building. There was a dusty, closed window. Suddenly a Quechuan man's face appeared behind it looking very uneasy. It was the entry guard. He disappeared from the window and opened the door. "Harvester," he said in a thick accent.

"Sendero," Nipper responded. Then in Quechuan, "You saw nothing. You heard nothing."

The frightened guard managed a stiff nod. Nipper dug into a pocket and fished out a fat envelope of US dollars. The guard took the money and, fawning, shuffled backwards into the entrance building.

Nipper grabbed a headset with a tiny camera attached over one ear from a bulging utility belt. He put it on. He spoke softly into the microphone, "Arrival OK. Hut man OK. Commencing preparations."

The bustling, colourful main square of Plaza de Armas in Cuzco was already in action in the early morning sun. The ruddy buildings almost glowed. Locals in vibrant

Peruvian clothing traded in market stalls. Llamas and children posed for recently breakfasted tourists. Hawkers wandered amongst them looking for the faintest sniff of business. And Massimo Colombo plus wife and two heavies, Vincente and Paulo, paused to buy some trinkets before getting into a shabby waiting car. They swept out of the square. The car drove through the streets up through San Blas towards the railway station.

The car deposited its passengers outside the dilapidated ticket office...

A girl sat behind a desk-cum-counter. Colombo walked up and fired off his needs in a New York Italian drawl, "Hey, lady. We want the day trip to Machu Picchu. They tell me it's good so we gotta do it."

Without a word, the girl prepared four tickets.

And so the Colombo party was treated to one of the most spectacular railway journeys in the world. Climbing steeply up the never-ending zig-zag out of Cuzco the red and yellow tourist train eventually made its way past the awesome vista of Mount Veronica and into the Urubamba river gorge. Glimpses of trees clinging to the vertical rock faces hinted at the majesty of the cloud forest to come. Through Ollantaytambo station – and then a descent into the gorge with views of the white water river in angry spate.

At last the train pulled into Aguas Calientes station – the nearest stop to Machu Picchu. The Colombos and their two minders boarded one of the many charabancs to do the hairpin ascent to the main tourist entrance of Machu Picchu – a thrilling, snaking journey.

Finally, after the ticket scrimmage they made it through the wooden hall to the first, never-to-be-forgotten view of Machu Picchu. It was two-thirty in the afternoon. Even the hard-bitten Colombo had to pause at one of the wonders of the world. "Say, Christ. This is just awesome," he said under his breath.

Quinn waited silently inside the walled ruin with its false door closed. Nipper hid in another nearby building.

The Columbo group split up to explore the ruins. There were few tourists about. One of Colombo's heavies, Vincente, started padding around the crumbling buildings perhaps twenty metres from where Nipper was hiding. Nipper produced a small, hand-held dart gun - similar to those used for anaesthetising wild animals. He extracted a small gas canister and screwed it into the rear of the gun. The device held a clip of eight tufted darts. Vincente meandered closer to Nipper. Nipper poised to shoot, aiming intently at the man's fat neck. The trigger was gently squeezed and, near-silently, the dart gun fired.

A tufted dart sank into the side of the Vincente's neck. He brought his hand up to the small wound and turned to find the source of the short hiss. He stood, frozen, as the toxin did its work. Nipper took no chances and fired another into his target's throat. The man buckled at his knees, looked ahead and slumped straight forward – quite dead.

"Tango Delta down," said Nipper into the mic.

"Roger that," came Quinn's response into his headset.

The false door opened and Quinn appeared. Vincente's body was perhaps thirty metres from Quinn. Looking about, it was clear to walk quickly over to the body. Still checking all around, Quinn dragged the body back into his hiding place and started to seal the door.

But Paulo, Colombo's other protection man, caught a glimpse of Quinn dragging the body out of sight from afar. Just as the false door closed, a pair of tourists appeared from round the corner of the walled ruin and passed by the slatted door completely unaware that anything had happened.

Paulo sprinted across the site to where Colombo and his wife were standing. Calmly, he explained what he had just seen. Mrs. Colombo walked away, on her own from her husband. Colombo and his man scanned the ruins for any activity.

Nipper, senses sharp, waited and watched through some small binoculars in his hiding place. Into the headset, he spoke, "Colombo's been alerted. His wife has left the group – probably moving to safety. Colombo and his man are still looking towards us."

Spanbauer's voice crackled flatly over the headset. "Ignore the wife. We have to take out Colombo."

Nipper shuddered and gurgled and suddenly blood appeared from between his lips. He keeled over. Mrs Colombo stood behind him with a bloody knife in her hand. She had stabbed Nipper through the neck. She bent down and inspected the headset. She removed it from his head and crushed the tiny camera under a nearby stone.

In Spanbauer's operations room Nipper's camera feed blinked to a fuzz of interference. Another screen next to it stayed on showing the back of the false door in the windowless ruin.

Spanbauer sat back in surprise at the loss of signal and started to fiddle with some controls - but to no avail. He slammed a fist down in annoyance. "Nipper, where are your visuals?" There was no answer. "Nipper, answer me. I've lost your video link... Nipper? ...Quinn, what's happening?"

A compressed radio voice answered, "I don't know. If he's not responding, I have to assume he can't. I'll have to finish this alone. Out." Quinn threw off the headset, stamping on the microphone and camera. He paused and gritted his teeth, deep in thought as to his next move.

Colombo and Paulo stealthily approached Quinn's windowless ruin. They both had silenced automatic pistols out and ready. Quinn was inside, dead still, listening intently. He moved to one side of the false door, his back to the wall, dart gun ready in his right hand.

Colombo and his man made their move and taking up positions on either side of the false door, their backs to the wall. Quinn waited and listened. Colombo began to signal something to his henchman but suddenly a group of tourists appeared. In a flash, Quinn's would-be assailants concealed their weapons and started to inspect the ruin putting on a vaguely comical act of extreme interest in the stones of the 'drainage control' building. The tourists gave them sidelong glances.

After the tourists had disappeared Colombo and Paulo resumed their positions. Colombo started to silently signal touching his watch and showed five with his hand - four times - twenty seconds. He held up his hand to show 'wait'. He motioned his hand to show that Paulo should go round the back of the ruin and climb over the back wall. He showed he would stay at the front and burst in. Signalling twenty seconds again he meant these moves should be synchronised.

Paulo confirmed his understanding. Colombo counted three, two and one with his fingers in TV studio floor manager style. On the beat after 'one', Paulo made his move round the back studying his watch as the seconds counted down.

Colombo's gaze was now fixed on the second hand of his watch. The heavy round the back of the ruin started to silently scale the wall...

...five...four...three...two...one...

With a mighty lunge, Colombo heaved into the false door - it broke down easily and he was in.

Paulo leapt over the back wall and he was in too. The weapons were let loose as bullets slammed into the black-garbed figure who was standing, back to the wall, by the doorway. The bullets were driven in and the body crashed to the floor.

Colombo and his man paused to exchange a fleeting triumphant smile but, as they did, the prostrate, dead body of Vincente turned and fired tufted darts into their necks. The targets gagged, then froze and fell to the floor.

Quinn sat back – heart racing – having exchanged clothes with the dead man and played dead himself. Quinn had propped up the poisoned man and dressed him in his own fatigues to take the bullets meant for him.

Quinn, in the dead Vincente's gross tourist clothes, exited the ruin and made good the false door. As he did so, yet another party of tourists passed by. He paused as they shuffled on their way. Mrs Colombo had joined the group and had effectively melted away. She gave a surreptitious glance at Quinn wondering how he survived.

Quinn made his way towards the Central Plaza of the ruins and stood in the middle. From his pocket he produced a small, black box with a button on it. Seconds later, the small helicopter rose up from below the level of the ruins much to the surprise of the tourists milling around. The craft hovered over the Central Plaza and a ladder was thrown down to Quinn.

In seconds he was on the ladder and the helicopter rose into the air with Quinn on the end of the ladder sweeping through the tree-clad mountains.

Twenty minutes later the aircraft tracked in to a helipad which seemed part of an Inca complex perched on the side of a perilously steep mountain covered in jungle. It was as if a stone castle had been tacked onto the vertiginous cliff. The characteristic smooth hewn, perfectly butted rocks made up the walls. The only elements betraying the construction's authenticity was an outcrop of small aerials and satellite dishes in a cluster on top of one of the complex's blocks.

Further inspection revealed rooms almost terraced over each other. At each corner were pill boxes of the same stone construction - manned gun emplacements. Though not overly obvious, the place could be very well defended.

Overall, the edifice looked like a series of stone Lego blocks covered with creeping plants erupting in trails from holes in the walls. A curved, wide sweep of half-silvered glass formed what looked like a viewing area across the nearby mountains.

This was Spanbauer's 'Inca Temple' - deep in the heart of extraordinarily difficult terrain.

As the helicopter landed, guards stood around the site at a discreet distance.

Spanbauer, a guard and Anastasia waited to greet Quinn as he emerged from the craft. Ducking the whirling blades, he ran towards them. He was still dressed in the tourist clothes.

Spanbauer, noticing the clothes, greeted him warmly, "Good holiday, Martin? A well-executed job - pity Nipper had to die but, as you know, it comes with the turf. Losing his edge anyway."

"Colombo paid his dues," Quinn replied.

"Come, a celebration drink," said Spanbauer; then to the guard, "Set concealment."

"At once, Harvester." The guard disappeared down some steps.

Spanbauer, Anastasia and Quinn strolled back towards the building.

There was a low hum combined with a strange rustling and scraping. Quinn paused to notice what was happening.

The trailing plants which emerged from the myriad of holes in the walls expanded as though pushed out from within. Each trailing plant enlarged such that the buildings become obliterated by a verdant patchwork. In seconds, nothing visibly remained as the structure melted away into the jungle-clad mountainside.

In the glass-walled lounge champagne was served by a servant of Quechua type. Spanbauer raised his glass to Quinn as Anastasia looked on.

"Colombo's replacement has been in touch about the shortfall. The extra gold will be delivered to 'Cornucopia' tomorrow along with some...er...compensation."

"In the form of...?" ventured Quinn.

"Mrs. Colombo's eyes. I felt that was the least they could do, don't you? You see, I had one of my own put out with a glowing poker - by the section of La Cosa Nostra Colombo worked for. It was during a 'meeting' where they felt my conversation 'lacked depth'. An eye for an eye." Spanbauer gazed at the sweeping view beyond the glass.

"You didn't strike me as a bitter man, Spanbauer," commented Quinn.

"No, just fair. It is a lesson to the people who buy my information that I am not to be played with. I thought you would have understood this by now."

"Believe me, it is completely clear."

Changing the subject, Spanbauer said, "I have arranged more comfortable accommodation for you. You can change those ridiculous clothes and we will discuss your next mission." He pressed a button on a table at his elbow and the servant appeared again.

"Take Mr. Quinn to his suite."

He motioned Quinn to follow the man. Quinn got up. Just before they reached the door Spanbauer said, "I trust you're still in the game, Martin... My game..."

Quinn looked Spanbauer right in the eye - a steely, cold gaze, held for just too long and slightly aggressive. Then Quinn's face broke into a mischievous smile.

Spanbauer cast a conspiratorial look over to Anastasia who did not quite return his gaze.

Quinn was shown in to his 'suite' by the servant. The room was the equivalent of a top hotel suite with opulent fixtures and fittings. All his things had been brought over from the Sheraton - including a smart tablet which sat on a small desk.

The servant departed closing the door behind him. Quinn paused and then tried the door. Locked, of course. He padded around the room looking for the usual bugs.

He expertly moved around the room. Peeking behind the pictures on the wall he found nothing. His eyes caught an odd-looking object on the top of a bed post. He carefully studied it, tapped it and thought for a second. He then pulled it from the top of the post only discovering it to be entirely ornamental. Somewhat disappointed, he carried on with the recce.

Moving into the bathroom, he still could not find anything suspicious. He returned to the main room and picked up his tablet.

Opening it he switched it on. It booted up to a Windows-type screen. Pressing the U,K,G and B keys simultaneously, a menu popped up. He selected 'Room Sweep' from the option list. A graphic showing the layout of the room filled the screen (as well as some adjoining room layout). The picture quality was similar to that produced by a medical ultrasound scanner. A overlaid cursor blinked as a green scanning line moved across the display. A message 'ENVIRONMENT CLEAR' flashed up.

Quinn's face was encouraged. He switched off the tablet and started to get changed.

CHAPTER 19: Job Offer

The rain gently washed the London streets. It was very late. Most commuters had long gone to their homes to eat their hurried dinners. However, Cadogan was still in his office as usual.

Opposite him sat Edmondson. "Still nothing from Quinn. Should we send someone out? Kramer was the last to see him."

Cadogan's mind was elsewhere. "No. Quinn has only gone for a while. He must be onto something. Leave it forty-eight hours."

"I wonder what he's up to..." said Edmondson almost to himself.

There was no answer from Cadogan. Speculation was not something that he thrived on.

Back in the Peruvian clould forest at Spanbauer's operations centre, Quinn, Slitz, Anastasia and Spanbauer sat around the main table. Spanbauer held court. Then, to Quinn, he said, "Life is a matter of trust. Trust is risk. Risk is opportunity. There can be no opportunities without trust. The question is, do I trust you?" He paused.

Quinn sensed a little dangerous edge to Spanbauer's words.

"You acquitted yourself well at Machu Picchu - a significant level of danger applied. Under changing circumstances, you thought well on your feet."

"There is no success without opportunity. And how can you measure trust? Do I have to do one or a hundred operations for you? Doesn't my implant guarantee my loyalty even without trust? What choice do I have?" Quinn countered.

Spanbauer's mood swung rather unnervingly into a strange, positive energy. He had made a decision. "Your use to me is threefold. Yes, as a field operative, you have proven yourself. As a purveyor of British intelligence, I await some golden nuggets. As a recruitment officer, you also have potential. Perhaps the latter skill is your strongest."

"Meaning?"

"Recruitment, Martin. Recruitment. I sell government information. Terrorist groups are, generally, exceptional payers. Look around you." Spanbauer gestured expansively. "The UK has certain strengths - a listening post on the world - the biggest bug on the planet. Your GCHQ and ECHELON are but two jewels in your information crown. But access to filtered, considered information can get so difficult. Can you see what I'm driving at?"

"Go on..."

"Haven't you guessed? Your department has responsibility for foreign affairs. Who's in charge? Who decides what's sensitive? Who asks for more detail when he needs it?"

A light came on in Quinn's head. "Of course, Doc's mission was nothing to do with me."

Spanbauer smiled as if a favourite nephew had done well at school.

The pieces fell into place. Quinn began, almost for his own understanding, "You needed someone who has precise knowledge. Someone who can access specifics - to order. Doc - as Devereux - was to...er... 'recruit' Cadogan. Inspired."

Spanbauer beamed. "Welcome to the world of international terrorism. Now we can see eye to eye. Now you will bring him to me."

Much later Quinn was in bed fast asleep. It was almost totally dark. There was a faint buzz at the door. A shaft of light gushed in swinging round the room. Quinn stirred slightly - but he was still asleep.

The shadowy figure entered and closed the door. The shape moved across the room and paused, looking over Quinn. The shape then lost her dressing gown and Anastasia slipped into the bed beside Quinn. This time he stirred violently - in a reflex action his hand went under his pillow to find the gun that wasn't there. She put her finger to her lips and pointed at his implant scar. They must be dead silent.

They embraced. Then kissed in a near frenzy, exploring each other - but without a sound. Their bodies writhed and entwined under the covers.

In a small control room a solitary guard dozed. An array of security monitors were ranged before him showing no movement at all. Barely audible was the faintest rustling and breathing from a speaker set into the desk with a red light on it. The LCD display underneath glowed: IMPLANT 603. There was a sudden female yelp of delight. The guard stirred but they had got away with it.

Sunrise in the cloud forest was always an event. The orientation of the high mountain walls and gorges gave the increasing golden glow an opportunity to play its shifting light magic through the layered mist, onto warm yellow rock and dark green leaves. Spanbauer's Inca 'temple' appeared out of the lush vegetation on the steep mountainside as the trailing cloaking was withdrawn into the walls.

The forest of aerials and radio dishes on the top of the complex begin to move - aligning themselves into new positions.

Quinn awoke. The sun peeped in though the curtains giving his suite a gentle, golden glow. Anastasia had gone. Quinn was now fully alert. He got out of bed, still confused. Throwing on a gown, he immediately walked over to the door and tried it. It was still steadfastly locked. The windows, after a quick test, were also stuck firm. He peered around the room. There was no way of escape. A small air vent, only fifteen by twenty centimetres and high up on the wall, caught his eye briefly but was dismissed with mild irritation. Sitting back on the edge of the bed, he resigned himself to wait to be let out for breakfast.

In the silence he heard the faintest sounds of talking. He listened intently. Spanbauer's voice interspersed with many other voices with different accents was barely audible – but definitely there. Distorted chatter floated through... "Number 23, welcome, you're through... Harvester, I have you on sound only... Number 4 on channel one-three-three... China, can you read me? Vision and sound, OK, number 27... Hold for a little longer, number 10, number 35..."

Quinn could not make out where the sound was coming from. He strained to get a fix. Slowly, he realised that the noises were coming from the air-vent. Pulling a chair over to the vent and standing on it he got his head closer to the source. Even so, it was still extremely difficult to make out any meaningful sentences.

He paused for an instant and then picked up his tablet. Using a nail file, he gently prised open what appeared to be a line in the moulding of the outer case. A tiny hatch swung open. Quinn tipped the palmtop at an angle into his hand and a polished blue-black metallic object dropped out.

It was about a quarter of the size of a credit card. Wafer-thin metallic wings were attached to the small torpedo-shaped unit. He placed it on the smooth dressing table surface. Quinn closed the tablet 'hatch' and booted it up. He accessed a 'Surveillance' menu and a picture of a deodorant canister appeared. The metallic object was sitting next to the same spray can on the dressing table.

He donned his earbuds and plugged them into a socket in the side of the tablet.

Using the nail file again, he prised up a tiny metal spigot. Pressing a key the shiny object emitted a low continuous buzz. The tiny silver plastic wings became a blur. A push on the spigot and the minute metallic 'beast' started to move forward across the dressing table. It then took to the air - a tiny robot 'insect' drone with a micro video camera on board.

Quinn controlled it around the room - the picture transmitted from the device as it flew was displayed on the tablet screen. It hovered in front of the air vent. Quinn then deftly manoeuvred it to fly into the darkness. Another key press and the robot insect's on-board light came on. Images of the interior of the air vent piping appeared. Quinn guided it through the shafts toward the source of the babbling voices. The rear of an air vent grille came into view – instinctively Quinn switched off the on-board light as the insect hovered into the room beyond...

In the vaulting cathedral that was Spanbauer's video conferencing facility, another auction had begun.

Spanbauer stood eerily lit at his centre podium. His movements were almost god-like as he set the controls.

All the screens facing him were on - each with an unpleasant looking face leering out - including a Chinese gentleman by the name of Zhenxi Thaxoi.

Spanbauer spoke, "Ladies and gentlemen. Welcome to a very special 'harvest' of information. I have a particularly tasty morsel to lay before you. He grasped the lectern.

The robot insect hung in space relaying it's picture and sound back to Quinn.

Spanbauer continued, "The enormity of what I have could be the ultimate... er... key, shall we say, to achieving your ends." He leaned back. The letterbox mouth gabbled on, "I have come by some extraordinarily specific information regarding the United States' nuclear capabilities. I offer a remote control to activate and target at least fifty, live nuclear warheads - on intercontinental delivery platforms. The added advantage is your representatives don't even have to be near the launch sites in question." A dramatic pause. Then, "My reserve price is one billion U.S. Dollars! A bargain for ultimate power wouldn't you agree? Until the next time... enjoy your fantasies!"

Quinn's brow creased. He sat stunned for a moment. He glanced at his watch, then flew the insect drone back and replaced it into the tablet. He selected COMMUNICATIONS from the options menu.

He started to initiate a link to London. The protocols crawled up the screen...

    COMMS: Tx

```
    TX ENABLED.
    TYPE LINK DESTINATION
        INITIATING TX LINK MOD/49X4JZ DEPT
CENTRAL
```

The screen paused...then flashed:

```
        ESTABLISHING LINK MOD/49X4JZ DEPT
CENTRAL
```

Another pause.

```
    LINK ESTABLISHED
```

The intercom on Cadogan's desk buzzed into life. "Sir, Quinn's through on the uplink."

"Get Edmondson and Dovey now." Cadogan looked at the comms feed.

In seconds Edmondson and Dovey came into the office. Dovey, a young, spotty tecchie, was carrying a tablet similar to Quinn's.

Back in Peru, Quinn's tablet scrolled the next series of received protocols:

```
    DEPT CENTRAL
    LINK ACKNOWLEDGED
    REPRESENTATIVE: 49X4JZ:
    GO AHEAD:
```

Quinn typed hastily...

```
        PERFORMANCE IMPAIRED BY IMPLANTED
DEVICE -
        TRACKS LOCATION AND SOUND.
        ANY IDEAS?
        TROUBLE IF LATEST OPPOSITION
        DEAL GOES AHEAD.
```

```
          INFO BEING SOLD TO OTHER INTERESTED
PARTIES,
          HENCE NO PATTERN TO PREVIOUS EVENTS.
          ICBM TRADE IN USA.
          REMOTE LAUNCH SEQUENCING BY THIRD
PARTIES POSSIBLE.
          LITTLE TIME AVAILABLE.
          'WORKING' FOR OPPOSITION.
          PLAN TO CAPTURE MANAGING DIRECTOR.
          TEAM REQUIRED TO PUT OPPOSITION    OUT
OF BUSINESS.
          USE LOCATOR.
```

Cadogan, Dovey and Edmondson sat impassively looking at their screen. The following appeared on the display:

```
          PERFORMANCE IMPAIRED BY IMPLANTED
DEVICE - TRACKS LOCATION AND SOUND.
          ANY IDEAS?
          TROUBLE IF LATEST OPPOSITION DEAL GOES
AHEAD.
```

And then...

```
          PARITY INTERRUPT ERROR = 0
          TX FAIL
```

"Blast, the link's gone down," said Edmondson. More text came across the London screen...

```
          ERROR CHECK OK: CONTINUING:
          HOWEVER, ALL UNDER CONTROL.   SUPPORT
TECHNICIANS NOT
          REQUIRED.
          CONTACTING YOU AGAIN 48 HRS.  49X4JZ.
```

Spanbauer sat calmly typing at a console. And on the monitor, clearly...

```
SIGNAL INTERCEPT STATUS: OK
RESEND NEW MESSAGE:
    HOWEVER, ALL UNDER CONTROL.  SUPPORT
TECHNICIANS
    NOT REQUIRED.
    CONTACTING YOU AGAIN 48 HRS. 49X4JZ.
```

Spanbauer sat back. Another line appeared:

```
TERMINATE INTERCEPTED SIGNAL?
PRESS 'ENTER' TO TERMINATE.
```

He pressed the 'ENTER' key on his keyboard, leant back in his chair and steepled his fingers. Softly, he spoke to himself, "There is a fine line between loyalty and stupidity, Martin."

In London, the Secret Service team was pleased. Edmondson broke the silence cheerily, "He seems to have the situation well under control."

Cadogan, with the wisdom of years felt uneasy. "But what about this 'implant' - it could seriously undermine our man's effectiveness. Any thoughts, Dovey?"

"Well it sounds as though it's a simple transmitter, probably very low frequency and quite powerful. Apart from a surgical removal of the device, the only thing that might disable it in situ is a very strong magnetic field."

"Well don't tell me - get the info back to Quinn," spat Cadogan impatiently.

Quinn sat looking at the tablet screen...

```
INCOMING MESSAGE: DEPT CENTRAL:
49X4JZ:
METHOD TO DISABLE DEVICE
MIGHT BE TO....
```

A pause...

```
UPLINK ERROR> TX TERMINATED
END OF TRANSMISSION
```

Quinn stared with blank annoyance at the LCD screen. He typed...

```
REINITIATE UPLINK
```

Another pause. Then the system responded:

```
NO SATELLITE CHANNELS AVAILABLE.
PLEASE TRY LATER.
```

Quinn shook his head, angry and bewildered.

Meanwhile Spanbauer sipped a coffee from an ornate cup and on his feed the reassuring message appeared:

```
ILLEGAL TX 10478: STATUS: JAMMED
```

His thumb gently tapped the side of the coffee cup. He had a decision to make.

CHAPTER 20: The Client

The West always remembers the significance of Tian'anmen Square; the horrors of that dreadful day in June, 1989. Perhaps thousands were killed. We will never know. But for the normal Chinese citizen the memory has all but been erased by careful management of the truth by China's all-seeing, all-powerful government. The huge square itself is an impressive tourist magnet in central Beijing as well as a vast meeting place for the residents and workers of the capital city. But, even today, there is a feeling of 'something-not-quite-right' about the impressive space. Visitors are searched before they can enter. There are also a preponderance of fire extinguishers dotted around the hundred acre site. The locals all know what they are for - "In case someone sets fire to themselves," they will cheerily tell you.

The general prospect is rather bleak and austere. Because of the great size of the square itself, the buildings on its flanks, though impressive architecturally, are diminished. The area sucks out the energy of its perimeter.

People bustle around; tourists, military men, women in coolie hats, bicycles, snacking workers and friends saying hello.

On either side of the square, set back a little, are two enormous government buildings...

An office of a high ranking party member overlooked the expanse. An ornamental fountain tinkled in the centre of the room. The theme was rich scarlet and gold - very pure traditional Chinese in design. And not the slightest hint of western influence. On the wall was a massive golden relief picture of a Chinese Dragon breathing fire with teeth and claws extended. Two men took tea. They sat side by side on a wooden seat.

One was General Yucchi in full military regalia - obviously very high ranking and, strangely, a little nervous.

The other man was Zhenxi Thaxoi. He wore his heavy thick glasses. The General scrutinised him a little closer. He was pale – his complexion as pure as a waxwork. The youthful oriental features did not sit well with the deep set eyes. He looked a little too thin as though he had been told by his parents to avoid seconds from an early age. He had deep, longish, black hair cut into the typical Chinese precision mop. He sat confidently with an unnerving stillness.

The exchange was intensely polite, laboured, serious and probing. It was almost as though they were having an inscrutability competition.

General Yucchi began carefully. "My superiors would not condone this unofficial meeting with a so-called terrorist, Zhenxi Thaxoi."

"You said your superiors needed my assistance," the pale, bespectacled man responded.

"Well let us say that there is an unofficial grouping of like-minded individuals."

"General Yucchi, you have few superiors."

"In the military, that is true."

"Like-mindedness often spawns risks... ...opportunities."

General Yucchi paused choosing his next words. "The thoughts of a minority can often be, shall we say, more correct than the majority."

"But thoughts are nothing without actions, General."

The General prepared himself for the reason for the meeting. "This like-mindedness calls for unofficial action against the United States. True Chinese patriots are tired of Imperialist American decadence leading world opinion. Zhenxi Thaxoi, you may hold a useful, unofficial key."

"Are you looking for the key, the pick or the lock itself?" replied Zhenxi Thaxio earnestly.

"The lock opens the door to a room were the United States is embarrassed and vilified. They should be made weak upon the world stage - shown in a spotlight of incompetence. A super-power belittled and humbled." General Yucchi stared unblinkingly at the younger man before him.

"So, what, exactly, had you in mind for me to accomplish?"

Yucchi continued, "We look for the US to make a terrible mistake - a blunder of global proportions. We want you to provoke the Americans in making that error in the eyes of the world - but it must never be linked to our minority like-mindedness. Your group, Hounan, has connections."

"If certain of your superiors found out, General Yucchi, you, and your colleagues, are dead men. This is not official Chinese foreign policy."

"The risk... ...opportunity is all mine. I lose or gain - but the wager is safe enough for me."

Zhenxi Thaxoi considered the conversation in silence.

At length he said, "Then I will consider some options for you. But I will need in excess of one billion US dollars - or equivalent monetary instruments."

The General mulled over the enormous figure. "It would not be impossible to arrange, Zhenxi Thaxoi."

General Yucchi got up to leave. Zhenxi Thaxoi stared forward in intense concentration not even acknowledging the man's departure. Yucchi, concerned at the lack of recognition, walked, hunched, out of the room.

CHAPTER 21: The Steel Gantry

On the other side of the world, breakfast was in full swing. Spanbauer, Quinn, Slitz and Anastasia ate together.

Spanbauer rounded on Quinn, "I trust you slept well, Martin."

"Most comfortable," replied Quinn.

Anastasia flashed a look over to Quinn. Spanbauer did not see it.

"You will have to move your attentions as to how Cadogan will be joining us," said Spanbauer not looking up.

"He's very shrewd. The faintest error will alert him."

"But, tell me, which subordinate cannot fool his boss from time to time?" Spanbauer hoped the double meaning was not lost on Quinn.

"Oh, I agree. There are always weaknesses," Quinn casually responded.

"As a boss, I try to eliminate all weakness. Thoroughness is the technique." Spanbauer changed tack. "If Cadogan is as shrewd as you say, won't he be expecting some communication from you?" With this, Spanbauer leant forward on his elbows.

"Oh, on any mission he realises that is not always easy for a field operative."

"Communication from here would, no doubt, cause problems - not least for the location."

Quinn paused for thought. "Indeed..."

Flatly, Spanbauer hit, "Indeed. Have you tried to communicate yet?"

Quinn chewed a mouthful of breakfast, his mind racing. "I'm sure you are thorough enough to know the answer to that. Cadogan is astute - there must be no surprises, no anomalies."

"For your sake, I hope you are still in the game," countered Spanbauer.

"Perhaps Machu Picchu wasn't proof enough?"

"Consistency is all. A stable pattern. Reliability. That is what I need."

"I fully understand," said Quinn trying to close the conversation.

The breakfast was over. Spanbauer got up. "Slitz, please show Mr. Quinn back to his suite."

Spanbauer left the room. Slitz stood up and looked expectantly at Quinn. Quinn gave Slitz a sheepish glance. Anastasia stood too. Quinn submitted and rose from his chair.

Quinn, Slitz and Anastasia made their way along a corridor. A guard stood outside a door. The group approached it.

Quinn's eyes constantly flicked around looking for some opportunity. His eyes latched onto a sign on the guarded door. It read: 'VIDCONF 1'. Anastasia noticed him looking at the sign. Quinn's eyes met hers.

They arrived outside Quinn's suite. Slitz slid a card into a reader to one side of the door. The door released and swung open. There were a series of locks and the corresponding holes in the door frame. The door had a steel edge which suggested the door was solid metal covered by a wood veneer.

A secure, but comfortable, prison.

Slitz motioned to Quinn that he should enter the room.

"Oh, that's a pity, Slitz. I had hoped you'd be taking us on a tour of the facilities," joked Quinn casually.

Slitz motioned his hand towards a scabbard containing his curved knife under his jacket. Quinn complied and entered the room. Slitz pulled the door to. Another card swipe and the sound of the locks seating home was heard.

Slitz turned suspiciously toward Anastasia who returned her most disarming look. They walked down the corridor together, side-by-side. Suddenly, she stopped and bumped into Slitz, blinking furiously.

"I've got something in my eye. Aaargh - I must find a mirror," she said.

She was about to turn on her heel going back the way she came. Slitz gazed at her seeing through the ruse - but she picked up on it.

"Come with me to the ladies room if you like. You know it's more than my life's worth."

Slitz grunted, shrugged his shoulders and walked on in his original direction.

Anastasia continued back to the bathroom. She turned into the corridor where Quinn's suite was. Her squint miraculously recovered and she broke into a run towards Quinn's door. She produced a swipe card - it was Slitz's! She took it from him when she collided with him. She swiped Quinn's door. It swung open.

In a firm whisper she said, "You've got five minutes - possibly less."

She then raced back down the corridor to where she bumped into Slitz, dropped his card and continued on her way.

Quinn could not believe his luck. He span round grabbing his tablet and gingerly left his room, glancing at his watch. It was 9:00 a.m. precisely. He carefully looked up and down the corridor before padding off gently - retracing his steps.

A guard sat reading a cheap paperback book in a control room. He had a suite of screens before him showing security camera views of rooms and corridors. He did not notice one of the monitors showing Quinn making his way along a passage.

Quinn made his way through a minor labyrinth of passages. At each turn and junction he paused, senses taut. He fumbled in his pocket and withdrew a cufflink. He pushed one of its surfaces. A hinged cover slid back to reveal a small, circular mirror. He pulled the two halves of the cufflink apart. What appeared to be a small connecting rod between the two faces extended telescopically to perhaps eight centimetres. He carefully angled the mirror and pushed it out on its short metal stalk beyond the corner of the passageway at floor level. He then checked the next corridor. All clear, he rounded the next corner.

He trod stealthily in absolute, controlled silence. He got to the final junction before the 'VIDCONF' room. His mirror revealed a burly guard outside the door.

Quinn paused. Glancing at his watch the second hand sweep showed forty-five seconds past 9:00 a.m.

He dropped to the floor and pulled out the small tablet. He called up the secure menu he selected 'LASER'.

The cufflink mirror appeared from around a corner into the guard's section of the corridor. A bright violet, pulsing shaft of intense UV laser light bounced from the mirror and struck the guard in the temple. He fell to the floor as the bloody sizzle wormed its way into his brain. Quinn emerged.

He yanked the guard's swipe card from his belt - glancing at his watch - 9:01:20.

A quick swipe into the metal groove and the door to the 'VIDCONF' room swung open onto darkness. Nervously glancing up and down the corridor he dragged the guard's body into the room. He closed the door. He was in.

Back in the control room the surveillance operator still has his nose in his book. A monitor, unnoticed over his shoulder, showed Quinn dragging the lasered guard into the VIDCONF room.

The gloom was a sharp contrast to the brightly lit corridor. Quinn listened and waited for as long as he dared for his eyes to become accustomed to the darkness.

Less than one inch away from his head was the faintest beam glowing red. He recoiled to avoid breaking the light and setting an alarm off. Slowly, he realised there was a criss-cross network of beams laced across the entrance to the main conference hall.

Quinn exhaled, whistling silently. He's been lucky not to have set off an alarm already.

He felt in his pocket and produced a small penlight torch. A shaft of bright white light darted around the facility - the banks of monitors reflected shapes onto the walls as the light caught them. Spanbauer's central console was now picked out by the torch. Another glance at the watch - it showed 9:02:15. He switched off the light to assess the alarm beams glowing faintly - too high to step over and too close together to step through. The watch showed 9:02:35.

On came the torch again. There were banks of photocells set into the walls of the narrow entrance opening sending and receiving beams. There were no panels to unscrew or any visible control mechanisms.

Just behind Quinn was a chair. Clipping the tablet to his belt, he seized the chair placing it next to the array of red beams. Standing on it, there was still not enough height to get over it. He paused again. 9:02:55.

Getting back on the chair, with great precision, he started to get a footing on the upright back of the chair to gain extra height. The chair wobbled, nearly toppling, sending Quinn leaping blindly back onto the floor. Still no beams had been crossed. Flicking the torch on once more, he noticed a second chair. He placed this back to back with the original to stop it falling over. Once more he climbed up. Now perched in near darkness, balancing crouched on top of the backs of the chairs he raised himself to his full height very, very slowly - arms outstretched, trembling to maintain his balance.

He stretched a little higher. There was a dull clunk as his head made contact with something above his head. The surprise made him lose balance and, once again, he jumped for the floor - still not crossing a beam. He flashed the torch above him. There was a simple light fitting dangling down from the ceiling held by a single electric cable above him. Getting back on the chair backs he could just reach it.

Would it be strong enough to hold his weight?

Precariously teetering on the chairs he reached up and tried to test the lamp. Suddenly he slipped clutching air and then, a split second later, he made a grab for the fitting. The chairs crashed over. He was now suspended holding the lamp. Plaster powder floated down from the ceiling - the particles lit by the beams as they drifted down.

The ceiling rose sprang to one side as something gave. Quinn jerked down two inches - but the single wire still held him. Very gently he started to swing his legs. His movement increased as he swung back and forth like a pendulum. At the highest point of the swing on one side he had to lift his legs to clear the beams. Sweat popped up on his forehead.

Maintaining his swing, he set himself up for the motion that was going to allow him to leap over the beams by letting go at the right moment. But another judder and the lamp extended downwards another couple of inches. The ceiling rose housing broke and travelled down the wire to the main lamp fitting. The wire connections were now exposed. The wire was simple two core electric cable. All that was holding Quinn's weight were two tiny brass screws clamping the wire to a small junction box. One of the cores started to slip through. Quinn had to keep swinging on the cable to increase his momentum.

Another judder and one of the two cores broke free.

He looked up anxiously. He had to make his move. He was now supported on a single wire held by a tiny brass screw in a tiny junction box. With a final, desperate lunge, Quinn let go at the apex of the swing and leapt into the darkness beyond the beams. He was through.

On with the torch again and a glance at the watch. 9:03:40. He sprinted up to the centre console. There was a screen on it. Under it was a computer-style housing.

In another part of the complex the surveillance guard lowered his book as he noticed a movement on a screen. He leaned forward with interest. A monitor showed Slitz walking along a corridor. The guard, recognising Slitz, was at ease again. He settled back in his chair and continued reading.

Slitz walked along familiar corridors. He reached a closed door. He stopped. Something wasn't right. He felt for his door access card. It was not there. Now suspicious he turned and started retracing his steps with a cruel, determined smile.

Quinn frantically looked around the computer box under torchlight. There were no visible ports save a cable to the monitor and a cable running into the body of the console pedestal. The watch displayed 9:04:05.

He dug into a pocket to retrieve a tiny screwdriver which he used to prise open the computer casing. The lid popped off.

Slitz, face set, made his way through the corridors.

In the video conference room Quinn switched on the computer using a switch on the console. The screen flashed: ENTER PASSWORD.

He typed in: HARVESTER

The response: PASSWORD ERROR. TRY AGAIN...

He typed: HARVESTER OF EYES

The response was still: ERROR.

The surveillance guard looked up as a screen view changed to a view of the video conference suite. Quinn happened to be behind the centre podium hidden from view. The guard put down his book and reached for a packet of cigarettes. The monitor view changed again and Quinn suddenly was in full view on the screen - but the guard was pre-occupied lighting his cigarette. As the guard glanced back at the screen, the view changed back to the one where Quinn was obscured.

Back in the video conference suite Quinn's mind was racing. He tried entering another word:

ANASTASIA

PASSWORD ERROR. TRY AGAIN...

He glanced at his watch – 9:04:30.

Slitz stopped abruptly in a corridor, looking down. He bent to retrieve his access card lying casually on the floor. He then turned to walk back the way he came but after a couple of steps he paused - still sceptical. He turned again and retraced his earlier steps past Quinn's suite.

Quinn looked desperate now. At the centre console he typed: CORNUCOPIA

    PASSWORD ACCEPTED.
    ACCESS SEQUENCE...
    HARVESTER HARVESTER HARVESTER
    CHOOSE OPTIONS:
    UPLINK SEQUENCE
    FINANCIAL TRANSACTIONS
    INFORMATION SOLD
    INFORMATION FOR AUCTION
    CONTACT DATABASE (IMPORT)
    CONTACT DATABASE (EXPORT)
    BID HISTORY

He heaved a silent sigh of celebration. He had just struck gold. The watch showed 9:05:15. Quinn's relief changed to near panic. He slipped a side panel open on the tablet and pulled out a wire bundle. There were some sixteen wires each ending in a tiny crocodile clip.

He moved back under the console to the computer box. He located the disc and control electronics. With meticulous accuracy he connected the wires to various wires and solder points around the disc and disc control.

Returning to the tablet he called up a menu:
    'DISC SIPHON'.
    ACTIVATE?

He hit the 'Y' key. There was a pause.

A message popped up:
    UNABLE TO ACTIVATE SIPHON.
    CHECK SECTOR PARITY SETTINGS
    CHECK HOST POWER POLARITY
    CHECK DISC ACCESS TIMES
    ENABLE SEEK PROCEDURE

Quinn started to type frantically on his tablet.

Meanwhile Slitz stopped at the guardless door to the Video Conference Room - now very wary.

Within, Quinn was still typing.

And the surveillance guard smoked his cigarette and read. Casually he glanced at the monitors. Quinn was in clear view again - but, as he was not moving in the low light, the guard failed to spot him.

Outside the video conference room Slitz pulled out his door card - and his knife.

Quinn stopped typing. The tablet monitor sprang into life...

DISC SIPHON ENABLED.
COPYING FOUND DISC DATA.
CONTENTS BEING READ SUCCESSFULLY.
COMPLETE SIPHON WILL TAKE APPROXIMATELY:
04 MINS 56 SECS

As the seconds counted down Quinn smiled faintly. And then a click and a buzz at the door. Once more he focused. He hid the still connected tablet to the side of the computer box and swiftly half-replaced the lid. He switched off the monitor only. The computer discs, however, were still whirring.

He whipped round the back of the centre console. Out came the cuff-link mirror once more.

Silence.

The door opened and light flooded into the room. Quinn watched Slitz carefully enter the room in the mirror.

Slitz stopped at the dead guard's body and the fallen chairs. The photocell beams still gently glowed. He produced a small key which he inserted into a tiny hole in the wall. The beams died. He turned the key again and the room was flooded with light.

Cautiously, Slitz, brandishing his surgical steel, advanced forward.

Quinn remained crouched and hidden on the opposite side of the centre console.

Slitz gently made his way further into the facility. He moved towards the centre console, ready to pounce - ready for anything. He slowly passed one side of the lectern console and Quinn had to stealthily move, crouched down, around the opposite side to avoid being spotted.

Slitz then circumnavigated the central plinth and, as he did so Quinn had to keep hidden behind the opposite side. As Quinn moved his shoe creaked. Slitz stopped dead at the noise. In absolute silence, Slitz readied himself to leap to one side of the console. He struck – but Quinn had disappeared. A handle on a door in the base of the console swung gently. Slitz's man has obviously hidden himself in the base.

Slitz stood preparing to pounce - his weapon glinting. With his free hand he grabbed the door handle with the lightest of touches. He listened carefully. In a swift move the door was open and Slitz stabbed wildly at the contents of the base - jerking the knife manically backwards and forwards. Then a pause. The base was full of old dust covers which looked like the back of a man. Quinn was not there. Slitz recoiled half in anger, half in surprise.

He whipped round scanning the rest of the room. There was just the faint whirring of the console computer - but this he ignored.

Quinn was standing, pressed flat behind the bank of monitors. As Slitz passed slowly in front of the screens. Through the gaps his shadow played on Quinn. Quinn was frozen.

Slitz paced along the front of the screen bank - knife held forward. As Slitz moved along, Quinn moved in the opposite direction behind the stacked screens. Slitz reached the end and turned behind the bank. Quinn had gone - he moved around to the front of the monitors.

Slitz spotted Quinn's shadow moving at the opposite end and allowed himself a confident smile. Slitz waited as the shadow progressed towards him. It looked as if Quinn was moving directly for him. Slitz watched and waited behind the far end of the stacked screens. The shadow got ever closer... ...really close - but it stopped - waiting. And certainly not close enough for Slitz to gain the advantage of surprise. Then the shadow started to move again - but very slowly.

Slitz wheeled round to the front to intercept the, now close enough, form. He jumped round stabbing wildly - but into a rending of cloth and air. Quinn had attached his jacket to a curtain track running the length of the monitors and had used the drawstring mechanism to animate his jacket along to where Slitz was waiting. Quinn was still nowhere to be seen.

Once more Slitz scanned the room – now very cautious and alert. His senses had been ratcheted up as twice his adversary had eluded him.

Slitz crept down to the other end of the monitors where the drawstring in the curtain tracking was controlled from. He made it to the other end and, with a great deal of care, knelt to look round the back of the bank. He peeped round just a fraction - and still, no-one was there!

Quinn, had made his way up high onto the top of the bank of screens. He looked down on the kneeling Slitz. However, there was not enough room for Quinn to drop cleanly on top of Slitz to knock him out. Quinn waited.

Slitz started to move his head up to peer above and his eyes met Quinn's. Slitz was onto him now and powered himself up the side of the monitor stack. Quinn had no weapon and had to retreat along the top – some six metres up.

In the surveillance room Quinn was in full view at the top the monitor stack in the video conference suite. Slitz could be seen climbing up the side of the towering screens.

Slitz was now on the top too - but at the opposite end to Quinn. They stared at each other directly. Quinn made his move. He leapt off the top onto the steel lighting gantry and climbed higher. Slitz was after him. Quinn swung hand to hand across the gantry.

Now Slitz was on the gantry. There were some control cables running over pulleys by which the structure's configuration could be changed. Slitz used his knife to cut some of the cables. The unit that Quinn was hanging from suddenly swung out uncontrollably as its tethers were now ineffective. Quinn was swinging over a fifteen metre drop - too high to let go. He had to swing back to another part of fixed construction - towards Slitz! Slitz moved to intercept him. They both raced for the same spot.

Slitz got there first...

Quinn stopped, hanging in mid air. He was almost out of Slitz's reach but Slitz tried a swipe and a slash anyway and caught Quinn's chest with his knife. Quinn's clothing gaped open at the slash - his bare chest revealed. A thin, bloody line started to ooze but it was only a surface wound.

Quinn made to retreat lurching backward. Losing his grip he needed to climb up on top of the swinging gantry to make better progress. In doing so, he gave Slitz time to start to inch out to meet him from above - Quinn had to move fast but he was tiring. Slitz could make better progress crawling above.

Slitz was nearly upon him. Then, Slitz's gaze drifted noticing more supporting cables. He wielded his knife again on another cable track. The severed cable whipped from the release of tension through the structure narrowly missing Quinn. As it was a major supporting cable, the whole swinging structure dropped a full three metres in a sickening judder ending up lop-sided at a crazy angle. Quinn, who had nearly made it to the top of this portion of gantry, was nearly thrown off - hanging by one hand and clutching air with the other.

Slitz started to work on yet another cable. Quinn decided his only option was hand to hand combat and painfully started to make his way back towards Slitz.

TWANG! THWACK! CLANK! The gantry slipped downward again nearly causing Quinn to fall off again as the cable flashed centimetres from his face.

The structure was now supported by only two cables - one at either end. It was swinging wildly. Slitz perched on a solid piece of gantry. Quinn's progress towards Slitz was better than Slitz had imagined so he started to use his knife with renewed vigour on the two remaining cables. Quinn inched ever closer.

Slitz focused on driving the knife across the two steel cables. They started to fray and stretch. Quinn was still not close enough. The steel threads started to untwine as the strength of the hawsers failed.

Slitz's eyes met Quinn's. He kept rocking the blade over the cables as he spoke, "You must be looking forward to seeing your wife again..." He laughed.

Quinn's face froze as he gazed at Slitz. The shock was too great for him to understand. His brow furrowed and set in recognition. Barely able to form the words, Quinn mouthed, "You... the knife man... nine years ago..."

Slitz returned a knowing smile.

The cables split apart as the machined blade succeeded in its work. One cable, as the strain was removed, snaked out and, in a flash, coiled itself around Slitz's knife arm.

The force of the cable pulled his arm and knife towards his upper abdomen - the blade plunging inwards and dragging across. A bloody mess gaped in his midriff as the knife ploughed through. He looked down in horror as he started to witness his own demise.

But more was to come. The two cut cables supported the gantry that Slitz was on. The structure lurched downwards in an arc towards the bank of monitor screens. Slitz, perched on the free end, smashed into the screens in a shower of sparks - the full weight of the gantry driving him into the tinkling, exploding mass.

Quinn still hanging on looked on as his adversary was consumed in the pyrotechnics. The gantry arm swung back hanging vertically leaving Slitz, sizzling and twitching, supported on the broken monitor wall.

On a surveillance screen Slitz hung, broken, in the sparking monitor rig. The surveillance guard came back into the room drying his hands on a paper towel which he tossed in a nearby wastebasket – contented that his bladder was now empty. His eyes shifted to the screen – his brain trying to work out what he was looking at.

Two patrolling guards passed the open door to the Video Conference Suite - their suspicions immediately raised. They entered - automatic weapons at the ready.

Quinn scampered down from the top of the monitor stack as the two guards made their way in. He darted behind the screens as the guards came to terms with the mayhem they had happened upon. They stopped to look at the dead comrade's body on the way in. Quinn watched them through gaps in the array of screens. They moved towards one end of the stack. Quinn went the other way. As the two guards turn round the back of the stack, Quinn slipped round to the front, keeping low diving for cover behind the central console.

Quinn peeked at the still connected tablet. The display read:
SIPHON: EXECUTING DOWNLOAD:
TIME REMAINING: 02 MINS 19 SECS

He slowly peered round the side of the console. The two guards emerged from behind the screens and started looking at the damage of the still fizzing monitor array, Slitz's mangled, smoking body and the gantry.

Sense at last took hold of a guard. "Get Dr. Spanbauer now," he barked at his colleague. The other guard snapped out of it and raced towards the door.

The tablet display showed:
TIME REMAINING: 01 MIN 56 SECS

The remaining guard started to make a more detailed assessment of the damage. He seemed convinced that there was no one else in the room and started to methodically inspect the damaged area. He moved behind what was left of the screen bank.

Quinn, under his breath, looking at the tablet display, desperately chanted, "Come on, come on," as the seconds leisurely counted down:
TIME REMAINING: 01 MIN 33 SECS

The guard reappeared from the back of the screens and turned towards the central podium where Quinn hid, frozen. Gently, Quinn replaced the tablet to its hidden position. The guard circled the central console and Quinn had to circle round the opposite side to remain hidden from view.

The guard then walked off and took up position in the doorway blocking any escape - the short-nosed automatic rifle casually slung at his side.

Quinn now seized his chance. He retrieved the connected tablet. Less than a minute to go. Faintly, he could hear the distant, panicky bustle of more guards approaching through the corridors.

Spanbauer and three men arrived outside the video conference facility. "No-one has entered or left the room since we arrived, sir," said the guard.

"And when did you arrive?" snapped Spanbauer.

"Must be two minutes ago, sir. The door was open and the guard was not on duty. We entered and investigated. Then we discovered the guard - dead - and..er... Mr Slitz, sir."

"Come! Show me!"

The party entered the room. "What the hell happened here?" exhaled Spanbauer as he took in the scene. "Search the place from top to bottom."

The men split up and started a search. Spanbauer remained in the room near the entrance. Over his shoulder, behind him, Quinn gently dropped from the ceiling above the doorway and scooted out, unnoticed, into the corridor, tablet in hand.

The first guard had climbed up to where Slitz was hanging. "Sir, he's still alive!" Spanbauer sprinted towards where Slitz was still pinned into the bank of monitors - perched vertically. Spanbauer clambered up over the debris.

"Slitz. Slitz! What happened? Speak to me!"

Hardly alive, in a bubbly, hoarse whisper Slitz shaped a word, "Q... Qu... Qui..." He trailed away into silence.

"Hold on, Slitz." Spanbauer fixed him. "Tell me what happened."

Slitz stared vacantly into Spanbauer's eye. "Quinn," he said as he breathed his last. Slitz's head slumped forward – quite dead.

Spanbauer wheeled round. "Get Quinn - now! Bring him to the main lounge."

Quinn pushed his suite door to with a click. Out of breath, he tried the door. It had locked itself solidly. He darted around the room checking for any evidence. He placed the tablet in his suitcase, kicked off his shoes off and lay on the bed - waiting.

In a second, there was a buzz and a click at the door. Quinn feigned sleep as two guards burst in. "You are to come with us – now!" shouted one. Quinn blinked as if just woken.

"What? I was asleep. What... what's the problem?" said Quinn stretching.

"Come with us. Now!"

"Hold on. Let me wake up, *please*."

A guard moved to grab him.

"Take your hands off me. I'm coming," said Quinn, cold and assured. He got up off the bed in his stocking feet and walked out of his suite with the guards.

Quinn stood, flanked by the two guards, in front of the seated Spanbauer.

"Sit down, Mr Quinn."

"Why am I brought here in such an uncivilised manner, Spanbauer?"

"Tell me what you did after breakfast."

"I got back and was locked in my suite. Became bored. Lay on the bed. Fell asleep. Then I was abruptly woken by these two primates. Why?"

Spanbauer looked intently at Quinn as though searching for some little shred of evidence. "It would appear Slitz ran amok in one of my facilities here. He appears to have killed a guard and launched himself to his own, somewhat spectacular death, after stabbing himself. Can you shed a more accurate light on the circumstances?" Spanbauer paused menacingly. "Or will it be necessary to use other methods to extract an answer?"

Spanbauer's hand moved towards a panel set into a nearby table.

"I really don't know what you're talking about, Spanbauer. Slitz and I weren't exactly best buddies - but I acknowledged his professionalism. Perhaps he was a little unstable?" Suddenly Quinn screamed and shuddered - dropping to his knees from his seat as Spanbauer activated the implant from a panel of switches on his side table.

"His last word was 'Quinn' - you see? He wasn't quite dead when we found him. Strange that he should utter your name as he died, wouldn't you say?"

Quinn recoved enough to speak. "I'm sorry, I don't understand what you're talking about. I never left my room. I can't leave my room. Are you telling me your security, your thoroughness, is weak?"

Quinn noticed Spanbauer react everso slightly to this barb.

"Unless you were, of course, assisted in some way." Spanbauer leant over to a small intercom. "Anastasia, you can come in now."

Anastasia entered. She had been beaten up. Her once beautiful face was now puffy and bruised. Red wheals were pricked with blood - her hair a mess.

Spanbauer continued, "It was unwise of you, Anastasia, my dear, for you to succumb to Mr. Quinn's charms. Entrapment is one thing. Involvement, entirely another."

Softly, through her swollen mouth, she replied, "He's dirt to me, Marius. I brought him to you - for what? This?!? Marius, you see too much."

"You lie. Get out of my sight!"

She gave Spanbauer a scowl and left the room.

"And what am I to do with you? Torture you for a few trivial secrets? Then kill you at the flick of a switch like an ant? Or believe you? That Slitz went mad? Then killed himself? That he has a fixation with your name such that he, in total insanity, speaks it as his last word?" Spanbauer softened. "Then nothing has happened. You work for me. I pay you well. But perhaps this is fantasy." And then, almost to himself, "But, then, I have information so powerful that I don't need you...or Cadogan."

"I'm genuinely fascinated. What information could be so important and of such a high value?" Quinn ventured.

"You flatter yourself that I would need to tell you." Spanbauer got up and turned to the guards. "Take him back to his room and guard him. I need some time to plan his death in an entertaining way. Get some resource to clear up the Video Suite - and look for any evidence." And then to Quinn, "Until our final meeting, good-day."

Quinn was roughly deposited back in his suite, the two guards standing watching over him. Quinn sat at the desk typing at his tablet. He looked up. "So, gentlemen. Prospects good for career progression working for Spanbauer - or will you always have to share rooms with guests?"

The guards did not react.

"Well you must have names. The condemned man should at least have basic social needs catered for. What are your names?" As he spoke, he slowly, but casually, moved the tablet aligning it to where the two guards were standing. The options menu was up. The line saying 'LASER' was highlighted... "I just don't know how you can be so cold. I am about to die and you offer me no conversation."

"Shut up, Quinn," mumbled one of his overseers.

Quinn ploughed on. "Do you like computers? I find them most useful for erasing bad data."

With this, Quinn turned the tablet laser onto the guards. The luminous violet shaft leapt from the computer into their chests - sparking and sizzling as it found its targets. They keeled over to the floor. Quinn, tablet in hand, took a door access card from one of the dead men, swiped it - the door opened - and he was into the corridor.

Suddenly, another guard appeared round a corner. He pulled up his machine gun ready to loose off at Quinn, but Quinn was too quick. The laser cut down his opponent and Quinn moved on.

After padding through some lengths of corridor he reached a lift door. He heard the muffled roar of a high performance lift passing the doors going up. He moved on stopping at another, glass panelled door. Using the cuff-link mirror, he saw a team of seven guards walking in his direction towards the door. They were heavily armed – no way forward.

He paced back to the lift doors. Checking the tablet display, the legend read:

LASER POWER - 03% REMAINING

Quinn sucked his teeth considering his next move. He decided. He blasted the lift control panel with the last of the laser power.

Quinn clipped the tablet to his belt and proceeded to prise the lift doors apart. The guards were about to come past. Quinn strained at the doors trying to separate them - but to no avail.

The guards appeared - surprised to find Quinn so easily.

Quinn removed an SD card from the tablet with his best magicians' sleight. He then opened the tablet cover keeping it retracted.

"Gentlemen, hello. Before you capture me, would you just wait here for five seconds?" Quinn casually let go of the memory card and then pelted down the corridor.

"Hey! Stop! Or we fire!" challenged a guard. They cocked their weapons.

BLATT!!! The memory card exploded. It was a

compact grenade.

Quinn hid round a nearby corridor corner.

He returned to the lift doors, which had been blown open, and the pile of motionless guards. There was a draught of air from the shaft as the lift plummeted down from above. Quinn made the choice. In a noisy rush, the lift swept past the open lift doors. Quinn jumped through the doors down the shaft. He plummeted in uncontrolled free fall down the lift shaft. Like a rag doll, he occasionally bounced on the shaft sides or tangled in the lift cables. Floor lights whizzed past. The downward velocity of the lift was so high that he fell towards the roof at a relatively low speed. With a gentle thud he half landed, half sprawled onto the lift roof, the wind whipping his hair.

Spanbauer and Anastasia were in the lift. The noise caused Spanbauer to look up. "What was that?"

"Marius, it's a noisy lift," soothed Anastasia.

He seemed convinced.

The lift started to slow. They waited patiently for it to come to a stop. The doors slid open into Spanbauer's underground shuttle. Spanbauer and Anastasia proceeded to buckle themselves in to the leather seats of the transit vehicle.

"Next stop Cornucopia, my dear," said Spanbauer.

Quinn slithered down the side of the lift cubicle into a small underground cavern hewn out of the rock. The lift was connected to the outside of the shuttle capsule. The capsule sat on a peculiar track. The track disappeared into a black tunnel.

Quinn inspected the track as he climbed onto the back of the shuttle. There were no real handholds save for a light cluster upon which he stood and a thin lipped panel seam to which his fingertips barely gripped.

By the track was a notice:

DANGER: HIGH VOLTAGE: INTENSE MAGNETIC FIELD.

Inside the shuttle, Spanbauer pressed a button on a control panel marked 'LEVITATE'. There was a loud electrical hum and the shuttle capsule lifted by about five centimetres off the 'MagLev' linear motor track. Quinn clung on to the rear of the unit. As Spanbauer pressed another button marked 'START TRANSIT', the background hum became more intense. There was a judder as the craft started to move. The shuttle began to accelerate off into the darkness of the tunnel. Blue-white electric arcs flashed from under the vehicle as the power contact shoe skipped the live rail.

Quinn's foot slipped with the increase in speed - but he regained control - clinging on for all he was worth as the speed dramatically increased.

The capsule powered down the tunnel with very little clearance between the craft's skin and the walls. Quinn gritted his teeth as he barely kept hold. The speed piled on as the vehicle snaked through the smooth rock tube. Considerable air turbulence buffeted Quinn and his fingers started to slip. The shuttle lost a fraction of its speed and Quinn's white fingers slipped a little more. He could take the pain no longer. There was simply no strength left. He lost his grip and tumbled onto the 'maglev' track, rolling and thumping into the tunnel walls. He fought to keep himself tucked into a ball – amazed he had not contacted the live metal rail running to one side of the metal pathway. After what seemed an eternity all was mercifully still. He didn't dare move as he started to think about the damage his body must have taken. The tail lights of the capsule disappeared far down the tunnel. He started to test his body. A gentle move of the foot, the slightest twist of the torso, the tiniest contraction of his thigh muscle.

The shuttle came to a halt. "Anastasia, your bags are packed and waiting." Spanbauer unclipped his seatbelt. The capsule doors slid back onto opening lift doors which would take them up to 'Cornucopia'. He got up. Anastasia followed.

Quinn lay motionless across the 'maglev' track. There was a distant sound and a minute flurry of a breeze. The airflow got stronger and then turned into a gale. Suddenly the hurtling shuttle came into view, headlamps glowing. The capsule was on its return journey. Quinn did not stir as he lay directly in the path of the oncoming vehicle. The headlights became dazzlingly bright.

Anastasia emerged from the 'Cornucopia' shopfront carrying a small suitcase. A car waited. She leant towards the driver, "Aeropuerto." She climbed in the back and the car set off off in a cloud of Lima dust.

The shuttle came to a halt and Spanbauer, alone, unbuckled.

Through the gloom of the tunnel, pieces of the smashed tablet computer littered the 'maglev' rails.

But Quinn was nowhere to be seen...

CHAPTER 22: Rotors

"Quinn's escaped?" Spanbauer nearly yelled at the senior guard who had to tell him the news.

"He must have had some sort of beam weapon. He killed his guards."

"Where's his location from the implant?"

"We lost his signal. The signal just weakened, then disappeared," the guard gingerly admitted.

"You are responsible for the security of this facility. This lapse will NEVER happen again, understood?" But Spanbauer knew that Quinn may now have an advantage.

"Sir!" retorted the guard, relieved that it was only a verbal dressing down.

"Set implants 603 and 341 to kill."

"Two implants, sir?"

"Yes. There was a back up in our friend Quinn. Get to it." Spanbauer stalked off.

Anastasia approached the check-in desk. The clerk smiled her practised smile, "Can I have your tickets, please?"

Anastasia handed them over. The clerk studied them and then, "OK, that's Los Angeles... ...with an onward connection to...er...Beijing."

"Yes," replied Anastasia through a moment of stress.

The senior guard stood bent over a small panel. There was a small screen. It read...
ENTER IMPLANT NUMBER:
The senior guard typed in 603.
SET IMPLANT ACTIVATION LEVEL (8 = MAX):
He typed in: 8
ACTIVATE IMPLANT? Y OR N
The senior guard's finger was poised over the 'Y' key. He pressed it.
IMPLANT ACTIVATION
SIGNAL SENT
ENTER IMPLANT NUMBER:
He typed 341.
SET IMPLANT ACTIVATION LEVEL (8 = MAX):
He entered: 8.
ACTIVATE IMPLANT? Y OR N
He pressed 'Y'. There was a pause. Suddenly he reeled backwards, arched and screaming. His body then stiffened and quivered dreadfully. His eyes stared locked in horror. The quivering stopped and he crashed to the floor, eyes still staring. Two guards and Spanbauer entered the small room.

Spanbauer spoke calmly, "Dispose of the body. Learn well."

Spanbauer left the frightened guards to do his bidding.

Back in his lounge the sun was setting. Spanbauer looked out of the panoramic floor to ceiling tinted windows across the helipad where two small helicopters sat silently. And then to the magnificent view beyond over the lush green mountains. The sky deepened into a rich orange glow down the valley. Amidst the peaceful scene Spanbauer was relaxed but contemplative. He closed his eyes and planned his next moves.

Outside, from around a low wall, a shadowy figure darted over to the helipad. The shape ducked behind an auxiliary power unit close to the larger of the two helicopters.

A guard stood quietly by the open door that led from the main lounge into the rest of the complex. A rather battered Quinn silently appeared behind him. In the swiftest of moves, Quinn's hands, holding a short length of wood at each end, whipped over the head of the guard from behind. In complete silence Quinn strangled the guard.

Spanbauer continued to sit – eyes shut.

Quinn removed the dead man's gun. Without a sound Quinn took up position directly behind Spanbauer training the gun, two handed, police style, and aimed at the back of Spanbauer's head.

"Put your hands on the top of your head and turn round very slowly."

Spanbauer's hands obediently did Quinn's bidding. He then slowly swivelled his chair round to face Quinn.

"Ah-ha. My trusted, loyal servant returns. We thought you were dead."

Quinn spoke softly, "For a while. I only just missed the train. We haven't got long together."

Spanbauer gave a bored sigh. "Because you didn't kill me instantly, I assume it is information you want. Whether you kill me or not, my final *pièce de resistance* remains intact. To know that I have already succeeded is an epitaph enough. You may kill me now."

"But the world would never know the full story. You

wouldn't want that, surely, Spanbauer?"

"My 'angel of death', Anastasia, is on her way even as we speak. She is to collect one billion dollars for a transaction of information. They say information is power."

"What, no compassion? I saw your auction. You pulled the nuclear stuff out of the dying Lesko to sell to terrorists." Quinn hardened. "You end the lives of millions for what - some mad, minority faction - who wouldn't have a clue what to do with the 'power' once they get it. You're sick...."

Spanbauer gave a hearty laugh. "Hardly a minority interest. This represents the will of one thousand two hundred million people."

"So you deal with governments too. That is having your cake and eating it - but what a cake!"

"More accurately, Martin, elements of governments. There will always be the rebels who know best."

"One billion dollars. You can't spend that in a lifetime."

"The irony is you could have so easily have been part of it..." Spanbauer dropped his gaze and prepared for death.

In the surveillance room, a guard sat at the console. A video feed from Spanbauer's main lounge clearly showed the scene. Voices were heard over the speaker...

"As I squeeze my trigger, Spanbauer, I'm trying to think of a country with so many people... But of course - China..."

The guard hit a red button marked 'MAIN LOUNGE – ALERT'.

In the lounge Spanbauer became testy, "Come on, Quinn. Finish it."

"So Anastasia's gone to China to tie up the deal. I have enough. Remember I told you about job satisfaction..."

Quinn started to squeeze the trigger. There was a click. A guard had just released the safety catch of a gun - the barrel one inch from Quinn's temple. Quinn paused...

"But I would prefer to live to see the fruits of my labours." Spanbauer turned to the guard. "What kept you? Kill him."

In a split second Quinn's arm flashed up underneath the guard's gun arm. BANG! The gun went off just over Quinn's head - the guard's gun clattered to the floor.

Quinn span round and loosed a round off into the guard's chest. The guard sprawled backward. Spanbauer, who was surprisingly fit, dived for the loose gun on the floor. Quinn spotted this action but before he could check Spanbauer, two more guards appeared in the doorway brandishing automatic weapons.

A deafening torrent of gunfire spat from the machine guns. Quinn dropped to the floor and rolled for cover. The noise was heightened by the shattering plate glass of the panoramic windows – razor sharp shards flew everywhere.

"Kill him!!!" Spanbauer bellowed from the floor.

Another barrage was loosed off. Quinn made it to the cover of a substantial looking sofa. The guards moved forward into the lounge. Spanbauer shuffled behind the line of fire. Quinn seized a chance and raced out of the lounge onto the helipad. More gunfire. As he ran out of the lounge, Quinn managed a couple of shots back towards the guards - but to no effect. More blasts from the machine guns answered Quinn's pitiful effort. Suddenly, there was a tiny lull as some of the guards paused to change ammo clips.

In that second, Quinn got into one of the parked helicopters. He started the engine. The guards had nearly reloaded. A hail of bullets broke from the lounge. Quinn tried to lift the chopper off the ground but the revs were too low. The machine skittered along the ground avoiding the blaze of ammunition. Mercifully the revs increased and Quinn was in the air.

Spanbauer and the two guards emerged from the lounge and made for the other helicopter. It was a considerably more powerful machine than Quinn's – and also festooned with armaments – underslung missiles and a couple of beefy looking cannons.

Quinn's helicopter was already flying off down the valley.

Spanbauer's helicopter's engines started up and they were airborne in pursuit. A guard piloted it, Spanbauer and the other guard sat on the front bench seat alongside the pilot.

Spanbauer was closing on Quinn. Spanbauer fired off a tracer volley - but Quinn's helicopter, though slower, seemed more agile and the fire missed. Spanbauer's helicopter wheeled round in a tight bank chasing after Quinn. Spanbauer took control of the missile aiming device. He lined up the laser guided target onto Quinn - the red launch button pressed. Two missiles spurted from Spanbauer's craft. They were on a direct line for Quinn - but not heat seeking. Quinn saw the problem in the very nick of time. Both missiles missed but one actually passed through the spinning rotors - avoiding the whirling rotor blades by some miracle.

But Spanbauer had the advantage of speed and rounded back on Quinn. The helicopters weaved earthwards in an ever tightening spiral as Spanbauer tried to get his prey back in his sights. The ground rushed up and both helicopters had to break out of the chase to avoid crashing.

In an instant, Spanbauer was tailing and gaining on Quinn in a climb. Quinn didn't have the power and had to peel off. More tracer fire from Spanbauer. The helicopters lurched and shuddered in the chase. Quinn ducked as tracer whistled and cracked though the cockpit plexiglas. More tracer leapt from Spanbauer's helicopter. The luminous stream of bullets shattered half of the cockpit dome. Quinn recoiled - his arm up shielding himself from the flying splinters. His helicopter pitched violently.

The two helicopters danced a vicious aerial ballet in the glorious sunset. Missiles and tracer bullets lit up like some unearthly firework display.

Quinn's mouth was set hard as he wrestled with the controls.

Spanbauer yelled commands at the guard flying his helicopter.

In the back seat area of Spanbauer's helicopter, huddled on the floor, gripping on tightly, was Anastasia. She was the shadowy figure on the helipad earlier...

The deadly gavotte continued. Quinn's helicopter was now some height above Spanbauer. The choppers were flying along the same track but in opposite directions.

Spanbauer climbed up and back over forming the start of a loop. The helicopter was now in a vertical position and starting to turn upside down. As the loop continued, Quinn was directly in the sights of Spanbauer's nearly upside down machine. Anastasia hung on in Spanbauer's near-inverted helicopter behind the front seats.

Quinn was unaware of Spanbauer behind him. However, Quinn started frantically looking for his pursuer.

Spanbauer at last had his target and released more tracer and two more missiles. They hit Quinn's helicopter which exploded in a sickening kerosene fireball.

Spanbauer's machine, now upside down, continued its loop. At the apex, his helicopter actually passed through the centre of the fireball from Quinn's helicopter -

meanwhile the burning wreckage of Quinn's aircraft dropped from below the fireball in an arc forwards and downwards as it had lost power and speed.

Spanbauer's helicopter emerged from the other side of the fireball, blackened but unscathed, to start to complete the loop.

Quinn's burning helicopter started to plummet to the ground. Inside Quinn was surrounded by flames and smoke - panicking to release his seat belt but completely disoriented as the chopper started to spin. The mangled wreckage continued its plunge earthwards. Quinn just managed to get free of his belt and now pushed wildly at what remained of the the door. Suddenly, it opened in a rush of buffeting wind. He fell out through a sheet of flame into mid air - free-falling towards the ground. He vaguely thought how useful a parachute would have been as his situation became more surreal.

Spanbauer's helicopter was still completing its loop. The aircraft was in a vertical downward position travelling at high speed. Quinn, falling through the air seized his tiniest opportunity and, in a chance in a billion, grabbed the landing strut as he fell past.

Quinn held on with all his energy as Spanbauer's helicopter finished the loop with tearing G-forces to get back on the horizontal, original track. Spanbauer and the guards watched the burning wreckage pile into the ground with another billowing, crimson explosion. Spanbauer smiled broadly and gave an uncharacteristic a thumbs up sign to the guards. They were totally unaware of Quinn hanging underneath. Spanbauer signalled to return to base.

Quinn struggled to gain a foothold on the landing strut and, after a muscle-tearing effort, he succeeded. The turbulence was considerable. He carefully stood up slowly to his full height - level with the rear passenger door of the helicopter. He hung onto the door handle while standing on the strut. With his 'free' hand he fumbled in his belt for his gun. He tugged at the door. It swung open.

Spanbauer and the two guards swivelled round in surprise. They reached for their weapons. Quinn fired through the open door. BANG! The first guard was taken out. BANG! The second guard, the pilot, was out - his face disappearing in a bloody red plume. Blood spattered on the cockpit window behind him.

CLICK! CLICK! Quinn was out of ammunition and worried. The helicopter started to swing and dive out of control.

Spanbauer smiled and trained his gun towards Quinn's head. "Die, Quinn!!!!" shouted Spanbauer over the noise of the helicopter as his finger tightened on the trigger.

Anastasia appeared from behind the seat and jabbed a syringe into Spanbauer's hand holding the gun. The toxin paralysed his hand. Spanbauer realised his terminal predicament with horror - the poison creeping up his arm. Using his other hand he grabbed his gun from his disabled, quivering hand.

He waved the gun madly in his other hand towards Quinn. But the neurotoxin was finding its way into Spanbauer's body. Quinn and Anastasia looked on in dreadful fascination as the poison got to work. Spanbauer shuddered in agony - his face contorted into a scream. His eye wide - rolling, staring. Muscles and veins stood out on his face. His limbs shook and his body bent violently - the head thrusting backwards.

Then, all was still. Spanbauer slumped stiffly in his seat.

Anastasia smiled at Quinn - but there was no time. The helicopter was now way out of control in a violent spin. Quinn struggled into the helicopter. The ground was coming up fast. He threw himself forward into the front seat amongst the bodies and started to wrestle with the joystick. But the control column was jammed by the inanimate pilot's body. Quinn heaved the corpse into the back seat - Anastasia helping. The ground was perilously close.

Quinn wrenched the stick trying to get some control. At last the helicopter started to pull up - but only just as treetops entangled in the landing struts. With the narrowest margin possible, he regained control.

"Where's Spanbauer's base?" Quinn shouted to Anastasia.

"It'll be cloaked - we'll never find it."

"I don't suppose you know where we are?"

Anastasia, looking concerned, shrugged her shoulders helplessly.

"Let's try south. We don't need this excess baggage..." And with that, Quinn shoved the bodies out of the open rear door. The mortal remains of Dr. Marius Spanbauer and two of his guards tumbled down like dolls to the green canopy below.

CHAPTER 23: Happily Ever After

Quinn, Cadogan, Edmondson, Anastasia and Dovey sat together in Cadogan's office. On the table was an opened, nearly empty, bottle of champagne surrounded by half-finished glasses on the table. The atmosphere was jovial - even a mood of celebration.

"Well, Quinn, as they say, mission accomplished. Congratulations." Cadogan raised his glass to Quinn and Anastasia. Cadogan happily embraced the reflected glory - he continued, "The PM's very pleased. Dovey, any progress on getting the data off the tablet hard disc?"

"Well, that's the last piece in the puzzle. Obviously severely damaged in the shuttle tunnel. We're still trying to reconstruct it but I don't hold out much hope."

Edmondson spoke, "When we got into Spanbauer's hideout via 'Cornucopia' all the data was gone, rather strangely. Must have been the few men left covering their tracks."

Anastasia turned to Quinn, "How did you disable the implant?"

Quinn picked up the small device that had been removed from the table in front of him. "Nasty little bug. I must have got lucky."

"Isn't it obvious? Magnetism, Quinn. Magnetism!" Dovey chipped in.

"Well it's the first time I've charmed something to fail!" Quinn responded with a smile.

"No. Your implant was knocked out by the intense magnetic field from the linear motor track of Spanbauer's shuttle. You were lucky to be in that tunnel," explained Dovey.

"Lucky??!!?! I was nearly crushed by that underground shuttle. There was only just enough space to lie down by the rail to avoid it," retorted Quinn ruefully.

Cadogan returned to his task. He swung himself round to face Anastasia. "So you 'missed' your Beijing rendezvous. But the Chinese trail seems to have gone cold. I know you've had a thorough debrief - but is there anything at all which seemed odd or might help?"

"At the airport I decided enough was enough. The way Spanbauer was treating me - it just wasn't worth it any more. I took back the tickets and turned round. It had to stop. All I had was the name of a hotel in Beijing and a time to wait in the lobby. I assumed, like before, it was a simple payment pick up. Spanbauer did all the information exchange electronically..."

Quinn interrupted Anastasia, "I assume the Beijing 'office' has checked the hotel out."

"Yes - but the perfect cover, of course," Edmondson said.

Quinn appeared lost in thought, "Spanbauer said 'all was in place' and he was ready to die - unless he was bluffing. I assumed the information had already gone to China - so we still might have a real problem as far as Spanbauer's US nuclear offer at his 'auction.'"

Anastasia cut in, "No. He'd been duped before and

payment first, info later was always the rule."

Cadogan spoke, "Although Chino-U.S. relations are frosty at their best, Beijing has no need to precipitate anything of nuclear proportions. World trade is far too important to them at the moment."

"What knowledge did Dave Lesko have?" asked Edmondson.

"Everything. In the US nuclear hierarchy he was one of the most highly placed. And there, maybe, is our hidden strength. There was so much detail, Spanbauer probably didn't have time to assimilate how any of it could be used," said Cadogan.

Quinn added, "The U.S. cannot change all their procedures. There's physically too much to do. And if we can't find the information in Peru - it could have been destroyed along with the rest of the evidence."

"Well let's hope so." Cadogan continued, "Edmondson, keep an eye on developments - get Beijing to increase their watching brief. Alert me if there's a change."

Quinn motioned to go. "Well, I have to get on and prepare for the next problem in my 'in' tray."

Cadogan raised his hand. "Wait, Quinn. You need some leave. The M.O. says you took a bit of a beating. Miss Montero might like to join you - she has some historical involvement to answer for - though I think it can wait. We're grateful for her help. Go somewhere and relax for a while."

"Well...er..."

Anastasia gave Quinn one of those looks.

"Well, perhaps a few days ... but where?"

"Mmm, how about getting hooked in Singapore?" said Anastasia.

A Singapore Airlines Airbus A380 settled on the main

runway at Singapore's Changi airport, airbrakes, spoilers and flaps extended – its Rolls Royce Trent engines protesting with reverse thrust.

Sir Stamford Raffles would be astonished at what happened in the 200 years after his treaty with Sultan Hussein Shah of Johor. Singapore was a port of convenience for the British East India Company whom Raffles represented. So important was this trading centre that in just a few short years the British government made the Sultan an offer he could not refuse and Singapore became a Crown Territory.

Before Raffles got there in 1819, only 1,000 people lived on what was to become Singapore Island. In just forty years that grew to over 80,000 owing to the explosion of Malay rubber exports around the globe.

Apart from the three-and-a-half years of Japanese occupation during the second World War, faltering steps towards independence, subsequent skirmishes with the Chinese, a few riots and a couple of dances with the Federation of Malaysia, Singapore was – and is – the Asian by-word for free trade.

Now, with five-and-a-half million inhabitants, the city-state has become the world's fourth biggest financial centre. A somewhat repressive government with a questionable record in freedom of speech and a dim view of civil liberties has resulted in successful Singaporeans loving every minute of living and working in their crowded, urban island.

The bustling, human energy coupled with a nod to colonial manners makes Singapore an exhilarating place to visit.

And one of the very best restaurants is Jaan – sitting on Level 70 of the Equinox Complex...

Quinn and Anastasia sat back to take in the awe-inspiring, electric view of the Singapore late evening skyline. From their table-for-two right by the room high plate glass they were masters of all they surveyed – the water of the marinas doubling the reflected majesty and intricacy of millions of lights from office blocks, apartments, streets, docks, ships, cars, aircraft and bridges. Ten minutes they stared without conversation until the next two courses arrived.

Jaan didn't disappoint. Smaller than Quinn expected it was the perfect viewing platform. Plain wooden tables highlighted the spectacular 'artisanal' food. The only design feature were two parallel crushed metal chandeliers that ran the length of the dining area like some great tinfoil tubes festooned with lights.

They tucked into their Dover Soles Meunières with gnocchi drenched in butter and Hokkaido leeks. This was followed by Venison Saddles sitting in mulled wine with celeriac and sauce poivrade. A Mersault Clos de Mazeray white burgundy went with the former, a Château Moulin Riche St-Julien bordeaux partnered the latter.

"Missions never usually end like this, Anastasia," commented Quinn wistfully.

"Oh, Martin. And we've got ten days of this! I'm simply hooked, Martin."

"Mmm, hooked in Singapore..." Anastasia drifted away as the view caught her attention once more.

They kissed across the table. The moment was broken by the arrival of the Chestnut Delice.

"Martin, please excuse me for just a moment," said Anastasia picking up her bag and getting up as if to go to the restroom. She walked across the restaurant until she was out of sight of Quinn. She checked behind her - her face set in stone. She opened her bag, retrieved a small envelope and, as she passed a table, casually dropped the envelope in front of a diner. She walked on. The diner had a pudding bowl of straight black hair and a thin, humourless face. Zhenxi Thaxoi cast a glance at the envelope through the milk bottle spectacles – stretched a bony hand out to retrieve it and placed it in his inside jacket pocket. He then returned to his hay-roasted pigeon with liquorice.

Anastasia entered a toilet cubicle. Closing the door behind her she lifted the cistern cover. There was a small package and a gun taped under the lid. She put the gun and package into her bag. She then replaced the cover, activated the flush and exited.

Anastasia walked back to the table but, to her surprise met Quinn walking towards her by the side of Zhenxi Thaxoi's table. They stopped.

"The bathroom seemed a good idea too," said Quinn jovially.

Anastasia laughed - but there was the tiniest uncertainty in her manner which Quinn noticed.

"You OK?" he asked.

"Oh, absolutely fine. See you back at the table," said Anastasia, composure regained. She flashed an endearing smile.

Zhenxi Thaxoi got on with his meal but, as Quinn passed, the Chinese man eyed him carefully. Quinn did not notice at all.

Quinn and Anastasia left the restaurant, arm in arm. A low-slung black limo started to move out of the shadows down the street towards them. The snout of a machine gun poked through a half-open window aiming at Quinn. A cacophony of automatic gunfire filled the street. Passers-by dived for cover - including Quinn and Anastasia. Anastasia screamed.

"Run for it!!! It's me they're after!" shouted Quinn.

Anastasia rolled across the pavement and, in an athletic move, sprang towards and into a taxi waiting close by.

"Just get me out of here!!!" roared Anastasia at the driver. The taxi squealed off.

CHAPTER 24: Hooked

Quinn raced up the street, weaving from side to side to avoid the hail of bullets. He suddenly leapt off down a side alleyway. The following black limo screeched to a halt, the doors opened and four Chinese assassins spilled out chasing Quinn on foot. They followed Quinn down a narrow road between the seedier side of some high rise blocks. He kept ducking and weaving to avoid the zinging bullets.

He raced across a busy road dodging cars into a boat marina filled with moored yachts, motor launches and assorted opulent craft. There was a network of board-walk jetties connecting to a series of concrete piers.

Quinn, pursued, darted into the maze of walkways. He jinked through the silent boats - but his would-be killers were nearly upon him. He boarded a motor launch filled with partying guests and proceeded to crash though the centre of the gathering sending drinks, food and displays tumbling to the floor. As if this was not enough, the assassins wreaked even more havoc amongst the outraged guests as they followed.

Quinn was across and through to the other side of the launch - but there was no jetty on this side. He noticed a smaller yacht across a small stretch of black water. Hearing the approaching commotion behind him, he took some steps back and leaped off the edge of the launch only just making it to the deck of the lower yacht. He tumbled aboard.

The assassins repeated his move too, pausing to fire off a few rounds at the fleeing Quinn. One man did not make the jump and splooshed into the water. He swam and tried to clamber up the side of the yacht to no avail. However, three of them had made it. They were still perilously close to their quarry.

At the back of the yacht was a small inflatable tender attached by a single rope. Quinn jumped into the craft and untied the rope. He used a small paddle which to move in an ungainly fashion away from the yacht. The assassins, seeing this, fired more shots into the gloom - missing Quinn but holing the inflatable in two places. There was a rush of air from the holes and the craft began to rapidly deform, water slopping in over the weakened sides. Quinn's paddling became frenzied as he made for a large pier directly ahead.

The three assassins continued lamely firing into the darkness.

The rubber tender was nearly useless. Quinn got soaked as he ploughed on. He only just made it to some barnacled supports under the pier as the boat turned into a mass of rubber sheeting half floating on the water. Quinn clung to the slimy poles and noticed some steps up. After carefully negotiating the interlocking beams he made the steps. He relaxed as he had finally escaped.

He continued up the wet steps only to be greeted at the top by a small crowd of waiting Chinese thugs.

Quinn lashed out flooring two of the men. He ducked as the group rounded on him. He dummied from side to side missing their lunges – threw himself to the ground and under the feet of more of them. Somehow he got through the group - but as he rose to his feet to sprint away, they had turned and were already after him.

Out of the corner of his eye, Quinn spotted a pedal cycle propped up against a wall. He tore towards it, mounted and moved off only just in time. It was not a performance bicycle and his pressured pedalling only kept him a whisker in front of the chasing group.

As he cycled, the pier became part of the more commercial area of the harbour - merchant vessels towered up into the darkness festooned with floodlights and signals. There was more activity now as dockers marshalled containers and goods around the quayside.

Quinn still pedalled hard. He was easily twenty metres ahead of the thugs now. But, as he rounded a bend, out of the gloom, yet another group of Chinese heavies emerged in front of him barring his path. Shots rang out and, ducking the fire, Quinn fell off his bicycle. A little stunned, he took his time to get up. The men had blocked off any escape routes and started to close in on him. Quinn came round with a start. Close by was a metal ladder leading up a support leg into a quayside loading crane. It was his only hope.

With a powerful lunge he grabbed the ladder and hauled himself up - shots still whizzing past his head. Three heavies started to ascend below him.

After a supreme effort up the ladder, Quinn made it to the control cab. It was empty. He sat down and looked for a 'start' button. The controls were marked in Chinese. He tried buttons and switches randomly. The cab suddenly span around as Quinn turned a wheel - the crane was alive.

The three heavies continued to clamber up the access ladder. The crane's load - a stack of large metal girders in a parbuckle – started to swing on the end of the load cable.

Back in the cab, Quinn seemed to have gained some control over the machine.

The crane moved in a full arc and the girders began to swing outwards. A bunch of men milled around the base firing shots up at the cab. Bullets sparked off the metal structure near to the cab. One shattered the glass. Quinn was now exposed to the open air. More bullets whistled and ricocheted close to his body.

And then they were upon him. The first heavy had made it to the top of the ladder, entered the cab and started to grapple Quinn from behind trying to strangle him. Quinn grabbed the man's arms trying to pull them away from his neck – but without success. Quinn started to gag - his tongue and eyes starting to protrude. He desperately tried to swing this way and that to shake off his opponent.

The other two were now at cab level. They were big, muscular and athletic.

Quinn's struggling weakened as the pressure on his neck stayed ever tighter. He collapsed. In the moment of the collapse, the first heavy loosened his grip a tiny fraction. This is all Quinn needed as his move was a feint. With a powerful forward lunge, Quinn lifted the man off his feet, upside-down and over. As the first heavy toppled forward into the glassless void in front of the cab, Quinn grabbed a handrail inside with both hands. The man was launched into the air but he had still got his arms locked around Quinn's head. The first heavy was now hanging in mid-air from the cab suspended from Quinn's head while Quinn clutched the rail in the cab to prevent him being dragged out too.

The situation was now very dangerous as Quinn's neck could break at any instant. The first heavy struggled to climb up Quinn to get back into the cab.

Quinn let go of the rail with one hand and stretched for

a screwdriver in a clip close by the rail. His fingertips were just millimetres away. He squeezed the last gram of energy into his outstretched hand and his fingers make contact. He grasped the screwdriver and now jabbed it wildly into the arms of the heavy.

The man's grip started to slacken and, with a scream, he fell towards the concrete surface of the pier, bouncing on the crane's structure before he hit the ground, sickeningly, in front of his colleagues below.

Quinn drew himself back into the cab with great effort. He swallowed hard and shook his head trying to regain control. He took the controls once more. The crane lurched round. This caught the second and third heavy off balance and they nearly slipped off the ladder by the cab. This bought Quinn a couple of valuable seconds.

Quinn aimed the girders at the bunch of his assailants below as the load swung round. As the girders tracked towards them, he threw the crane into the opposite direction. The load tugged and strained at its restraining cables. The steel beams slid out from the end of the load cable and they tumbled earthwards. There was no time for them to run. The metal girders crashed on top of them bouncing on the concrete pier.

Quinn checked behind him. The second heavy had entered the cab and was about to squeeze the trigger of a hand gun to shoot Quinn. Quinn turned raising his hands to the ceiling of the cab in surrender but the man continued to pull the trigger. Quinn jumped upward, his raised hands grabbing a support beam on the cab roof and thrust both feet into the heavy's chest. The gun went off as the second heavy fell backward into space out of the cab door.

One man left - but already he was in the cab brandishing his gun. Quinn jumped towards the open cab window grasping the upper horizontal lip of the metal frame. Bang! Bang! Two shots just missed Quinn as he clambered outside and up onto the cab roof. Bang! The heavy fired up into the roof but the metal skin was too thick - the bullet just dented it.

The man paused as he listened for Quinn moving around on the roof – planning his next move. Quinn, on the cab roof, lay dead still, waiting.

The heavy made his move. Very carefully he got out of the cab down the metal ladder keeping close to the structure such that he was below the angle of view from Quinn on the roof. Under the cab he moved sideways off the ladder and onto the main crane structure. He looked up. The criss-crossing metal slats lead up in a column up, past and by the side of the cab. He started to climb, gun tucked into his belt.

Quinn cautiously peered over the side of the cab – but he couldn't see anything.

The heavy continued his ascent. He drew level with the cab roof so that his eyes just skimmed over the edge. Quinn was squatting, looking over the far side of the cab - his back towards his assailant.

The man gently rose higher over the roof level and aimed his gun squarely at Quinn's back. In the polished cuff-link mirror Quinn could clearly see the threat behind him.

In a swift move, Quinn back kicked the man's hand sending the gun spinning into the air. Quinn whipped round to face his attacker. The man climbed up fast onto the cab roof to face Quinn. Now it was hand-to-hand combat to the death as the two men circled each other.

The fight ensued – viciously wrestling, punching and kicking. They were evenly matched landing blows with equal ferocity. The balance of the fight swung back and forth, both men nearly falling off the cab roof at various stages.

Quinn sent his man crashing down onto the roof. Quinn then made a leap onto the crane structure and scrabbled upwards. His opponent was back on his feet and clambered after him. They climbed up the outside of the crane superstructure - Quinn only just ahead.

They finally reached the main horizontal crane arm and Quinn moved to the end supporting the thick metal cable - the hook swinging thirty metres below.

The fight went on - the men perched precariously at the end of and on top of the tubular steel arm.

Quinn, just as all seemed lost, managed to land a powerful punch to the side of his attacker's head. The man started to topple over the end cable pulley point of the crane arm. He staggered backwards fixing Quinn in his gaze. He fell but managed catch and hang onto the steel crane cable. He was now dangling about a metre below where the cable emerged. The thick, rope-wound, metal cable glinted in the surrounding docks' floodlights. A moment passed. Quinn lay down on the top of the crane arm to see the assailant hanging below – but too far away to reach. The men stared at each other - hate filled the heavy's eyes.

Slowly and deliberately, the man started to inch his way up to Quinn. The effort of the move did not seem to drain the attacker's energy. Slowly, he pulled himself up.

Quinn crabbed back across the crane arm and looked around for some weapon to stop him. He paused at a small service hatch undoing the metal catches. Inside were some highly greased gearwheels, assorted tools on a small shelf and a palm-sized can of oil. Quinn moved on, still searching...

The heavy started to make progress. He now only had about half a metre of cable to go before he could climb back onto the crane arm. Quinn now started tugging a loose strut hoping it would make a suitable weapon - but it would not budge. The heavy now had only centimetres left on the cable.

Quinn lurched back to the service hatch and grabbed the can of oil. He moved as fast as he could to the end of the crane arm. He leaned over looking down on the heavy. Quinn frantically worked the pump handle on the oil can and a glistening, golden fluid started to drizzle from the nozzle. Quinn placed the tip of the nozzle onto the shiny cable and sparkling globules of oil trickled down the cable and on the heavy's hands. Quinn kept on pumping and more oil dribbled down the wound steel threads.

His assailant's hands started to slip as the oil disabled his grasp. Panic crossed his face as his slimy hands no longer had any purchase. He began his dreadful slither down the steel rope. His eyes, wide in fear, stared skywards as his speed increased as he slipped down. He scrabbled for some grip – any grip - but the his drop was too fast. Now the cable was whizzing through his hands until has fall was abruptly and terribly checked by the crane hook ripping up between his legs and into his abdomen and chest. He hung, motionless from the hook swinging in mid-air.

Quinn's mouth curled down in horror. Looking away he muttered, "Hooked in Singapore."

He paused to get his breath back and started to shin down the crane.

CHAPTER 25: Hooker

Across the city, a taxi drew up outside a shabby entrance. Anastasia emerged from the car, paid the driver and rang on a buzzer by the door. A slit opened in the door and a pair of oriental eyes peered through for an instant. The slit shut and the door opened. A Chinese lackey beckoned her into a dusty, dimly lit hallway. Anastasia followed the man towards a large inner door. He pushed it open and motioned for her to go in. The door clicked to behind her.

She found herself in a highly decorated Chinese sitting room awash with ornaments ranging from cloisonné vases and ginger jars to beautifully carved ebony dragons – and everything in between. Brass, porcelain, glass – all neatly arranged on stands or shelving. Zhenxi Thaxoi sat, cross-legged on an oriental deep pile rug in the centre of the room. He was dressed in a rich, embroidered, Chinese robe. He looked straight up into Anastasia's eyes.

He spoke. "Anastasia, you risk a great deal coming here."

"If you kill Quinn, it won't be the end. I've been into the heart of British Intelligence. Quinn is only a field agent."

"Quinn is being dealt with as we speak." He paused, and then, with some weight, he said, "So is the British Secret Service." He regained his controlled, smooth delivery. "Relax, Anastasia. I have the co-ordinates, the frequencies and the coding. You have your money... ...your love of money is... er... quite breathtaking."

"The money ensures my excellent service."

There was an urgent knock and the lackey entered without waiting for permission.

"I have to inform you that the man, Quinn, has escaped."

Zhenxi Thaxio turned to Anastasia. "It may be that I shall need more of your excellent service." Then, back to the lackey, "I want all Singapore Hounan looking for Quinn."

In a downtown street Quinn walked along keeping a low profile. He kept checking he was not being followed. However, he did not notice a streetcleaner watching him as he paused to look into a shop window. Nor did he think anything of the young couple who brushed past him. Nor an aged street flower seller. A man in a doorway lit a cigarette as he passed.

He did notice the small crowd of Chinese youths emerging from around a corner behind him. He wondered if they might be following him. Their intentions were confirmed as he turned into a side street. They turned too and, looking forward, he saw a second group of youths appearing round a corner in front of him.

He was trapped - in front and behind. He tried a door as he was passing but it was locked. The youths closed in on him.

A very ordinary, small saloon car passed by and Quinn took his chance. He ran alongside the car and pulled the driver's door open. A startled, but very attractive woman, glared at him.

"Please - I need your car - otherwise I'm dead. Can you live with my death on your hands for the rest of your life?" he pleaded.

The car stopped and the woman moved into the passenger seat. "Mmm. I could live with you for the rest of my life. Are your legs tired? You've been running through my mind all day." She fluttered her eyebrows.

As Quinn got in she started to move back onto Quinn! "Can I sit on your lap and see what pops up?"

Quinn pushed her gently back. It was clear that the woman was obviously a hooker – and a little desperate for business. As Quinn stamped down on the accelerator, screeching off, her hands were already all over him.

Two following cars were commandeered in less subtle ways by some of the youths who gave chase. Their vehicles were of greater performance.

Quinn's car screeched down the road but the chasing vehicles, even at this stage, were coming up behind them much faster. The first car bumped into the back of Quinn's car as it started a left hand turn. This sent it spinning into the midst of some slow moving traffic travelling in the opposite direction.

After a couple of collisions, Quinn deftly weaved the car through the traffic and dived off down another left turn. The two chasing vehicles got round too without incident.

The chase continued down some brightly lit streets turning down a one way street. Oncoming traffic was avoided by mounting a pavement. Street furniture was knocked over as pedestrians jumped out of the way.

Quinn and his hooker turned right – their pursuers making contact with the car's back end all the time. The woman started to fondle Quinn's tie. "Nice tie, it matches my duvet..."

Quinn tried to push her away. "Does this car go any faster?"

"I've never driven it this fast before. But am I fast enough? This shirt would look great on my bedroom floor."

"Certainly, but we need a better car," said Quinn through gritted teeth.

Quinn swerved the car and crashed it into a garage back lot smashing into and through the rear wall of a car showroom. The vehicle was badly damaged surrounded by bricks and dust.

The chasing cars squealed to a halt and their occupants got out and raced toward the scene. Quinn and the woman slowly came round. Quinn's shirt was fully unbuttoned.

Quinn snapped into life but she was still delirious. He gave her a powerful kiss which partially revived her. "Thanks for the lift - but I've got to trade up..." And with that, Quinn exited the car.

The woman suddenly became very indignant as she came round and shouted, "You men are like toilets - vacant, engaged or full of..."

Quinn raced over to a sporty looking vehicle in the brightly lit showroom. He got in slamming the door covering the word 'crap'. There were no keys.

Youths from the chasing cars were picking their way over the rubble and into the showroom itself. Quinn was desperately looking around the car for some way of starting it. He felt behind the driver's sun visor. There were the keys. He fired the ignition with a look of 'Why didn't I look there first?' Glancing in the wing mirror he saw a reflection of the hooker and the youths stomping towards him. Throwing the car into drive, he sprinted off directly into the plate glass showroom window and out onto the street beyond. There was a shower of splintering glass.

Three of the youths realised Quinn was escaping and had turned on their heels back to their car. The remaining youths tried starting other showroom vehicles.

The woman, incandescent with rage, got into a small but powerful car in the showroom. The youths managed to start another performance vehicle and shot out through the broken window. The hooker started hers and revved off behind the youths.

Quinn snaked in and out of slow moving traffic. The showroom youths were in hot pursuit followed by the woman in her sports car. From round a corner, the original youths also appeared and join the chase behind the woman.

The procession continued, swerving this way and that, through a series of streets until Quinn turned off down a side street. It was a dead end - but not quite - there was an exit lane to a hotel car park.

He crashed through the exit barrier to meet the bright headlamps of a vehicle trying to leave the car park. The slip road was only one car wide and had walls on each side. The road curved downward into the underground car park...

Quinn slammed his foot to the floor and his car lurched forward. Steering it up onto the kerb the car bounced upward so that one of the front wheels started to climb the wall against the curve. The car was pitched on it's side at 45° as it crawled along the wall. The other car moved to the other side of the slip road and, incredibly, Quinn passed without a scratch.

Quinn whistled down into the basement level 1 of the hotel car park.

At the car park exit, as the car Quinn had passed left, the showroom youths entered the slip road, just missing each other.

Back in 'Basement Level 1' Quinn slammed the squealing car into a tight corner. To his surprise, coming directly for him, were the original youths in their car. Quinn performed a perfect handbrake J-turn and launched the car back 180° back onto its original path. The showroom youths appeared directly in front of him. And, again, he was trapped.

Quinn noticed a gap in the row of parked cars to his left coming up. He drove into the gap. Directly in front of him was a small flight of steps leading up to some double glass doors with a corridor beyond. Over the glass doors there was a sign reading: 'Singapore Imperial Palace Hotel - ENTRANCE'. He trod on the accelerator and mounted the steps - crashing through the glass doors into the carpeted corridor beyond.

A roar of engines drowned the soft hotel muzak playing in the empty corridor and Quinn's car appeared from around a corner. As he turned, he scraped the nice wallpaper and destroyed some occasional chairs, coffee table and ornaments. From around the same corner the showroom youths' vehicle appeared.

Quinn drove on clipping a solid-looking laundry cart. The cart swung into the path of the showroom youths who smashed into it. Sheets, pillow cases and bathroom replenishments flew everywhere upon impact. One sheet lay itself over the showroom youths' windscreen and they continued blindly, guided by a wall. One of the young men leant out of the side window and yanked the offending fabric off the windscreen.

Quinn's vehicle screeched into a mezzanine bar, sending tables and chairs into the air. Residents sprinted out of the way.

The youths in the originally hijacked car drove at top

speed past the devastated laundry cart.

The showroom youths' car swept through the bar enhancing the devastation.

Quinn hurtled along a balustraded section of the mezzanine floor which looked down onto the main lobby area. There was a grand, sweeping staircase at the end of the balustrade and he made the turn down the staircase as hotel guests leapt out of the way.

He was closely followed and both cars race down the ornate, wide curving staircase into the lobby.

An angry looking woman in a sports car drove at speed past what remained of a laundry cart.

An ornamental fountain played in the middle of a circular pool in the centre of the lobby. Quinn drove round this with the showroom youths on his tail. The cars circled it twice as Quinn looked for his next chance. In the meantime, the original youths' vehicle came down the staircase as the woman in the sports car passed by the mezzanine balustrade.

The original youths tried to block Quinn off as he emerged round the fountain by slewing their car round sideways. Quinn had no choice but to avoid them slamming his car into a gift shop, glass-sided on two sides. He took out the bulk of the gift shop's souvenir stock as the glass exploded under the impact. He went straight through the other side. The showroom youths swerved and followed.

Quinn now faced another apparent dead end. He passed signs to 'HEALTH CLUB'. There were a series of full height glass windows along one side of the corridor with a view to a gym beyond. He smashed the car into the gym. Ahead were some glass doors and a sign pointing to 'POOL & TERRACE CLUB'. He pushed the car through these, shattering them in his wake and drove along the poolside towards a large glass window leading to an exterior terrace.

On the terrace a formal business party was in full swing with a band, dancing and drinking by the outside part of the floodlit pool. With a crash, Quinn's car appeared through the glass from the inside pool onto the terrace area. Guests yelled and screamed but the overly loud band played on oblivious. He screeched to halt. The showroom youths appeared behind him entering the indoor part of the pool. There was no way forward.

Quinn slammed on the power and launched himself towards some more balustraded wall at the edge of the terrace...

The hotel's immaculate floodlit gardens sloped away from the terrace wall some six metres below the Terrace Club level. Quinn's car smashed though the wall. It was in mid-air as it sailed earthwards, thumping down onto the slope below. Amazingly, the car was still operative and Quinn continued into the gardens. Just seconds later the showroom youths crashed over.

Quinn's car ripped through terraced flower beds. The showroom youths followed. A series of Chinese Temples loomed ahead in the headlights and both cars swerved to avoid them. Quinn wrested his vehicle round and made for some closed, arched gates set into the high, brick-built garden wall. He piled on the power, the engine screaming for mercy, just missing some garden statues and smashed through the wooden gates. He was closely followed.

Quinn found himself in a narrow back street. He had to turn violently to the left to prevent himself going straight into the opposite wall. The car skidded sideways and crashed, side-on, into the wall - but it was still working and he pressed on.

His pursuers were nearly upon him. Quinn screamed

out of the back street onto a main expressway narrowly missing traffic. But on the other side side of the four lane road the original youths waited. They set off across the traffic giving chase - followed by a woman in a sports car.

The speeds rapidly increased on the expressway as the cars made their way past slower traffic. They went by a slip road signposted 'Power Station Only'. They continued ever faster. By this time, a couple of Singapore Police cars had joined the chase.

Ahead, an overtaking lorry blocked both lanes and there was no option but for Quinn to slow. As he did, the showroom youths rammed him off-centre from the rear sending him spinning back on himself so he was now travelling the wrong way down the carriageway directly towards oncoming traffic. He threw the car this way and that, occasionally clipping vehicles - including the police cars. He could not cross the central reservation as the carriageways were separated by a high concrete wall.

Meanwhile, the rest of the chasing vehicles had turned round too and were now following.

The exit slip road for the power station approached. Quinn's pursuers were gaining on him - the showroom youths were close enough on his tail to nudge him. At the very last minute, Quinn dived down the power station exit slip road such that the showroom youths and the hooker in the sports car could not follow. However, the original chasing car made it some seconds later down the slip road after Quinn.

The showroom youths handbrake turned into the entry slip road for the power station. The woman had to slow right down and also succeeded in turning towards the power station.

Quinn drove into the power station complex, straight through the closed exit barrier to the consternation of some security guards. He turned into a maze of service roads in amongst low electricity pylons. The station was floodlit with orange sodium vapour lights. Masses of crackling high tension wires and insulators criss-crossed above. Quinn paused - straining to see headlamps behind him in his mirror.

The two cars taken by the youths entered the maze – their headlamps off. They split up and proceeded cautiously in different directions.

Quinn drove gingerly past a series of electric shock warning notices - his headlamps still on.

And so the cars began to play cat and mouse amongst the pylons and cables. The sodium floodlights gave everything a surreal orange monochrome feel.

As the cars moved nearer the complex perimeter, the grid of service roads became progressively less well lit. Still no-one had seen each other.

Suddenly a pair of dazzling headlamps appeared round a corner shining directly into the windscreen of the original youths' car – momentarily blinding them. With the swiftest reactions they stopped and exited their car as the lights came towards them. They opened up their automatic weapons into oncoming vehicle with an intense barrage. The car swerved, uncontrolled, into the base of a pylon and stopped. Some of the metal struts holding up the pylon deformed under the impact. More instinctive gunfire. Then silence.

Hissing steam and leaking fuel, the bullet-riddled car came to a halt. Inside, a dead body was slumped over the wheel. It was the hooker.

The young men realised their mistake. With no concern they simply got back into their car and continued their search for Quinn.

Nearby, the showroom youths spotted Quinn, lights off,

just as he was sneaking off down yet another service road. They paced him, hanging back so as not to be noticed. Quinn continued, oblivious to the fact that he had been seen. He drove on to see the crashed car. The high tension cables were now sagging across the middle of the road because of the deformed pylon. He stopped his car under the sagging wires recognising the woman's vehicle. He got out to investigate. He knelt down by the side of the car to see if the hooker was alive. He was greeted by the dead stare of the bullet-riddled body. He briefly closed his eyes at the unnecessary death and went back to his car.

As he shut the door, the damaged pylon yielded a metallic groan and leaned over more. One of the high voltage cables touched his car roof. Nothing happend - the vehicle's tyres were earthing sufficiently. Quinn looked up and out of his window seeing his predicament. The wire crackled faintly. It was still live.

Through his rear view mirror he noticed the showroom youths' car approaching. He felt the gun still in his waistband. The car stopped about ten metres from the stationary vehicles. Quinn sat dead still. There was a pause. Slowly the youths emerged brandishing their weapons. Two of them split and approached Quinn's silent car from the rear - one either side. The two remaining youths covered them. Quinn has his gun ready.

The two young men were alongside the driver and nearside passenger doors. On a signal they both grabbed the door handles to open the car. As they touched the metal, they completed the circuit and they both lit up as the blue-white arcing voltage shot through their sizzling bodies. They screamed - but they were unable to move their hands from the car. They froze, smoking and faintly glowing orange around their wounds - then silently sagged to the ground.

The other remaining two looked on aghast but became intensely alert as the new situation arose.

Quinn who watched the gory spectacle from the safety of his 'Faraday Cage' that his car had become.

Quinn seized his moment and shot his rear window out and fired at the two young men. One dropped to the ground as Quinn's bullet found its target. The other returned a hail of automatic fire. Quinn dropped down behind his seat for cover. The automatic fire stopped briefly and Quinn managed to loose off a grab shot. It found its mark. One car down.

Quinn paused in thought as to how to get out of the car without completing the circuit and frying like the others. He turned the key, slammed his foot down and drove off - the high tension wire spitting and sparking as the car moved. The cable was left swinging in mid-air. The supporting pylon collapsed towards his car, crashing to the ground - but with inches to spare - Quinn made it avoiding the fizzing steel struts.

Quinn allowed himself a sigh relief at having escaped. He drove on down the network of dimly lit service roads.

Without warning, from a side road with a loud, deep crunch, the original youths' car broadsided Quinn's passing car and sent it spinning into a small utility building.

Quinn inside his car was semi-conscious with the impact and tried to rouse himself. A young confident Chinese man pulled open the door.

The youth spoke. "A gift from Hounan..." With this, he punched Quinn violently across the face. Quinn was out cold.

CHAPTER 26: Field Work

At the Changi Airport International Cargo Centre cargo pallets were being unloaded from an elderly 747 under the airport floodlights. One pallet was placed to one side. At the security gate a flatbed pick-up truck drew up. An airport official emerged from a hut. The Chinese truck driver wound down his window and eyeballed the official. The security man took one look at the truck driver and hurried, scared, back into his hut. The gate obediently lifted open and the truck was airside.

A short drive and the truck pulled up alongside the pallet. Three Chinese cargo handlers opened the container. They unloaded a large wooden crate measuring about three metres high, two metres long and about a metre wide. They used a small fork lift to transfer the crate onto the waiting truck.

The truck left the airport as quickly as it had entered and rumbled off into the darkness.

After nearly an hour the truck pulled off a road onto a dirt track through a swampy area dotted with the occasional low tree. The deep throb of a large helicopter grew steadily louder. The Mi-17 came into view – its searchlight following the truck - and gently sank to the ground ahead of the vehicle, engines still running. The truck came to a halt and perhaps six men dropped out of the helicopter from a large sliding side door. They raced towards the truck and man-handled the wooden crate into the aircraft. The deep pulse of the engines increased, the searchlight extinguished and the chopper lifted off into the night.

Across the moonlit open sea the Mi-17 flew low towards a small, strangely shaped island. It swooped in grazing the waves and landed on a make-shift helipad fashioned on the beach. The island was part of the Kepulauan Tambelan archipelago off the Borneo coast. In the dim neon lighting, a group of men rushed out of a small hanger-like building and speedily unloaded the crate from the helicopter.

In a trice the lid of the box was crowbarred off revealing a metal inner lid. There were a series of locks and sliding bolts. Once opened the metal lid was removed. Inside there was what appeared to be a bundle of cloths. Grimy hands pushed the rages aside to reveal a gas cylinder with tubes running further into the interior of the crate. More packing was removed. Suddenly a dead still human hand was revealed as the cloths disappeared - then an arm strapped to a tubular, polished metal chair - then a torso. Up the torso ran a corrugated rubber tube similar to a scuba diver's. More was hastily removed. The tube ended at a semi-transparent mask similar to a lightweight anaesthetist's mask. Gently it was removed revealing the nose and mouth. Another cloth was taken off the eyes and there, sitting unconscious, was Cadogan.

He half sat, half lay, strapped into a tubular metal seat. A white-coated technician stepped forward, pulled up the sleeve and injected Cadogan with a syringe. Slowly he came round.

The helipad burst into activity again and another helicopter landed. The men rushed forward to meet the arrival and an unconscious Quinn was bundled out of the aircraft.

Elsewhere on the island Zhenxi Thaxoi sat meditating on a sofa - his eyes closed. A soft knock and a Chinese man entered.

"Sir, they are here."

Zhenxi Thaxoi gave no reaction save for opening his eyes. The Chinese man bowed and left softly closing the door behind him.

Some hours later, Quinn and Cadogan were crudely, but securely, tied to basic wooden chairs, back to back. They were awake but looked gaunt and haggard. They were sitting under a bare electric light in a room which looked like a parts store - basic shelving units stretched away into the dark corners. Zhenxi Thaxoi straddled another wooden chair and scrutinised them. He got up and started to circle - still studying his prey.

And then he spoke. "Quite remarkable - your thoroughness and the late Dr. Spanbauer's planning. It seems you are the two people in the world furthest down the trail. A servant and his master - somehow equalised at the present moment, wouldn't you say? I would like to assure you that your deaths will occur. One way, is the road of pain. The other; the road of peaceful repose. Which road you choose entirely depends on the confidence you give me that the trail ends with your demise."

"The British Secret Intelligence Service and the CIA have complete knowledge of Spanbauer's plans and contacts. And of yours," Quinn lied.

"With deep respect, Mr Quinn, you do not even know who I am."

Zhenxi Thaxoi turned to go but Anastasia entered.

"Hello, Anastasia. Double crosses, yes, but the art of the triple... I'm impressed," hissed Quinn.

Anastasia cooed, "Martin, I'm sure you'll understand. I hate to see information go to waste - but a billion dollars can turn a girl's head."

"Easily tempted, Anastasia."

In mock embarrassment, she said, "Martin, I know. Isn't it simply dreadful..." Then she hardened, "...and you've no opportunities left."

Zhenxi Thaxoi and Anastasia motioned to exit. Anastasia turned and blew Quinn a kiss.

Quinn muttered, just loudly enough, to Cadogan, "I wondered how long it would take for Hounan to surface again."

Cadogan, instantly picked up on Quinn's line, "Its good to know that the Beijing Station is on it's toes. A billion dollars buys a lot. It's the sort of money only governments can put up."

"Which tends to make Hounan a mere instrument," Quinn added.

"Exactly, Quinn. Exactly."

Zhenxi Thaxoi stopped dead and turned round. "Anastasia, it would seem our plans need a little acceleration." They departed.

"How on earth did you know it was Hounan?" said Cadogan under his breath over his shoulder to Quinn.

"It struck me at a power station."

Zhenxi Thaxoi and Anastasia marched out to a waiting helicopter - its engine running. "Give me your mic," he said to the pilot as he climbed up the ladder. A loudspeaker crackled into life blaring out across the facility. "Kill Quinn and Cadogan as soon as you have time. There's no more use for them. Bring forward all plans forty-eight hours. Ready the jet."

CHAPTER 27: The Cavalry

Dovey was hunched over a desk in his lab working at a computer terminal. Edmondson appeared.

"Any progress?"

Dovey looked up. "Yes, the disk's mostly reconstructed. Watch this..." He typed in a password - CORNUCOPIA - and the screen sprang into life. A menu appeared divided into Contacts, Projects, Accounts, Bids and the like.

"We've got to work very fast. Try contacts..." Edmondson blurted.

Dovey clicked on the 'Contacts' app. A long list of names, arranged alphabetically, dropped out with a single number in a repeating format. At the top of the list was:

Acanthus 0481609N0241958E

"Those numbers are global co-ordinates. Have you got a search program?" asked Edmondson.

"Shall we try Singapore?" replied Dovey with alacrity.

A program opened in another window. Dovey typed: SINGAPORE.

The display pinged back:

Singapore 1° 17' N 103° 51' E

NO MATCH FOUND

"Widen the search," said Edmondson.

Dovey entered some more figures. A pause, then:

Zhenxi Thaxoi (Hounan 15)   0010738N1065210E

Edmondson's eye's widened. "Hounan – that's amazing..."

"Interestingly, there's is a tiny, island showing at that exact co-ordinate."

Edmondson turned. "I think the Singaporean Air Force ought to take a look. Hell of a flap about Cadogan's disappearance – must go."

Zhenxi Thaxoi's and Anastasia's helicopter landed at a rough landing strip, hewn out of the deepest Borneo jungle,. A small, long range executive jet waited close by, the engines running and its door open ready to receive passengers. They dashed out of the chopper and into the plane.

"Anastasia, Arizona calls us," he shouted above the jets as they mounted the steps.

Quinn and Cadogan were still tied up.

"I thought you were paid to be resourceful." Cadogan was miserable.

Quinn looked at the shelf in front of him. "I've still not seen anything we can use to get these ropes off."

They then, almost comically, in a series of tiny moves, made enormously laboured, uncoordinated progress by a series of small, shuffling jumps. The chair legs clattered and squeaked.

Suddenly, a clanging grind as the main door slid open. Two guards appeared - both armed. They jabbered in Chinese looking down each aisle for Quinn and Cadogan. They located them and dragged them with little ceremony back to their original position.

A guard addressed them in broken English, "You are to die."

Both guards unclipped their automatic pistols from their holsters and flicked off the safety catches.

Quinn turned as best he could to Cadogan, "There's a certain amount of pressure involved in being a field operative."

"You know, I always hated sending men to their doom," Cadogan responded. But Quinn doubted this very much.

The two guards each rammed a muzzle into Quinn and Cadogan's temples. Despatching a couple of prisoners was obviously familiar territory to the guards. Quinn prepared himself. He vaguely wondered how much he'd feel when his brains were turned to a bloody spray. He could feel the sweat pricking his brow.

Cadogan considered how unfair it all was and then checked himself for being philosophical at such a desperate point in his life. He closed his eyes. Had it been a good life? A useful life? An enjoyable life?

Quinn clamped his teeth together as a reflex to prepare for the shock he would not even know about.

The guards looked across at each other. One nodded. They tightened their fingers round their triggers. The triggers were moving inward to the bodies of the pistols. In a fraction of a millimetre the tempered steel springs would be released driving the striking pins into the soft, round brass of the bullet bases igniting the cordite. The resulting confined explosion would drive the lead pellet at twice the speed of sound into the fistful of pinky grey brain and the lives would be extinguished.

BOOOMM!!!

A massive fireball ripped through the hanger. The

guards, Cadogan and Quinn were sent tumbling to the floor.

In the chaos, the chairs on which Quinn and Cadogan were tied were broken sufficiently for them to struggle free but the two guards were up on their feet. Quinn was tangled up in rope and pieces of chair wood. The building was on fire.

Singaporean Air Force fighter jets wheeled around in the sky over the island firing at the buildings. The Hounan men retaliated from gun emplacements. A full ground-to-air/air-to-ground battle ensued. One of the jets was hit by a guided missile and exploded in a intense fireball as it crashed onto the rocks. Explosions peppered the island.

Inside, a guard was on his feet and aiming his gun at Quinn. He fired and the shot whistled past Quinn as he ducked. Quinn grabbed a steel pole off a nearby shelf. The guard fired again, missing, as Quinn ran towards him.

The second guard was starting to come round from semi-consciousness.

The first guard fired again but Quinn just managed to dodge the bullet once more. With the pole, Quinn swiped the gun from the first guard's hand sending it skittering across the floor.

The other man was up on his feet and pointing his gun directly at Cadogan. Cadogan was still hampered by the ropes. The second guard fired - Cadogan rolled over - and he just missed - but started lining up for his second shot. Cadogan rolled again - in the opposite direction - on the floor and was just within reach of the first guard's gun. But as Cadogan's hand moved for it, the second guard loosed off another and struck the first guard's gun making it fly another metre away from Cadogan. Cadogan lunged forward again - and this time succeeded grabbing the gun. The second guard was upon him and he fired – Cadogan was struck in the shoulder of his gun arm and winced in pain. Cadogan transferred the gun to his other hand and pulled the trigger. The second guard crumpled as he took the full force of the bullet in his stomach. Cadogan fired again to make sure. The man sagged to the floor.

Meanwhile, Quinn and the first guard were locked in a vicious fist fight. Punches swung back and forth.

The ground-to-air battle continued as a series of bombs found their way to key targets around the island. The Hounan guards were putting up a good fight but were being pounded by the air assault.

In the hanger, the first guard got his hands round Quinn's throat. Quinn chopped him in the ribs and the grip slackened enough for a head butt. The man reeled backwards. Quinn landed an almighty blow to his head and the first guard fell backward on top of the second guard's body. Quinn sprinted over to Cadogan.

"Come on," yelled Quinn.

The first guard slowly he came to – unbeknown to Quinn. Very slowly the guard reached for his dead colleague's gun. His fingertips made contact and in a second the weapon was in his tight grasp. He aimed at Quinn's head.

BANG! Quinn span round – surprised to see the first guard land heavily on his back – arms splayed out, dead.

Cadogan had shot the man.

"I'm still constantly grateful for the intervention of my superiors," commented Quinn.

The battle continued to rage but the Hounan resistance was now weakened. The hanger took a direct hit from the Singaporean air power. A huge churning explosion ripped up into the dawn sky.

By some miracle, Quinn and Cadogan emerged from the smoking hanger. They clambered up some rocks away from the buildings. Sporadic explosions went off nearby but the air fighters were victorious. Helicopters appeared and Singaporean troops abseiled down from them onto the island mopping up. A few Hounan guards surrendered and the Singaporean soldiers took them prisoner.

Quinn signalled to a soldier coming towards them. As soon as the soldier is within earshot he shouted, "Hold your fire! My name's Quinn from British Intelligence. I must make contact with London."

The soldier grinned back. "Quinn? I hope you've enjoyed your stay with us. Your people tipped us off - we came as fast as we could."

Overhead, a descending Singapore Airforce helicopter drowned them out and landed. The soldier gestured for Quinn and Cadogan to get on board.

A medic instantly attended to Cadogan's shoulder. They donned headsets.

One of the flight crew crackled into the headphones, "We have a line through to London, Quinn."

"Hello..? Hello, Edmondson. How the devil are you?" Quinn bellowed over the noise of the chopper.

Back in London Edmondson leaned over a microphone. There was a speaker on the desk. Dovey was sitting beside him.

"Better to hear your voice, Martin. Cadogan's disappeared. We can only assume kidnapped."

"I have not bloody disappeared," cut in Cadogan from the helicopter. "And have you cracked that Quinn's bloody tablet disk?"

Dovey spoke, "That's how we managed to alert Singapore. We do try and function in your absence."

"So what's the next move, Edmondson?"

"The US are laying on some transport for you. The chopper you're on at the moment is heading straight for

Guam. There's more: Dovey's sorted most of the disk siphon data from Quinn's tablet. It's a fair bet that the leader of Hounan, a charming gentleman by the name of Zhenxi Thaxoi, is en route to a US nuclear base, probably Johnson's Field in Arizona. We're tracking aircraft movements to see if we can spot Zhenxi Thaxoi's jet. There was a woman with him...

Quinn interjected, "Anastasia Montero - greed won."

CHAPTER 28: Guam to Arizona

Zhenxi Thaxoi and Anastasia each nursed a Jack Daniels in the luxurious cabin of the executive jet at 40,000 feet.

"How long before we get to Arizona?"

Zhenzi Thaxoi snapped out of some deep thought. "There is only one more refuelling stop. I estimate another seven hours."

The Singapore Air Force helicopter wheeled in and landed at United States Air Force base at Guam. Quinn emerged dressed in a high tech G-suit suit for flying.

Doug Kramer raced out to greet him.

"Martin Quinn. Last time we met was in Langley! Welcome to USAF Guam. I see you're suited up and ready to fly."

A small jeep approached. It stopped. They got in. Cadogan caught Quinn's eye from the chopper's doorway. He almost gave a small salute. Quinn returned a wave. Cadogan really suited an office, he thought.

Quinn turned to Kramer. "I gather you've laid on some transport."

"You betcha ass. Now just take a little look over there."

A very weird, matt black, stealth-looking aircraft stood silently on an apron. It was similar to an F-117 but considerably more pointed and sleek. It had two cockpits buried in the top of the fuselage..

Kramer continued. "Fastest way to Arizona is one of these birds. Our brand new baby - the FX-5000R. A prototype and very exclusive. Service ceiling a cool 80,000 feet, cruises at a little over two thousand miles an hour. It'll seat two and, if you step on the gas a little, you'll be touching down at Johnson's Field in what, about 9 hours - including refuelling."

"Jeez," Quinn whistled through his teeth. It made a change from RAF stock.

The jeep as it trundled towards the plane.

"Powerful beast. How much for a new one?"

"I dunno - I guess around a billion dollars - for cash! Who knows?!"

"Mmm, I'll take it. I assume I'll be flying clean," Quinn said.

"Sure. With no external weapons you're looking at least a seven per cent increase in speed - and, even with your Top Gun-plus flying hours, we'll be flying you this time."

The jeep stopped by the plane and the Kramer motioned Quinn to climb a ladder into the rear cockpit. The forward cockpit already had a pilot sitting in it.

As Quinn ascended he looked back to Kramer, "I'm not used to a chauffeur."

"Sure, but you might be able to get some rest!"

Quinn was in his seat and, as he thrust his head into a flying helmet, the FX-5000R's engines roared into life. The cockpit canopy closed. In a few more seconds they were taxiing by the jeep. Kramer returned Quinn's acknowledging wave as they passed.

The FX-5000R lifted off the main runway with a deafening roar into a near vertical climb.

In Dovey's office a technician popped his head around the door and announced that Cadogan was on a videolink from Guam. Edmondson duly appeared and they turned to a nearby monitor with a webcam. Cadogan's face appeared looking much better and fresher.

And Cadogan's energy was back too. "So Quinn's *en route* to Johnson's Field. It is one of the most well protected bases in the USA. It is central - miles from anywhere and road transport is not swift. Any unexpected aircraft would be intercepted miles off. Therefore, actually capturing the missiles is not an option for Zhenxi Thaxoi - even if he knew the arming sequences. Would you agree?"

Edmondson and Dovey nodded.

"Maybe he plans to detonate the missiles at the site - but the loss of life, although reprehensible, would not affect more than, say, six thousand people," Edmondson offered.

"He could get far more bang for his buck by more insidious methods. Spanbauer's notes mention Zhenxi Thaxoi wanting to 'humiliate the Americans'." Cadogan paused for thought. "Unless he plans to target the missiles..."

"But he'd need some serious inside help. How thoroughly vetted are the military personnel at Johnson's Field?" said Edmondson.

A large proportion of the six thousand staff at Johnson's Field Nuclear Weapons Facility in Arizona were either thinking about or having lunch. It was 12:30 p.m. And there were a number of canteen facilities across the sites.

At one of the largest canteens, US military staff lined

up with their trays and empty plates ready to receive their food. It was slopped on their plates in large portions in true military style. Nearly all of the kitchen staff were of Chinese extraction.

In a cleaning equipment storage room some cleaning staff were also taking a lunch break, chatting and playing cards. They were all Chinese.

At a service vehicle maintenance depot on the site a group of mechanics were eating lunch. Others carried on working huddled over jeeps, light armoured vehicles and trucks. They, too, all seemed to be Chinese.

In the very heart of Johnson's Field, in a top security area well away from the main complex, rows of nuclear missiles stood in a high underground steel cavern - waiting. The actual destructive capability of these weapons was only known to a handful of technicians and high ranking military personnel. Each warhead was capable of delivering thousands of times the power of the Hiroshima atomic bomb to an unbelievable accuracy – not that accuracy really mattered when everything was flattened for many miles around the target epicentre. The range of the devices far exceeded the publicly available specifications. From lill'ol' Johnson's Field you could flatten pretty much any target you liked, anywhere in the world.

Because the base was so remote it had its own airfield as virtually all supplies were airlifted in. A chain of Boeing C-17's plied their trade each day such that the whine of their engines had become a reassuring noise to those posted at Johnson's Field. However, only a few noticed the black shape appear on final approach. It was the FX-5000R aircraft. With a delicate squeal of rubber on concrete it touched down.

In the surrounding lonely expanse of desert, curious

rock formations dotted the landscape. A tiny trail of dust could be seen seen in the far distance - a motor bike on a dirt road. There were two people on the bike, one riding pillion.

The bike pulled up at the base of a rock formation. There was an entrance to a well hidden cave. The riders dismounted and took off their helmets. Walking away from the bike, a helmet under each arm, Zhenxi Thaxoi and Anastasia entered the cave. They walked along a short rock passage into a natural chamber lit by temporary arc lights.

Chinese operatives scurried around. In the centre a radio transmitter with a dish was being assembled.

The operations manager walked briskly over to meet Zhenxi Thaxoi.

"Sir. Welcome."

"Why is the transmitter not yet finished?" barked the thin, bespectacled young man.

The operations manager was taken aback. "We are working as fast as possible. Please do not forget that you brought forward our orders by forty-eight hours."

"I expect you to be always ahead of schedule. That is why I chose you as Head of Operations."

"Completion is only a few hours away but we must test the equipment otherwise the operation may be in jeopardy."

"It is chance I will have to take. Get on with your work."

The operations manager bowed deeply and rushed back to his station.

Zhenxi Thaxoi looked at Anastasia. "Look at the power of your information, Anastasia. A simple, directable radio transmitter, people in place within the heart of Johnson's Field ready to eliminate their radio jamming capabilities and myself, poised to alter the affairs of the

United States so profoundly. The world-wide humiliation, the vilification, the embarrassment of America - their nuclear warheads 'mistakenly' targeted and detonated on their allies' territory. Oh, such honour."

He walked across the cavern to an island of computers and operatives. One individual stood up as he approached and bowed.

"Set target co-ordinates, New York, London, Tokyo, Paris, Berlin, Moscow and Johnson's Field. We test transmit tonight. Final codings transmitted at dawn. Now return to your station." Then to Anastasia, "All the evidence will be destroyed. Aren't you impressed with this finesse, Anastasia?"

"I'm impressed with one billion dollars - and a fast motor bike after the countdown starts," she replied.

CHAPTER 29: Missiles

The top man at Johnson's Field was General Chuck Woodward. An Iraq veteran of the Bush Snr. campaign who had risen through the ranks mainly because of a combination of zealous patriotism and not making too many mistakes. In his mid-fifties, his white hair was a close cropped marine. He was a big man, square head on square shoulders. His face was the weather-beaten from the dry desert air and sand - but a little pudgy owing to a pizza or two too many.

He was a focused, expansive individual – pragmatic to the point of inflexibility but he knew people responded better to him if he tried to be helpful.

He had been at Johnson's Field for fifteen years and knew the place like his childhood home. He'd moved his long suffering all-American wife out to Arizona on his appointment as a general. She was keen to support him at first and was prepared to give the project five years at the max. She longed to be able to get off the hermetically sealed base lifestyle. Taking the C-40 Clipper to Phoenix for a day's shopping was hardly compensation. Even for a general, the quarters were poky, basic and needed a good facelift.

Quinn found General Woodward engaging but knew he was irked that a Brit was coming on his patch trying to call a few shots. The two men sat in his office.

"General Woodward, I know Cadogan's briefed you - but are you sure your security is tight? Any loophole - any chink in your systems?"

"Nope, Mr. Quinn. Tight as a duck's ass here."

"Any areas of high staff turnover?"

The question seemed an unnecessary curved ball to Woodward. "Well...erm...only ancillary services and the like - you know, catering and housekeeping - routine maintenance, I suppose – just like any other big operation. But ancillary staff ain't got any access whatsoever to any...erm.. sensitive areas. Need-to-know - that's the regime round here."

"And your radio surveillance? Good?"

"Look, man, we're scanning every horizon here. I've given instructions to be interrupted day or night if there's anything not right."

Quinn ploughed on, "As you are aware, General, the threat is likely to be from a small, but powerful, portable transmitter."

Woodward was beginning to get a little tired of, what was obviously to him, old ground. "Yeah, the missile firing sequence can be initiated by R.F. - but it's highly specific stuff, ya know. Particular wavelengths, coded pulses, that sorta thing. But look, my facility is screened by the most effective jamming systems dollars can buy."

There was a knock at the door.

"Enter," Woodward bellowed, grateful for the interruption.

An officer walked in and saluted.

"At ease, Officer."

The man was bursting with a message. "Sir, we've gotta fix on a rogue radio transmission. Twenty miles due south of this base. Sir!"

Woodward flashed a quizzical glance to Quinn. "Get armed choppers over there now, Officer. Quinn, consider yourself scrambled."

Quinn was on his feet. "Thanks, General."

It was already dusk and a formation of five military helicopters took off from the floodlit apron. Quinn was impressed that only fiffteen minutes ago he'd been sitting in Woodward's office. The helicopters with their searchlights full on flew fast, skimming the dramatic landscape - set against the royal blue and orange dusk sky.

The pilot of Quinn's helicopter grabbed his attention as they sat side-by-side in the cockpit. On the helicopter's GPS display a fix on a radio source was displayed. The position of the helicopter was shown on the display relative to the fix. They were close.

The pilot pointed down - the searchlights were playing on a cave entrance.

Suddenly, a group of twenty Hounan operatives emerged from the cave mouth, automatic weapons blazing at the hovering helicopters.

One of the helicopters was hit and burst into flames, lost height rapidly and crunched into the ground. A few seconds later the fuel caught and the machine was engulfed. This aggression drew a stream of cannon fire from the remaining helicopters into the mouth of the cave. Explosions lit up the sky as mushrooms of flame appeared around the cave.

The aerial fire was unrelenting – a total domination of firepower. More explosions. The cave, personnel and contents must surely have been destroyed.

Quinn and the pilot gave each other a hearty thumbs up sign as they hovered over the afterglow of the attack.

On a small rock promontory overlooking the cave from perhaps half a mile away in the desert, Zhenxi Thaxoi, Anastasia and a group of operatives were sitting safely from afar watching the explosions. A small transmitter dish was perched on a flatbed truck is close by.

The helicopters unleashed a final, terminal blast onto the cave and flew off back to their base.

Zhenxi Thaxoi glanced at his wristwatch and allowed himself the smallest of smiles.

Back at Johnson's Field, two military personnel scanned the screens in the base's radio threat room.

One man stretched and yawned. "God, isn't this the most boring watch on earth?"

"Bob, tell me about it. Our orders are to sweep the airwaves for Uncle Sam. So sweep," came the reply.

"...and maintain complete radio suppression into this facility. Aw, Hell, I'm bored."

"Leave it, Bob. You got leave in forty-eight hours - then you change rota. What's the beef?"

As the man finished speaking, three Chinese housekeepers came into the room complete with the paraphernalia of office cleaning. One emptied the wastebaskets into a big black plastic sack, the second started to mop the floor and the third polished the door handles and brass fittings. The military guys were completely unconcerned by their presence - even acknowledging it.

The cleaners then, simultaneously, out of sight put on nose clips and tiny mouth-sized respirators. The second cleaner carefully reached into a pocket and withdrew a small glass vial. As he bent down to clean a door handle he crushed the vial under his foot. A clear liquid spread outwards.

The cleaners carried on, their backs to the military staff.

The radio scanning officers slumped forward, overcome as the liquid vaporised, the first man to go was nearest the crushed vial – his colleague maybe noticed the problem for only a couple of seconds.

The 'cleaners' turned round and expertly started to dismantle some of the control gear and typing in 'ABORT' commands into a workstation.

A message came back on the screen - 'RADIO SUPPRESSION SUSPENDED'.

Some small circuit boards were removed from a rack, broken in two and replaced. Other pieces of electronic equipment were hidden amongst the cleaning items.

Everything was back to normal save for the dead radio operators. The Chinese cleaners left as casually as they had entered.

On the other side of the base, close to the perimeter fence, a jeep pulled up by the base of a radio transmitter aerial.

By the structure was a small, deserted, clap-board maintenance hut. Two mechanics of oriental descent got out of the jeep - one carried a tool bag. They ran over to the hut, opened a door with a key and went in. They set to work disabling the transmitter. The unit was part of with the base's jamming capabilities. Various wires and power supplies were disconnected. Components were taken out and placed in the tool bag. They left, locking the door on their way out and drove off into the night.

A few hours later as dawn came up, breakfast was in full swing. Base personnel stood in line with their trays waiting for the food to be served in the large canteen.

A Chinese-looking kitchen staff member serving beans

shouted to the back of the kitchen, "More beans!" A Chinese kitchen assistant appeared carrying a steaming serving tray of beans using thick oven gloves to replace the empty one. As the full tray was replaced into the warmer, with a deft sleight of hand, the kitchen assistant emptied a small ampoule of clear fluid into the beans.

The bean server stirred them thoroughly. "Next in line!"

The helicopter pilot who flew Quinn's craft during the previous night's operation took a big plate of breakfast. A large helping of beans was accepted.

Another figure moved in for his breakfast, tray in hand. Again, beans were generously served as part of the breakfast. It was Quinn's breakfast.

Up next, a USAF officer - he too, took his breakfast - beans included.

Quinn and the helicopter pilot made their way to a table. Their conversation was lost in the noise of the canteen. Quinn eat a mouthful of fried egg - the pilot; a slice of sausage. They chatted briefly. Quinn had some toast. The pilot took a forkful of beans while Quinn sipped some juice. The pilot consumed more beans. Quinn paused from eating, talking once more. The other man drank some coffee, then had another forkful of beans.

Meanwhile on the promontory overlooking the cave the sun made some more progress into the sky. Zhenxi Thaxoi looked at his watch again. The transmitter now pointed towards Johnson's Field. A few operatives passed the time on folding chairs. Anastasia was asleep in a chair under a blanket. Their leader spoke, "Take positions... ...transmit." All became alert.

An operative's finger prodded a small button on a console. The transmitter hummed into life.

Within some silos in the high security missile launch

area on the base, klaxons sounded and missiles started to move slowly on rails to their launch positions. Red and amber lights began flashing.

In the missile control room, abject panic ensued as the controllers could not understand what was happening. "What in hell's name!!??" shouted an operator.

A supervisor leant forward, "I'm... I'm not sure but it looks like a launch sequence has started."

"God! We have no confirmation of initiation!" another yelled.

"Do we abort or continue? Where's the order? What's gives?! Is this authorised?!!?" the wide-eyed operator shouted looking for some guidance.

"It *must* be an exercise..."

The supervisor was shaking, "No, no. I confirm armed warheads."

"Auto-targeting has commenced. This is crazy!" another blurted.

In a silo an automatic loading jig hovered and stopped over a missile, the jig's load marked DANGER: HOT NUCLEAR MATERIAL with radiation hazard logos all over it. The jig lowered the warhead and transferred it to the top of a missile. Automatic clasps shut fixing the warhead atop the missile rocket. The jig returned for another live warhead and it eased over to a new, empty missile ready to receive its deadly load.

It was complete pandemonium in the control room. Switches were being flicked wildly to and fro but to no avail.

In the radio jamming control room members of the new shift arrived in the room to be greeted by the two slumped bodies over the control desks.

An officer dashed to a red phone and picked it up.

In General Woodward's office, the base commander

and three aides were answering phones ringing off the hook - there was panic here too.

Woodward bawled down a red phone, "No, this is NOT an exercise and NOT an authorised launch - I repeat, this is NOT an authorised launch!" He slammed the receiver down and picked up another, "Abort launch sequence. Yes, abort, abort, abort!!!"

Suddenly, with the telephone receiver still in his hand, the General bent double clutching his stomach. "Aargh, my... my... guts." He keeled over on the floor, whimpering.

An aide rushed over to his assistance but, he too, was suddenly taken over by the stomach wrenching pain.

On the tarmac the helicopter pilot dropped to his knees in pain, clutching his stomach, as he walked towards his aircraft.

In the missile control room three of the five controllers were writhing on the floor in agony. The two remaining controllers fought with the controls. One of the two opened an electronics cabinet. "The boards are bust - this is sabotage - wait, the ZL-40 board is missing - hey, we're screwed. Get a call over to Spares."

"I'm onto it," came straight back from the other man.

In the computer spares store a telephone rang unanswered. Two storemen lay motionless on the floor – their faces wracked with pain.

In the silos a row of six armed nuclear missiles stood ready for launch - klaxons sounding, lights flashing.

Across Johnson's Field the carnage was now obvious. Nearly two thirds of the base's personnel had succumbed to the toxic beans. Those who were left were in chaos trying to understand what had happened.

Quinn burst in to Woodward's office. He rounded on the General's aide, "What's happening?"

The man was no longer in control of himself – let alone

the situation. "It's just wild. We've got a full nuclear launch sequence activated - no authorisation. They're all dead or dying. Master launch control is sabotaged. No radio jamming capability. This is it..."

Quinn grabbed the man holding his head forcing him to look into his eyes. "Pull yourself together." He struck the aide across the face. "Did you eat breakfast," Quinn demanded.

The aide slowly regained control. "No."

"Great – that means you're fine and you're going to help me. Take me to the missile control room."

As they raced over, the automatic jig loaded another warhead onto a missile.

The control room had turned into a chaotic pressure cooker. Two controllers had not succumbed to the poison.

"How long have we got?" roared Quinn.

A controller blathered, "This is just way out of control. The arming sequence is nearly complete. Before launch can occur, the targeting sequence starts. The missiles have got their own internal navigational systems - but the target co-ordinates are already in the system."

"How long?!!?"

The controller calmed a little. "It's like a commercial airliner getting its navigational position exactly right before it takes off. The system runs guidance programs for exact routing. The first launch will take place around fifteen minutes from now."

"Where are the targets?"

"Seven missiles. New York, London, Paris, Berlin, Tokyo, Moscow and...er... Johnson's Field. That's one mother of a problem."

"How do we disable the missiles?"

The other controller found his voice, "Three ways. Radio jamming..."

Quinn interrupted, "But the systems are out of action..."

"Retarget the devices - again needs a radio signal - but even if we manage that, the missiles will be out of our range by the time we work out the coding sequences..."

"And thirdly?"

The man paused. His colleague answered for him, "Manual intervention."

Quinn recoiled at this. "Exactly what sort of manual intervention?"

"There's a procedure which can be applied... ...to the armed missile itself."

"Can we do seven? That's if there's enough time to take them out before launch? Within..." Quinn checked his watch, "...fourteen minutes? What are our chances?"

"Three chances - fat, slim and no."

"Then let's do the slim one," retorted Quinn.

A motor bike roared along a dirt track across the Arizona desert. Zhenxi Thaxoi and Anastasia were making good their escape.

Quinn and a controller, followed by the aide, clambered up a metal stairway which ran to the top of a support arm holding the missile in place on its launch pad.

They got to the side of the actual missile. It hummed and whirred as the various internal mechanisms powered up. The controller removed a panel from the side of the weapon. There was a mass of wires and mechanisms inside.

"We've got nine minutes before this one flies," said the controller in a surprisingly matter of fact manner.

"And only six missiles to go after this one," said Quinn ruefully.

"You need to climb in."

Quinn look quizzically – and with some trepidation - at the controller.

"Yes. I've got to patch wires on this circuit board here. You've got to enter keystrokes - with this terminal - and my colleague," he gestured to the aide, "has got to read from a Manual such that none of us makes a slip. Understood?"

Quinn nodded and started to ease himself into the hatch. "Quite disarming, I hope."

The controller gave Quinn a small QWERTY keyboard and attached LCD screen - not unlike a small laptop. The device had a multi-connector attached to it via a ribbon cable.

Quinn was into the body of the missile amongst the mass of circuitry. There was a socket for the connector in front of him. "I've found the socket for the terminal."

"Good. Quinn, you'll have to wait while I reconnect this." In front of controller was a simple plug board - similar to a mini telephone network patchboard.

The aide, standing by the controller, said, "OK, what's the serial number of this one?"

"I can see the identifier plate - it's X-M-four-six," said the controller.

"Hang on, I have to look it up." The aide riffled through the manual. "OK, got it. Unplug the following cables - green 16, blue 12 and red 26.

"OK - they're all unplugged," answered the controller tugging at the patchboard.

"Right, green 16 goes to socket 47. Check?"

"Check," said the controller.

"Blue 12 in zero four. Check?"

"Check."

"And red 26 in 38. Check?"

"Check. They're all in."

"OK, Quinn. Plug your terminal in," said the aide.

Quinn's voice came from inside the missile hatch, "OK, connected - the screen's on I've got a row of coloured LED's lit up now on the circuit board."

"You have to type in a password. For this unit it is a four figure number 4 - 4 - 2 - 1."

Quinn typed the numbers.

"There's another plug repatch. Orange 18 into 56, red 20 into 30 and blue 6 into 50."

The contoller did this, "Check."

A menu appeared on Quinn's terminal:
    ABORT
    RETARGET
    CANCEL OPERATION
    DELAY

"I have a menu and we've less than two minutes," shouted Quinn.

The aide continued, "All right. Use the up arrow keys to highlight the required option - abort. Then press 'ENTER'.

"It's come up with INCORRECT PASSWORD," said Quinn, clearly worried.

"Look, I don't understand what the problem is. The password is 4 - 4 - 1 – 2," said the aide.

"Congratulations, you got your digits swapped first time round," came back Quinn's pressured voice. He entered the new code and moved the cursor over 'ABORT' – then hitting 'ENTER'.

Quinn yelled, "Right, abort successful. One down, six to go - Go! Go!! Go!!!"

The three men raced back down the metal staircase from the support arm to the base of the next missile.

"How long have we got for the next one?" asked Quinn.

"Less time - I estimate six minutes max," said the controller.

The aide became serious, "We've got a problem. The next missile needs to be on the launch platform for us to get to the inspection hatch." He pointed to the spot high up the side of the missile.

"I need to speak to the control room," said the controller. He darted away to a phone and frantically dialled a number to his colleague still in the control room.

He ran back after the call to his man. "He thinks he can do it - but it'll take a minute or two."

The three men waited - the pressure ratcheted up another notch.

"Even if he moves this missile now, there just won't be enough time to do the other five. There has to be another way..." pleaded Quinn.

With a grind and wheeze, the gantry actuators heaved into life and the aborted missile moved slowly along its rails off the launch pad. Missile number two moved across and into place.

"Three and a half minutes," Quinn said breathlessly.

The three men again ascended the steps to start the hatch process once more.

And so the second missile, with its involved patching and password procedure was disabled. Quinn launched himself from the maintenance hatch. "Aborted. Two down. Move!!!"

The men sprinted down the steps. The controller made his call again to the control room - and missile two moved off the launch pad; replaced, achingly slowly it felt, by missile three.

Once more they raced up the stairs...

The abort procedure was repeated on missile three – but this time with only seconds to spare. But the launch sequence started as the supporting arm started to swing back leaving missile three free standing - hissing as pressure built up for lift off. The large metal door above the missile opened and daylight flooded in.

The controller and the aide made it back onto the gantry steps but Quinn had to leap across space as the arm moved away. He only just managed it. Suddenly the launch sequence reversed on the successful 'abort' input.

They hurled themselves down the steps...

"It doesn't get much closer," Quinn muttered.

"It does - next one is around two minutes," the controller retorted.

Missile four slowly slid into place.

Up the steps again and they started to disarm the device. As they did so, the controller's colleague from the control room entered with a handful of soldiers. He shouted up, "Seems these guys skipped breakfast!"

From the top of the steps the controller gave a terse update, "There are three to go, that one's the most pressing. He pointed to missile five.

One soldier produced a rope with a grappling iron on the end. He spun the rope with the hooks on the end and threw it aloft by the side of missile five. It hooked successfully on a cross member support in the roof and the rope was secured and guided into place. Two more soldiers climbed up the rope and start to work on the hatch setting the missile to abort.

Missile four was defused with seconds to spare - but a little less hairy than missile three.

Suddenly, just when aborting the missiles seemed 'easier' the missile track sprang into life. There was a problem. Once more, panic reigned as missile number six trundled on its rails into place and onto the launch pad. Quinn, both controllers, the aide and the soldiers scurried out of the way.

"How long before the sixth missile blows?" said Quinn.

"Seconds only," came the reply.

"We must try..." Quinn grimaced.

Quinn, the controller and the aide went up the metal stairs but as they reached the top the missile trembled. Again, the launch sequence had started and this was a live warhead. Smoke and steam began to billow from the base. Hissing and groaning came from within the giant metal tube as the rocket motors neared final pressurization.

The aide cried at the top of his voice, "We've got to get out. We'll be fried by the rocket engines."

They flew down the stairs.

"There's a safety bunker over the other side. Run!" shouted the controller.

The breathy whining of the missile changed into a thunderous roar - building as the missile started its launch. Flame billowed up around the sides of the missile and the silo tube. The missile slowly lifted off - the noise deafening. A wall of flame blasted out from underneath.

The men ran through the sheet of flame to get to the bunker...

They just made it - cowering from the searing heat - clothing and hair singed. Within the bunker there was an eerie yellow, flickering glow.

Outside, the rocket of death slowly rose between the steel lips of the silo into the sky. Now it was on its way to deliver its nuclear warhead to some unprotected city – innumerable lives doomed. An arc of billowing white smoke marked its trail skywards.

Amid the steam and smoke, Quinn and the controller emerged from the bunker. They paused briefly looking up through the smoke in awe. Through the circular missile silo launch door they saw the missile burning its way into the sky.

"What's the fastest way to the airfield?" Quinn called to the controller.

CHAPTER 30: Targets

The FX-5000R stealth research aircraft stood on the apron under the burning sun. Another first from the US secret military research and production facility, Skunkworks, this new aeroplane pushed the performance envelope to new levels. Its enormously high, near space, service ceiling coupled with its speed, incredibly low radar footprint and ability to carry a wide range of weapons made the FX-5000R the world's most potent military aircraft.

Quinn was already in the cockpit. No time for pre-flight checks, he flipped his smoked helmet visor down. Refuelled and ready to go he fired the engines. What was left of a ground crew gave a half-hearted thumbs up as he taxied toward the main runway.

Though it had been some years since his time in the RAF Quinn felt immediately at ease with the controls. Pure fly-by-wire, the glass cockpit immediately fed back all he needed about the flight systems. Much of the information was projected onto his visor meaning that there was no need to take his eye off the view ahead.

At the holding point, Quinn grabbed the throttle levers, piled on the power and released the brakes. He felt a massive punch in the back from the acceleration down the tarmac. The FX-5000R hurtled down the runway and in seconds he was airborne.

He looked across to the far side of the base. The deadly white plume of the missile tracked high into the sky. Quinn banked upwards and directly towards the missile to give chase.

He hit the throttles again - the engines protested with reheat and the g-forces kicked him back in his seat. The mach indicator rose sharply.

The sky was already becoming a deeper blue with the height. The missile raced ahead, sitting on it's intensely bright flame. He locked onto the weapon and climbed further

Below, the seventh missile broke from its open silo door and ascended majestically into the sky.

Zhenxi Thaxoi stood on top of a hill by the motor bike. He looked through a pair of powerful binoculars towards the missile base. Anastasia looked into the distance, her hand shielding her eyes from the sun. Zhenxi Thaxoi took the binoculars away from his eyes but he is still stared into the far distance at the giant white smoke stacks.

"Two out of seven is a result." He allowed himself a tiny smile. He turned to Anastasia. "Come, we must go. The last warhead is targeted on Johnson's Field. We still have some miles to make up."

Up in the dark blue sky the FX-5000R was slowly gaining on missile six.

The nuclear missile was clearly in the centre of Quinn's head-up display. He worked some controls and a message flashed up: TARGET ACQUIRED - LOCKED.

On the control stick, Quinn's thumb hovered over the

red 'FIRE' button. Now it was his turn to smile in satisfaction. His finger hovered over a red button marked 'FIRE'. The aircraft's tracking systems had locked onto the prey.

Down went the thumb on the red button.

A message came up on the flight display: NO WEAPON INSTALLED and an electronic voice blared in his ears, "No weapons installed. No weapons installed."

Quinn punched the instrument panel in frustration. Of course, he was flying clean. He remembered Kramer's response at Guam, "Sure. With no external weapons you're looking at least a seven per cent increase in speed."

The FX-5000R was still gaining on the missile. The plane climbed at about 65° attitude, sitting on its engines. On the head-up-display the digital altimeter showed 60,000 feet and rising. The engines started to gulp for air.

Now he was alongside the missile. He manoeuvred the plane closer and closer to the missile pacing its speed. The wingtip was now only a couple of feet from the rocket.

The altimeter now showed 77,000 feet.

The mach indicator displayed MACH 3.34. Must be over 2,200 mph, he thought to himself.

Quinn balanced the aircraft so that the wingtip made contact nudging the missile slightly.

A bead of sweat rolled into Quinn's eye. Madly, he flipped the visor and rubbed with his flight glove-clad hand. The plane slipped away a little from the missile.

Once again he moved the aircraft closer. The wingtip was now under the missile. There was contact again and Quinn controlled the FX5000-R such that the wing pushed the missile off line and closer to the vertical. Suddenly, Quinn was sitting in a rollercoaster of buffeting as the airflow over the wing was broken by the rocket. The automatic control surfaces flapped wildly in the thin air trying to correct the poor aerodynamics.

Somehow he managed to guide the missile into a vertical position pushing it way off track. He stayed with it for a few seconds – the plane bucking and lurching in protest - to ensure that it did not revert to its original course.

The missile's on-board guidance was sufficiently confused. As Quinn peeled away diving earthwards as the missile headed for outer space.

He put the aircraft into a vertical nose-dive. The plane started to buffet as he piled on more power. The mach reading was 3.96 and increasing.

Closer to earth, the seventh missile made progress skywards in a vertical attitude. Gradually, it started to level off and then turned downwards back towards the earth. It sought its target – Johnson's Field.

Quinn hurtled earthwards - the engines screaming - the plane shaking violently.

The missile was now heading directly for Johnson's Field. From Quinn's viewpoint above the rear of the weapon he could clearly see that it was on course for the pattern of runways, buildings and service roads that made up the base. He thought briefly about whether those already dead from the beans were luckier than being fried and blasted to dust by the atomic explosion. Another thought crossed his mind. What would happen to the hundreds of nuclear warheads stored at the facility? Would they too detonate? Or would they be sent up into the stratosphere as countless, highly radioactive particles? And then would the deadly cloud be sent around the globe through weather systems slowly killing and disrupting DNA to all in its wake?

Now Quinn could see the exhaust flame of the missile below - but it was still only a speck. The aircraft continued to vibrate with the extreme stresses of speed well beyond the plane's specification.

The black plane shot earthwards chasing the deadly rocket. The aircraft was getting closer - but not by much. Quinn became aware that he was getting much lower as more ground detail was apparent.

And suddenly, he was alongside the missile - but was there going to be enough height to complete the manoeuvre as before? The ground is started to rush towards him - the speed extreme.

The FX-5000R wingtip made contact just underneath and, slowly, started to correct the dive of the missile. There was simply no margin for error.

The ground rushed directly towards Quinn. He could now make out vehicles. Only seconds remained before he would smash into the ground alongside the nuclear missile.

In what seemed like an eternity, the wingtip progressivly flattened the missile's course as Quinn plummeted down.

The ground flashed by in a terrible blur of detail.

Still the trajectory of the rocket flattened. Quinn was now disorientated. Buildings flew by – he was impossibly close to the ground at desperately high speed. A number of hangers and office blocks lay in a cluster directly ahead – not that there was time for him to notice. There was a series of covered walkways connecting the buildings over service roads.

The jets squealed mixed with the deep, crackling roar of the missile rocket motor.

The aircraft was now at the flat base of the dive, travelling parallel to the ground and guiding the missile along - perhaps only fifteen feet above the surface.

Both plane and missile skimmed the roads as, in a split second, they flashed in-between the buildings and then under the walkways.

Quinn kept on correcting the missile's path such that it was back in a climb once more.

The wingtip was in contact with the missile. There was a sudden, sickening buffet of turbulence and the wingtip and missile crashed into each other. A flash of flame and the wingtip started to disintegrate - the aileron suddenly ripped off.

Quinn started to fight for control. The trajectory became vertically upward and the plane paced the weapon. Again, the sky turned a darker blue as they ascended. He maintained a course for outer space.

Quinn looked across at the white vapour trail as last missile headed for the deep blue sky. Suddenly the missile veered back towards earth – it had re-locked onto its target co-ordinates. As this happened, a cockpit warning klaxon screeched. The plane's electronic voice blared out, "Malfunction! Malfunction! Malfunction!"

Quinn glanced at the display screen showing the words 'Control surface inoperative! Port aileron! Port aileron!'

The plane now lurched from side to side. Quinn wrestled the controls. The plane pitched and wallowed. But his eyes were fixed on the missile as he wrenched the plane directly for it! Through the head-up-display the aircraft flew on a collision trajectory. The speed built. Quinn was soaked in sweat. The FX-5000R got closer to the missile. He used every ounce of his strength to maintain course. He left it until the very last minute as he flipped up a small yellow and black striped cover. There was a label to one side - EJECTION CAPSULE. A button was revealed - at last he pressed it. In a white flash and a rush of air the ejection capsule separated from the aircraft. The plane continued on its course, found its target and made contact.

An almighty fireball engulfed the capsule in a massive

blanket of flame.

In the cockpit capsule he covered his face with his arms. There was a long pause as the ejection capsule plummeted to earth. Suddenly, all went intensely white as the nuclear material detonated. The atomic flash died a little and then the capsule was pummelled by the shock wave – though less serious in the rarefied atmosphere at this great height.

And then the sixth missile detonated safely in near space. There were two bright balls of light of different sizes as the two missiles destroyed themselves.

The sky was a lighter blue. The speck of the falling capsule was gently jolted by the reassuring crumple and crackle of its parachutes opening.

Quinn looked up through the window at the two points of light. Then he glanced down at the console. There was a notice. It read:

> THINK OF THE NEXT GUY!
> Leave this aircraft as
> you would wish to find it!
> TIDY UP!
> REPORT ANY DAMAGE

Quinn give a relieved smile and closed his eyes as the capsule floated down.

CHAPTER 31: Loose Ends

Zhenxi Thaxoi sat alone on a seat in Tain'anmen Square as tourists milled around. General Yucchi approached and parked himself beside him.

After a short while, the General spoke looking directly ahead, "Good day, Zhenxi Thaxoi. One billion dollars is a high price for the deaths of a few US military personnel and some damage to an airbase."

"Your money will be returned, General Yucchi, but it will take some time. Hounan honours its debts."

"Debts can be both monetary and personal," added General Yucchi.

Zhenxi Thaxoi stiffened. "The man Quinn - he has a price to pay."

"Is wreaking revenge on one man enough recompense for your own failure?"

Zhenxi Thaxoi pondered for a moment. "It would help me to understand and live with my failure."

"Look after yourself, Zhenxi Thaxoi. Look after yourself." General Yucchi got up without another word and walked off into the crowd. Zhenxi Thaxoi looked at his feet.

The sun was setting over London skyline. Commuters found their way to trains, buses and cars. Another day in the city. Just like any other.

A key turned in the closed front door of Quinn's apartment. It opened and a shattered-looking Quinn entered carrying cases. He was home. He dumped the cases in the hall with a sigh and wandered into his lounge. Everything was exactly as it was. He took off his coat and jacket and then slipped off his shoulder holster. He walked over to the drinks cabinet and fixed himself a stiff brandy. He flopped into a sofa.

He considered for a moment how surreal life could get. One moment sitting in a US research aircraft flying at over two thousand miles an hour chasing nuclear missiles – the next, at home sipping a brandy.

He raised his glass into the middle distance. "Here's to baked beans." He took a sip. "Never could stand them."

He noticed the picture of Jayne and drank a deep swig. He stared at the photo for a while in thought.

Snapping out of it he got to his feet. "Food. What shall we have, Jayne? Oysters? Champagne? Truffles? ...Beans?"

He walked into his kitchen and opened the refrigerator door to see if there was anything still edible.

CRACK!!!

Zhenxi Thaxoi, naked and glistening - save for his loin cloth, delivered a massive karate blow to the side of Quinn's neck. Quinn sprawled on the floor. Zhenxi Thaxoi stepped out of the shadows.

Quinn groaned. He struggled up. BAM! Zhenxi Thaxoi kicked him in the chest. Quinn reeled back on the floor.

Quinn heaved himself onto all fours. Zhenxi Thaxoi waited, leering at him and allowed him to struggle to his feet. SMASH! Another blow and Quinn was sent spinning out of the kitchen into the hallway - stunned. But Zhenxi Thaxoi was unrelenting.

Quinn got up once more only to be knocked over by a vicious chop. He slowly, painfully got up again. BAM! Yet another blow.

This time Quinn was knocked to the floor, motionless. Zhenxi Thaxoi stood astride him - a coiled spring like some victorious hunter.

Quinn whipped his legs up to the exposed groin and Zhenxi Thaxoi bent double giving a series of little high-pitched whines.

Quinn regained a little strength and he was up on his feet again. As Zhenxi Thaxoi stood up, Quinn punched him hard and full across the face. It was the Chinese man who fell this time. Quinn swung again but missed as Zhenxi Thaxoi crumpled faster than he had judged. Now Quinn was off balance. Zhenxi Thaxoi lashed out with his feet connecting with Quinn's legs and Quinn toppled on him.

They grappled on the floor - no man gaining an advantage. In a novel martial arts move, Zhenxi Thaxoi leapt to his feet. He kicked at Quinn again but missed. Quinn was up and lunged at him. The force sent then both careering through the lounge door.

The hand-to-hand fight continued. They crashed this way and that causing much damage around the room.

They were on the floor again and, during a grapple, Quinn saw his gun in its holster by the foot of a sofa. He tried to stretch for it. Zhenxi Thaxoi spotted the move and grabbed the gun.

In a trice, Zhenxi Thaxoi was on his feet aiming the gun at Quinn. Triumphantly, he spoke, "You have caused me much loss of honour. I must now purge my life of you. You destroyed my missiles."

He squared the gun up aiming at Quinn with renewed commitment.

"Hardly honourable to shoot a defenceless opponent," blustered Quinn.

Then, much to Quinn's surprise, "You are right." With this, Zhenxi Thaxoi threw the gun at the window – smashing the glass and sending it clattering to the street below. He assumed a fighting stance. "Let us begin..."

Quinn got up, poised and taut. They circled each other. The Chinese man made the first move and lashed out at Quinn. Quinn blocked successfully. The sequence repeated.

Then, at the same moment, they lunged for each other like a pair of stags - hands round each other's neck.

They slowly started a mutual stranglehold but Zhenxi Thaxoi seemed the stronger. Quinn let go and transferred his grip to his opponent's wrists trying to relieve the pressure. To no avail. Then Quinn tried a karate two-handed chop to Zhenxi Thaxoi's midriff. But he could take it.

Quinn's eyes and tongue started to bulge - the veins standing out and pulsating on his forehead. He turned bright crimson.

With a free hand, Quinn caught the edge of a lamp table. Then his fingers connected with Jayne's picture. He grabbed the picture and smashed it. Still stuck in a piece of broken frame was a long glass shard. He carefully positioned his fingers around the section of frame and rammed the glass up under Zhenxi Thaxoi's ribcage into his chest.

The grip round Quinn's neck slackened slightly but Zhenxi Thaxoi was still staring at him. Slowly, Zhenxi Thaxoi's arms dropped and his eyes glazed. He slowly slid down the front of Quinn onto the floor. Quinn collapsed into a chair - nearly dead too. He stared across at the glistening heap of yellow muscle that was Zhenxi Thaxoi.

In Cadogan's office, Cadogan and Edmondson drank coffee. Cadogan was recovering well from his battering.

"Field work to your taste?" asked Edmondson.

"I think not. But everything seems to be mending as it should."

"The medics say Quinn is doing well but he's has actually said he'd like some leave for once!"

Cadogan smiled. "That'll be fine. I knew Quinn was good – I have to admit better than I'd imagined." He paused. "What of the Anastasia Montero?"

"Disappeared," said Edmondson. "Just enough money to get by I suspect."

"Mmm. I must let Dovey know that the data from the Quinn's broken tablet proved extremely effective..."

Seven unpleasant Muscovites sat in a smoke filled attic around a table strewn with empty vodka bottles. A single overhead bulb dropped a weak pool of light onto the wood.

A burly, unshaven man called Olav began speaking, "So, the next three bombing campaigns. Shopping centres first, then the government buildings and finally the transport infrastructure. Boris, as chief of staff, does the plan look workable?"

"Thank you, head of ops," replied Boris. "All the cells are already in place and tight. Armourer?"

Another unkempt man muttered, "The quartermaster assures me that the weapons and explosives caches are all in place."

"That is excellent, the Russian Mafia will become triumphant once again." Vladimir raised his glass again. He and the others followed suit.

The toast was interrupted by a loud battering on the

attic door. Within seconds, the door burst in and a tear gas cartridge scuttled across the attic floor. It spewed clouds of its debilitating vapour. The cartridge was closely followed by Russian policemen, special agents and soldiers wearing gas masks. The incapacitated Muscovites were handcuffed with only the minimum of force and led down through the attic door.

Three Hispanic types sauntered along a Washington sidewalk.

A group of five men caught up with them, whipping their guns out.

One of the five yelled, "Freeze! FBI. Rodriguez, Martinez and San Juan - out for a nice walk and all together. OK - on the floor, guys. It's been a long time but we get there in the end."

The Hispanic types complied.

Some unsavoury-looking men were frog-marched off a junk, at gun point, in Hong Kong harbour by members of the Hong Kong police. They were bundled onto a police motor launch moored alongside the junk. In a few seconds, the captured men had their hands in the air, handcuffed.

Two men, Fiorelli and Gasparini, were half way through an excellent Italian meal. The restaurant, Bradacchio, was rated very highly in most of New York's eating out guides.

Fiorelli began, grasping a big glass of a very fine Barolo, "You know, Snr. Gasparini, the protection I can offer you doesn't come better than this. Put business my way and you've got a friend for life."

They clinked the big glasses together in celebration.

"Mr. Fiorelli. This is the best deal I have ever had. And

I want to thank you for it." Gasparini's hands imperceptibly dropped below the table level. "But, you know, I have a confession to make. There is a gun trained on your private parts. I am, actually, from the FBI and this restaurant is surrounded. You either come quietly or I shoot."

Fiorelli raised his hands above his head in submission.

In a bustling market street in Beirut a swarthy man opened up the back doors of a medium-sized police van. A bunch of sixteen Lebanese thugs were herded into it by armed officials. The doors were closed and locked and the van drove off.

CHAPTER 32: Geneva

The Geneva seafront, though pleasant, could not be described as one of the great holiday destinations of the world. Like any other city there are some picturesque areas – undeniably the views out across Lake Geneva. The fountain gives it its trademark, but otherwise it is an industrial and financial place just like many other European second cities. There is, though, a strong whiff of private Swiss bank accounts. And the shopping areas seem to be entirely dedicated to no other items than watches.

The half-a-million people in the city itself enjoy the proximity to France and winter sports in general.

But Geneva is a great city to be in to go unnoticed.

A woman walked up to a clean, well-to-do but uninspiring terraced house somewhere in the inner-ring suburbs. She let herself in giving a furtive backward glance down the street before entering. She wore sunglasses and a brightly coloured headscarf but it was definitely Anastasia Montero.

She carried a medium-sized soft leather document bag.

The door closed behind her.

Anastasia made her way into the tastefully appointed lounge. There was a fire burning in a grate. She took off her coat, headscarf and sunglasses and threw them onto a low coffee table. She pulled a chair up to the fire, went over to a bookshelf and took down a carved wooden box around thirty-five by twenty-five centimetres and about ten deep. Fumbling in her pocket she produced a small key and turned it in the lock of the box - but she did not open it. She placed the box on a sofa beside the chair near the fire.

Then she pushed the fireguard aside. The leather bag was then opened and a sheaf of papers taken out. There was a passport on top. She took and opened it taking a quick look before throwing it onto the fire.

Anastasia's passport was slowly consumed by the flames. More identification papers followed from the leather bag – including birth certificate, driving licence and credit cards. All of these were added to the blaze.

Her face was lit by the dancing flames. A half smile played around her lips. The leather bag was now empty of its contents.

She waited until the fire had eaten the papers to ashes and then she slowly opened the carved wooden box. Inside were more documents. On the top was a Swiss passport. She picked it up and opened it. The name was clearly visible:

COLAS, Monique.

The photograph showed a different hairstyle but it was, definitely, Anastasia. She clutched the passport to her chest. Her smile broadened and she started to gently rock back and forth in her chair staring at the flames. She then put the new passport back into the box and pulled out more papers...

Scattered across the floor were all manner of share

certificates, Swiss bank statements and bearer bonds, all showing very high values. The name on each made out to 'MONIQUE COLAS'.

Her smile broke into a giggle as she rocked in the chair. Her eyes sparkled in the light of the flames. She had actually got away with it. The giggle turns into a full laugh as she leant back in the chair with self-satisfied joy mixed with a blessed relief.

"Hello, Anastasia." The voice was somehow very familiar. But then it couldn't be...

Anastasia's face froze in shock. Ghina stepped from a dark corner of the room with a gun, silenced, held in both, gloved, hands and steadfastly aimed at Anastasia's head.

Anastasia still held her papers. She could not move or speak. The shock changed to fear.

Ghina's emotionless voice continued, "For three minutes I was clinically dead. I was in a coma for two months. I could walk unaided only three weeks ago. But, you know, the knowledge of an address in Geneva somehow gave me the strength to carry on." The dull snout of the gun was held steadfastly unwavering.

Anastasia, half choking, could hardly form the words, "G...G...Ghina... whatever you want... you... you... can take. Take it all... I know how you must feel - but it's not like that... honestly, it's not. Here..."

Anastasia offered the papers in a trembling, outstretched hand.

"I can take whatever I want, can I, Anastasia?"

"Please, Ghina. Have it all... it's not like it seems... Trust me..." Anastasia pleaded.

"You know, I've changed. Life can be without the stress... without the evil... without the constant threat. But I'm still taking what I want." There was a pause. "Your life."

Anastasia's horrified face changed to a contented smile. "I failed when I didn't kill you. But I can still rejoice in your months of suffering." She laughed mockingly.

The muzzle of the gun spoke. THUD! THUD! THUD! THUD! THUD! THUD! Brief tongues of flame spat from the gun.

Ghina stood rooted – somehow mesmerised by what she had done - petrified by the horror before her. Tears started to stream down her cheeks. But perhaps tears of relief. Or tears of revenge.

Some time later, the front door of the house opened. Ghina appeared - both hands ungloved. She carried a small brown paper packet in her hand.

She made her way down the quiet, deserted street. There were a number of parked cars in a line. She stopped by one and got in. The engine started.

A black Jaguar saloon pulled out from the roadside between the parked cars.

She got into the passenger side. The driver of the right hand drive vehicle was in shadow - but it was, without doubt, a dark-haired man.

The car purred down the street. It stopped at a red traffic light next to a letter box being emptied by a postman with an open sack.

Ghina passed the small brown paper packet to Quinn. He glimpsed the sheaf of ornately printed papers protruding from it.

"One billion dollars," she said.

He inserted the packet into a Jiffy bag. He then produced a compliment slip - the wording clearly read, hand-written:

> SORRY ABOUT THE AIRCRAFT DAMAGE.
>
> USE OF ULTIMATE FORCE AUTHORISED!

He signed the document: *Quinn.*

He then sealed the Jiffy bag and turned it over revealing an address label...

>MR DOUG KRAMER
>c/o CENTRAL INTELLIGENCE AGENCY
>LANGLEY
>WEST VIRGINIA, USA

Quinn casually tossed the Jiffy bag directly into the waiting postman's sack from the open car window. The postman, in surprise at the accuracy, looked up to acknowledge Quinn but Quinn and Ghina were in a passionate embrace. They kissed and kissed and kissed. Oblivious. The postman gave a kindly smile and turned back to his work.

The lights changed to green but the car did not move.

Quinn and Ghina were completely absorbed in each other. Neither heard the hooting of cars behind waiting to go through the green light.

Then she said, "Martin, the lights are green..."

He said, "It's OK, Ghina..." He paused for another kiss. "...or should I say, 'Monique'?"

Suddenly, his hand gently pressed a button and the seats reclined as they continued their clinch.

A cacophony of car horns filled the Geneva street.

A stationary Jaguar was surrounded by a crowd of other cars inching past the obstruction and hooting wildly.